The Ornamental Hermit

Olivier Bosman

CONTENTS

CHAPTER ONE
The Wild Man of Sutton Courtenay

Clarkson sat at his desk, bent over his report, frowning with confusion. "'Ere, Billings, 'ow d'you write *very*?" he asked. "One *r* or two?"

"One," replied Billings who was sitting opposite him reading a book.

"You sure? Innit the same as *merry*? As in merry Christmas?"

"I'm sure."

Clarkson was not convinced and began reading out loud from his report. "'*The man was wearing a very long red coat…*' It don't look right," he concluded.

"It's one *r*, Clarkson. Trust me."

Billings was only half-listening to his colleague.

He was reading Robinson Crusoe and was currently captured by a particular phrase which he read over and over again. The phrase appeared in the passage in which Crusoe questions what it was that kept driving him from one tragedy to another: *'It is a secret overruling decree that hurries us on to be the instruments of our own destruction. Even though it be before us we rush upon it with our eyes open.'* How truthfully that phrase rang in his mind, then. And how apt the ensuing tale proved it to be.

"It were a striking coat, Billings," continued Clarkson. "Went all the way down to his ankles. It had a furry collar and it were bright red. Very conspi... conspu... what's the word I'm thinking of, Billings?"

"Conspicuous?"

"That's the one. 'Ow do you write it?"

"Don't write conspicuous."

"Why not?"

"It's subjective. Just write that it was long and red."

"He looked just like one of them Russian warriors. You know, with the red coats and the fur hats. 'Ow do you call them, Billings? These Russian soldiers?"

"Cossacks?"

"That's it. He looked just like a Cossack.

Probably was one, come to think of it. Bloody Russians! Ain't we got enough crime to deal with, without having to chase after foreign counterfeiters."

"You're at Scotland Yard now, Clarkson. That's what we do."

"Me feet are killing me, do you know that? I spent all day walkin' around the bloomin' city, shadowing me target."

Billings finally put down his book and glanced at the clock on the wall. It was ten minutes to six. His shift had ended thirty minutes ago and he had hoped he'd be able to spend a quiet hour reading his book before going back home, but Clarkson had put an end to that idea. He picked up his satchel from beneath his desk and started packing his book back into it when suddenly there was a knock on the door.

"Oh, bloomin' heck! If that's Jack..." Clarkson threw his pen down on his desk, spluttering ink all over his report.

A teenage boy opened the door and popped his head in.

"You better not 'ave a message from those coppers," Clarkson cried.

"I 'ave, sir," the boy replied. "They've arrested a man. They're asking will you come down and take a statement."

"No! It's ten minutes to six and I'm about to go home. Go back to those coppers and tell them there was no one here."

"But sir, 'tis a special one, this."

"Oi, hobbadehoy! Did you hear what I said?"

"But they say it's the Wild Man of Sutton Courtenay."

Clarkson went quiet for a brief moment and raised an eyebrow. "'Ow do they know it's him?"

"Well, it's a rough-looking man, with a dirty beard and..."

Clarkson lost interest and began cleaning the ink stains from his report with blotting paper. "Sounds like another shivering jemmy to me. Tell those coppers to let him go."

"But sir..."

Billings saw the boy become flustered. "It's alright, Jack," he said. "Someone will be down shortly."

The boy sighed with relief. "Thank you, sir." He marched off, closing the door behind him.

Clarkson looked up at his colleague and frowned. "I don't believe this! I've been runnin' around London all day chasing some bloomin' Russian, and when I finally get to sit down for a few minutes..." An idea occurred to him and he suddenly stopped talking. "Billings, me old mate." He flashed his colleague a smile and knitted his eyebrows over his pleading blue eyes.

Billings shook his head. "No, Clarkson. It was my turn yesterday and I've got my day off tomorrow." He put his satchel on his lap and tightened the straps.

"Go on, 'ave an 'eart. It's pork tonight." Clarkson got up from his desk and went towards him. "Me rib's waiting at 'ome for me with me sawney. The li'l ones are starvin', waitin' for their daddy to come 'ome." He leaned over his colleague's desk and stared at him with those baby blue eyes of his. "Be a sport, Billings, me old mate. You ain't got nothing to do tonight, 'ave you? The Wild Man of Sutton Courtenay, Billings. Fancy that. Sounds like an interesting case for you."

Billings had never heard of the Wild Man of Sutton Courtenay. He wasn't in the habit of perusing the papers like the other detectives did, preferring instead to read his novel whenever he got the chance. It astounded him how he had managed to acquire a reputation for being a smart, ambitious young officer within the force. He didn't consider himself smart at all, even though he was better educated than most of his colleagues. And he certainly wasn't ambitious. It was probably his willingness to stay on longer at work and put in the hours which led to this reputation, but of course, none of that had anything to do with ambition. He just didn't like returning to his sombre little room in Battersea.

"All right, then," he said finally.

A broad smile appeared on Clarkson's face.

"But you owe me."

"Oh, Sergeant Billings. It's you, is it?" PC Dwight sounded disappointed as Billings came down to the holding cells. Billings was not much liked by the uniformed men. They considered him to be arrogant. Aloof. An odd bird. "Weren't you on duty last night?" he asked.

"I was." Billings ignored the hostility in the constable's tone. "Who have you caught?"

"Oh, we got a big one, tonight. Didn't Jack mention it?"

"He mentioned something about the wild man of... uh..."

"Sutton Courtenay, Sergeant. Brendan Lochrane, The Wild Man of Sutton Courtenay. You'll have read all about it, no doubt."

"Well, I must confess, I..."

"Bloomin' heck, you bunch of dicks! I thought

Detective Constable Clarkson was on duty. Hadn't we better get him?"

"I'm on duty, Constable. Now, where is this man?"

"He's in the cell."

Dwight un-clicked a bunch of keys from his belt and walked towards the cells. Billings followed him.

"The Berkshire County Constabulary feared he'd find his way down to London and published a sketch in the police gazette . A patrol officer found him sleeping in the bushes in Battersea Park. It weren't until he tried speaking to him that he realised who it was."

"Why?"

"I'll show you why. 'Ere, Jack! Help me pin the suspect down to the wall, so I can show the Sergeant."

Jack, who was sitting at the entrance of the cellar, jumped up from his seat and ran obediently towards the cell.

As Dwight unlocked the cell door, Billings caught his first glimpse of the so-called Wild Man. The man was huddled down in the corner, sitting on the cold brick floor wearing dirty rags. His hair and beard were tangled together, knotted to each other like ivy to a tree.

"Alright Brendan," said Dwight as he slowly opened the door. "We're just coming in to have a look at you. Nothing to worry about."

The man didn't react and continued to gaze at the ground, passive and docile.

"You ready Jack?" Dwight whispered to the boy. "When I say go, you grab his right arm, got that?"

"Yes, sir."

"Alright... go!"

Dwight and Jack suddenly rushed into the cell and lunged at the man. They grabbed an arm each and stretched it out, disabling the use of his elbows. They then pulled the man up to his feet. The man screwed his face up in pain and a strange muffled roar emanated from his mouth.

Billings stood a few steps away from the cell and watched. It was an unpleasant scene to witness. A renaissance painting came to his mind (was it Rembrandt? Or Caravaggio?) of Jesus being raised on his cross.

"You hold him tight now, do you hear?" Dwight instructed as he attempted to prise open the man's jaw by pushing his cheeks together with his thumb and index finger.

The man let out that agonized roar again, which made Billings wince. "I say! Steady on, Constable!" he called.

"This is a dangerous man, Sergeant." With the man's mouth finally opened, Dwight turned to face Billings. "Do you see that?"

It was dark and Billings struggled to see anything of interest.

"Look closely, Sergeant. In his mouth. There's something not there that ought to be."

"My God! His tongue!"

"That's right."

"He has no tongue!"

"No tongue, Sergeant. That's our monkey, alright." Dwight let go of the man's mouth and turned to Jack, who was still desperately holding on to the Wild Man's outstretched arm. "Alright, Jack. At the count of three. One... two... three!"

They both dropped the man's arms in unison and staggered quickly out of the cell. The man dropped back down on the floor, pulled his knees towards his chest and continued to stare vacantly at the ground as before.

Billings squatted down before the bars and tried looking him in the face.

"Mr Lochrane?" he said gently. "My name is Detective Sergeant Billings."

A horrible stench wafted from the man's mouth and Billings was forced to look away.

Dwight rolled his eyes. "He don't speak,

Sergeant. No tongue, remember."

"But he can hear," said Billings, although there were no signs of that. The man continued to stare ahead of him with that bewildered look, ignoring him completely.

"There's no point, Sergeant. We tried talking to him ourselves. He won't respond."

"Then how do you know you've got the right man?"

"How do I know?" Dwight turned red with indignation. "'Cause he fits the description, that's how!" He picked the police gazette up from the desk beside the cell and looked for the corresponding page. "Here. 'A rough-looking man, about six foot three, shoulder length hair, unkempt. Brown and grey beard, most likely caked with mud. And no tongue!' There! Look for yourself."

He held out the gazette to Billings, but Billings didn't take it. He was still looking at the Wild Man, huddled in the corner of his cell, staring blankly ahead of him. How to describe that look? It was powerless, defeated, resigned. This was a man who had given up fighting and was ready to take whatever life thrust at him in the hope that it would soon put him out of his misery. "He's not quite six foot three," Billings concluded.

"What?"

"The police gazette describes him as being six foot three. He's shorter than that."

"This *is* our man, Sergeant. The Wild Man of Sutton Courtenay. We done our job. We caught our monkey. Now it's your job to gather the evidence and get him hanged."

Berkshire Aristocrat Murdered By Axe Wielding Wild Man

The Berkshire County Constabulary reports that on the 21st of October 1890, the body of Lord Palmer of Sutton House, in the village of Sutton Courtenay, was found lying face down in the woods of his estate, with a hatchet sticking out of his shoulder blades. The hatchet was identified as one belonging to Brendan Lochrane, a vagrant known locally as The Wild Man of Sutton Courtenay, who had been living and working in the woods on Lord Palmer's estate for almost a year. There were also large wounds on the back of Lord Palmer's head and the body had been robbed of five pounds, three shillings, a gold watch and a gold plated cameo ring. The whereabouts of Lochrane is currently unknown, but the police suspect him of being on his way to London. The Berkshire Constabulary describe him as being six foot three, with long, ruffled hair and a long black beard which he may now have shaved off. He is also described as having no tongue. The public are urged to report any sightings of an individual matching these descriptions to the police and under no circumstances to approach him themselves.

Billings read up on the case in The Morning Post that same evening and instantly cursed Clarkson for talking him into taking it. There is nothing more stress-inducing than to be saddled up with a sensational case which has captured the interest of the national press, he thought. His heart started trembling in his chest and his brain was pounding in his skull as he walked back to his rooms in Battersea. His hands were shaking and his knees were knocking so much that he was forced to stop on Chelsea Bridge to catch his breath. The tremors didn't usually start until around eight o'clock. He had taken that into consideration when he agreed to stay on longer at work. He calculated that he would be back home, safely cradling his syringe and his morphine ampoules long before any signs of his addiction would become visible. But the notoriety of the case and the expectation and responsibility with which he was now laden had aggravated his condition, and he was a complete wreck by the time he staggered up the stairs to his room.

Two hours later the morphine was rushing

through his veins, lightening his mind, soothing his vision and un-tightening his muscles. He was lying on his bed, propped up against his pillow, his eyelids were drooping and he was drifting slowly into that twilight state, somewhere between dream and wakefulness, when his landlady walked in to pick up the dishes.

He saw her frown when she saw him draped over his bed. "You taking that morphine, again? And you bein' a detective and all. Ain't you supposed to stay bright and alert?"

He used to be more careful. He used to wait until midnight. Make sure that he had locked the door and blown out all the lights before taking his dose. It used to be merely an aid to help him sleep, but over the years, he had become lax. The morphine had become a crutch and he found that he needed to take his dose earlier and earlier. Midnight became ten o'clock. Ten o'clock became nine. Now it was eight. Sometimes even half past seven.

"When you gonna brighten this room up a bit, eh?" his landlady continued. "It looks like a bloomin' prison cell in here!" She closed the curtains. "And when you gonna let me put some colourful drapes up for you? I've got an aspidistra in the lounge, you could have that. That'll cheer things up a bit. It's a good job you never have any visitors. I'd be too embarrassed to show them this room – 'ere, you ain't eaten any of my soup!"

What a disappointment he must be to fussy old Mrs Appleby, thought Billings. He used to be her prize tenant. 'Detective Sergeant Billings from the Metropolitan Police.' Now he was just a sad, miserable dope fiend she couldn't bring herself to turn away.

CHAPTER TWO

The Disappearance of Sebastian Forrester

My dear John,

(I may call you John, I hope. I have known you for so long and I have been following your life with such interest. I hear you have been promoted to the CID. Mr Forrester and I send you our warmest congratulations.)

You must be wondering why I am writing to you now after all these years. Something has happened which has upset us both very much and we need your help. It's about Sebastian. I do not want to put this in writing, but I would like to meet you. Could you come to the meeting house today at four? (Why don't we see you at the meeting house anymore? God is in you, John. Waiting for you to give him the opportunity to shine through. I hope you don't feel I'm being too forward or that I am in any way interfering, but there is so much of you that reminds me of our dear Sebastian. The same darkness that cloaked his life, cloaks yours, and I just know that God can help you lift it.)

Trusting to see you at today's meeting and wishing you strength and love,

yours truly,
Mrs Cecilia Forrester

The letter lay waiting for Billings on his breakfast plate as he came down that morning.

"It was delivered by an elegant lady," said Mrs Appleby as she appeared from the kitchen to pour his coffee. "She was dressed all in black. I told her you were in and she could deliver the letter to you herself, but she was in such a hurry."

The letter came imbued with the scent of Mrs Forrester's perfume and the smell of Mr Forrester's cigars. The aroma wafted up from the paper and triggered a flood of bittersweet memories in Billings. He instantly found himself in that dark little room on the top floor of the Forresters' Chelsea home, where the servants used to sleep. The fragrance of citrus and lavender reminded him of the linen on the large oak bed which he shared with his mother – linen which had been taken from

Mrs Forrester's own bedroom and had been moved upstairs for their use. The smell of cigars reminded him of the tobacco-stained pages of Mr Forrester's old books, which had been cleared from the study to make room for newer and more important works and which had been stacked into piles against the unpapered walls.

"An acquaintance of yours, is it?" asked Mrs Appleby, still standing before him with the coffee pot in her hands.

"No," Billings replied softly.

"She was awfully smart. Not a relative of yours, is she?"

"No."

"Just a friend, then?"

Go! Billings kept thinking to himself. *Go away and leave me alone!*

"She's the one who put us up when we returned from Africa," he said.

"Oh, when your father died?"

"Yes."

"Well, I should've insisted she'd come in then. But then she was in such a hurry." Mrs Appleby finally picked the dirty dishes up from the table, put them on her tray and carried them back into the kitchen.

Billings remained sitting at the table, staring

blankly at the letter without blinking until his vision glazed over and the curly black letters merged into one swirling blur. Suddenly he saw his mother again, pale and sickly on her bed, sore from all the coughing. She had caught consumption during the crossing from Cape Town. They had only been in England two months. Her last words, her last breath, were spent on utterances of gratitude and humility, so that none were left for her son. Billings understood now that she had persuaded Mr Forrester to look after him when she died and that this is what she was thanking them for, but he didn't know that then. At that time he just wondered exactly what he was supposed to be grateful for. He was a minor when he came to England. A thirteen year old boy with a rough and patchy education, orphaned within two months of arriving and stranded helplessly in a foreign land. It was surely Mr Forrester's duty to look after him.

'It's about Sebastian,' she had written. Billings suddenly felt that same roaring rage well up as when he was fourteen and Sebastian Forrester would come home from university. The glorious young Sebastian with his pensive blue eyes, his strong, broad shoulders and his alabaster skin. There stood Billings demurely in the corner, short, pale and scrawny, watching the Forresters kiss and hug and fuss over their beloved son whilst he waited his turn to pay his respects. Only a few months ago, he too had two parents who loved and fussed over him. Only a few months ago, *he* was the white demigod and all the Malagasy children looked at him with envy as he got to go home with his parents – their teachers – and they were forced to return to their straw huts and work the land or graze their cattle. Now he was just a ward. A protégé. An orphan.

Why did Mrs Appleby have to tell Mrs Forrester that he was in? He had no choice now but to go to the meeting house and meet up with her.

Billings stood outside the Friends Meeting House on St Martin's Lane. He couldn't bring himself to go in. He hadn't attended a meeting for many years. Quakers called them meetings because they didn't worship. They didn't preach or sing or pray. They just sat in shared silence, only ever speaking when they were moved to do so. Billings hated silence. It made him feel uneasy. He wanted noise around him. He needed distractions. God's presence could be felt in silence and he didn't want that.

The meeting ended and the congregation started to exit. Billings watched the men come out of the building first, with their plain, black clothes and their bushy whiskers. They shook each other's hands and patted each other on the back as they said their goodbyes. The women came out later. They were also dressed in plain, black clothes and their hair was tied tightly back. Quaker women never wore curls or ribbons. Nor did they wear perfume or jewellery.

Mrs Forrester rushed out ahead of the other women and looked around her. Billings called out her name.

"Oh John, you came," she cried. She ran towards him, wrapped her arms around his waist and squeezed him till it hurt. "Oh John! My dear, dear John!"

Billings couldn't remember the last time he had been hugged like that and he felt chills run down his spine. But then Mrs Forrester suddenly stopped.

"But you didn't come in," she said, looking accusingly into his eyes. "Why didn't you come in?"

Billings avoided answering the question. "Where is Mr Forrester?"

"Mr Forrester is at home. He's dying. But look at you. You look good. But thin. Are you eating? And when are you going to find yourself a nice young wife to settle down with?"

She went in for another hug, but Billings grabbed her by the shoulders and looked her straight in the eyes.

"Mr Forrester is dying?"

"Oh, he's been deteriorating slowly for the last few years. He won't last the year. That's why it was so urgent for us to see you."

"To see me about what?"

"I'll tell you on the way. Come, there's a cab waiting for us." She took his hand and pulled him towards the cab stand, where a row of hansoms were waiting to pick up the people leaving the meeting house.

"He's been ill for some time."

Mrs Forrester sat next to Billings in the cab, his hands sandwiched tightly in hers. Her eyes were still gleaming with the joy of seeing him after all these years, even when she spoke of her husband's ill health.

"He's never really been the same since Sebastian went missing. It's his heart, he's been suffering terribly from palpitations. I blame it on the stress and the expense we incurred in finding Sebastian. Do you know how much money we paid those incompetent detectives in Cumberland? We should have employed you."

"I was only a constable at the time."

"They profited from us!" She suddenly let go of his hands. "They milked us. Combing the hills, dragging the lakes. That's what hurts the most. That in the midst of our desperation, our grieving, somebody else tried to profit." She took off her gloves and stared out the window at the bare trees which lined the cobbled streets of Chelsea. "We got a letter," she said.

"A letter?"

"From him. From Sebastian. He's back in Oxford. He sent us a letter."

"I thought he was dead."

He realised his clumsiness immediately and cursed himself inwardly, but Mrs Forrester ignored the gaffe and turned back to face the detective.

"We were in Oxford last week. Both of us. Mr Forrester, sick as he was, insisted he'd come with me."

"How did you find him?"

"We didn't. We waited for a whole week at that tea room he'd suggested for our meeting, but he didn't show up. And we had no way of locating him. We inquired everywhere, but nobody could enlighten us. So we went back home. Mr Forrester thinks it may have been an impostor."

"An impostor?"

"Mr Forrester is dying, John. I told you that. There's a large inheritance at stake. Anyone can pretend to be Sebastian. It's been ten years."

She turned back towards the window and fell quiet. Billings tried to think of something to say, but couldn't come up with anything appropriate. Suddenly he heard Mrs Forrester sniff. Was she crying? He didn't know what to do and remained sitting silently and awkwardly next to her, until the cab came to a stop outside the old Chelsea home he remembered from his childhood.

"You must be quiet when we enter," said Mrs Forrester as she unlocked the heavy front door. "We put his bed in the drawing room, so he wouldn't feel alone. He's usually asleep in the evening so I don't want to wake him."

She pushed the door open and entered the house. Billings followed her into the dark hallway. The door to the study room was open and he peeped into it as he passed. This was the room where Mr Forrester used to sit and study and where he was not to be disturbed under any circumstances. There was that large oak desk with the lion claws carved into the legs; the heavy bookcase, stacked from top to bottom with his big leather-bound books; and the Persian rug with the beautiful intertwining patterns. It was just as he remembered it from his childhood, but somehow not as impressive. It seemed smaller now. And dustier. And the furniture was old-fashioned and heavy and dark.

"Freddy?" Mrs Forrester popped her head into the drawing room and whispered. "Are you awake? I've got John Billings with me."

Billings could hear a small crackling voice mumble a reply. "John?"

"You remember, dear. Gideon Billings's son. The detective. He's here." She turned to Billings and beckoned.

Billings approached slowly and saw an old man lying in a big oak bed in the middle of the room. It took him a while to fully recognize him but eventually, looking past the sunken cheeks, the glazed eyes, the weak skeletal arms which tried in vain to push his body up to a sitting position, he saw the great man he remembered.

"Hello sir," he said.

Mr Forrester didn't reciprocate the greeting. "Show him the letter!" he said, still struggling to sit up.

"Not now, dear."

Mrs Forrester rushed to his aid and began

propping a pillow behind his back, but he pushed her away.

"Show him the letter, Godammit! I haven't much time. I'm dying!"

"Oh, Freddy!" Mrs Forrester bit her lip then quickly ran out of the room.

It was only at that point that Billings noticed Mr Forrester's beard had been shaved off. That's what made him look so small. The great, impressive white beard was gone, making him look naked and vulnerable. Like a shorn sheep. Why did they do it? Perhaps it was easier to feed him.

Mr Forrester squinted at his guest. "John Billings, eh?"

"How are you, sir?"

"Come here. Step into the light. Let me have a look at you."

Billings stepped closer. Mr Forrester looked him up and down.

"Ah yes. I recognize you now. There's traces of your mother about you."

"I know."

"Nothing of your father."

"No."

"Good man, he was. Deep thinker. But morose."

"Yes, I think I may have inherited *that* from him."

"Did good work for our faith in Africa. And your mother too. Great shame it ended the way it did. What was it? Malaria?"

"Yellow fever."

"Did she tell you about the letter?"

"She told me you received one."

"We need someone to investigate."

"Yes, I understand that, but..."

"I'm dying. Did she tell you that?"

"Yes, sir, she did, but..."

"All expenses will be paid. Wages too, if you wish."

"I understand that, Mr Forrester, but I really can't leave London now. I've just been given..."

"We looked after you. Your mother was destitute when she came back with you from Africa. Not a penny to her name."

"I know. And I appreciate that, but..."

"I want to see my son again, John. I only have the one. And I want to see him before I die. I may not be around next month."

Mrs Forrester entered carrying a writing box.

"John's taking the case," Mr Forrester said to her.

Before Billings got the chance to argue, Mrs Forrester rushed towards him, grabbed hold of his face and kissed him on both cheeks. "I knew you would do this for us, John," she said. "You are the only one who knows Sebastian well enough."

"Well, I never actually knew him that well," he replied. "It was a long time ago and I only have very vague recollections of him."

"Oh, you remember him, John. He was an unusual child. Wild and stubborn and passionate. Do you remember, dear?" She turned towards her husband. "Do you remember how he used to run around the garden naked? Stark naked, he was!" She laughed. "We couldn't get him to put his clothes back on. And no type of weather could deter him. Rain. Snow. You turned your back once and there'd be a pile of clothes on the floor and he'd be out there, naked like a savage, enjoying God's world in blissful innocence. How old was he then, dear? Nine?"

Her husband didn't reply. He was looking away from her. Frowning. Impatient.

"I think he felt trapped," Mrs Forrester continued. "He felt trapped by his clothes. He felt restricted. He couldn't bear restrictions. I asked him once. I asked him why he did it. 'Because I want to feel the elements,' he said. 'Elements!' That's the very word he used. He wanted to feel the elements on his skin. 'If God wants me to be cold, I'll be cold. If God wants me to be wet, I'll be wet,' he said. 'But God doesn't want you to get ill,' I said.

'That's why he invented clothes.' Oh, he had a very special way of looking at things. Even at that age."

Suddenly one of Mr Forrester's pillows came flying towards her and hit her arm. "Will you shut up, woman!" her husband cried.

"Freddy!"

"He was weak!" he screamed. "That's why he couldn't hack it in the theological college! He was a dreamer! A romantic, quixotic fool!"

Mrs Forrester picked the pillow up from the floor and looked at Billings apologetically. "It's his illness talking. The constant pain makes him bitter."

"This is the devil's realm we live in!" Mr Forrester continued with his rant. "That's what he couldn't understand! This is the devil's realm and we are all stained with the devil's spore!"

Mrs Forrester rushed towards Billings and kissed him quickly on his cheek. "You had better go. He starts talking nonsense when he's tired. Here. Take this with you." She handed him the writing box. "The letter is in there. And others too, so you can compare the handwriting. Study them. They might give you clues. Thank you, John. Thank you for doing this for us. If anyone can find him, it's you."

After taking his nightly dose of morphine, Billings put Sebastian's writing box on his bed and studied its contents. It was an elegant piece of equipment. Approximately fifteen inches wide, nine inches deep and six inches tall, it was made of solid mahogany with a decorative brass strap binding it on either side. Beneath the lid there was a sloping leather writing surface. There was a small lever on the side of the box which, when pushed, caused the surface to shoot open and reveal a secret compartment. In the compartment Billings found a book, a notebook and some letters.

The notebook was filled with dates and terms of church history: 'Council of Nicaea – 325; Council of Constantinople – 381; Council of Chalcedon – 451' etc. Sebastian seemed to have made a half-hearted attempt at taking notes, but only the first few pages were filled in. The rest just had a couple of sentences hastily jotted on them or were covered with abstract drawings and caricatures of his lecturers.

The book, however, was much more intriguing. Bent, dog-eared and covered in fingerprints, it was obviously well read. It was called 'The Sayings of The Desert Fathers' and it appeared to be a collection of rules and quotes from early Christian monks who withdrew into the Egyptian desert in the 5th century. Billings dropped the book on to his bed and it fell open on a page where a particular passage had been underlined: *'Live as though crucified; in struggle, in lowliness of spirit, in good will and spiritual abstinence, in fasting, in penitence, in weeping.'* Billings was too hazy-minded and foggy to make much sense of it, but he had no doubt that this was significant.

As he returned the book to its drawer, it occurred to him that the box was too big and clunky for what it contained. He suspected that there might be another compartment hidden in it. After fiddling about with it for a while, he discovered a couple of buttons hidden beneath the sloping surface, which when pressed in succession, suddenly caused a small drawer at the back of the box to spring out. Inside the drawer he found a diary. Fifty or so pages, filled with writing – small, tightly packed, and often spilling into the margins. This must be a great discovery, he thought. The Forresters had made no mention of a diary. Were they ignorant of its existence? But it was the letters Billings was most interested in. The first one was sent ten years ago from Windermere, shortly before Sebastian's disappearance.

Dear Mother and Father,

You will by now have heard that I have left Oxford and that I am staying in the Lake District. Please do not worry. I shall try to explain in this letter what has driven me here. I have been at Wycliffe Hall for over a year now and I have become convinced that I can not leave England and go to Madagascar to teach, as you had wished me to do. I have nothing to teach. I am a wicked, selfish, ignorant fool and I only have things to learn (Father will know what I mean). At Wycliffe Hall they teach us to read and interpret the ancient texts, to decipher the parables, to explain the apparent contradictions, but in my view all this is futile. Religion is not a science. It is not a history lesson. Religion is about faith. This strange and otherworldly sensation which can fill your heart and drive you into a state of ecstasy. Faith can not be explained. It should not be explained. Faith is not about knowing, it's about believing. That is our only connection with God. Faith, as opposed to knowledge, can only exist if we live in ignorance of the facts. How can I explain God's words to another? It is impossible. God does not speak in words. He speaks in feelings, in instincts, in passions, and it is by these means that he has spoken to me. He has called me and I have decided to follow his call. I do not know to where it will lead or for how long I shall have to travel, but please do not worry. Just pray for me. Pray that I shall proof myself worthy for God to enlighten and redeem me (again, Father will know what I mean. He won't understand or agree, but he'll know). I shall write again soon. I promise.

Yours lovingly,
Sebastian

The second letter was written in Oxford and received only six weeks ago.

Dear Mother and Father,

You will be surprised by this letter after ten years. Much has happened to me since we last saw each other and I don't know where to begin explaining, but I should like to see you again. Please write back to me and tell me how you are.

Yours lovingly,
Sebastian

Billings observed some striking differences between the two letters, both in calligraphy and style. The first was written by a confident and flowing hand, whereas judging by the pressure applied to the pen and the missing joints halfway through the words, the second letter was written considerably slower and with much greater effort. As if the writing of it caused the author physical pain. He felt that this might also account for the abruptness of the style. However, the size, shapes, curls and dashes of the letters were consistent.

He dropped the letters on his bed. He would read them again later when he was sober. But he had already made a conclusion. In his current state of mind he was always unencumbered by the cluttered mess of anxieties which normally troubled him and he was able to make clear and reliable judgements. His inclination was to believe that the second letter was written by the same author as the first, from which he concluded that the writer was not an impostor and that Sebastian Forrester was still alive.

The Ornamental Hermit

CHAPTER THREE

The Vulgar Man

Billings strode down the Victoria Embankment on his way to work. A thin young man in a long grey overcoat and brown derby hat was leaning against the wall of the Scotland Yard building. He lit a cigarette and lifted his head as Billings approached. "Ah, Detective Sergeant Billings. So it's you, is it?" he said with an amused glint in his eye.

Billings stopped and looked at him, confused.

"So it's you who's been put in charge of the of the Lord Palmer case," the man continued.

"Do I know you?" Billings asked.

The man stood up from the wall and tipped his hat. "Jeremiah Rook, from The Illustrated Police News. How do you do. So he's been caught then, has he?"

"A man matching Brendan Lochrane's description was picked up yesterday in Battersea Park, if that's what you're referring to, but his identity has not yet been confirmed." Billings tipped his hat back at the reporter and continued briskly towards the entrance.

The reporter followed him. "Did he have a tongue?"

"I'm sorry?"

"The man you caught yesterday? Did he have a tongue?"

"No, he didn't."

"Well, then it's him, isn't it? The Wild Man of Sutton Courtenay."

"We don't know that for certain yet."

"You got a lot of suspects without a tongue in there, have you?"

"No."

"So it must be him. The evil axe murderer! The depraved cur! The vile beast!"

Billings stopped and frowned at the reporter's sensationalist descriptions.

"So what does he look like then, the Wild Man?" the reporter asked.

"You know what he looks like. It's been in the papers."

"Have you got him chained up to the wall?"

"What? No."

"Why not? Isn't he roaring and raging and rattling his cage?"

"No."

"Not foaming at the mouth, then?" The reporter smiled cheekily. "I hear he was found hiding in the bushes."

"That is correct."

"Digging his teeth into a little dead dog."

Billings frowned again. "What paper did you say you work for? The Penny Dreadful?"

The reporter laughed. "It was a joke, Billings. You can take a joke, can't you? Or have I offended *thy* delicate ears?"

Billings didn't understand why he was suddenly using that archaic pronoun and looked confused.

"Well, that is how ye speak, isn't it? Thou and all thy *friends*?"

It was after the reporter had emphasized the word '*friends*' that Billings realised he was referring to the plain speech used by the early Quaker fathers.

"We don't speak like that anymore," he said. He turned his back on him and resumed his walk.

The reporter followed him. "Well, come on Billings! Give us some details. What was he doing in his cell when you found him?"

"He wasn't doing anything. The man I saw yesterday was meek, tired and docile. He was confused and scared and…"

"Aha!"

Billings stopped and looked back. "What?"

"Sympathy! You felt sympathy for him, didn't you?"

"Yes, I did feel some pity for…"

"Your father was Gideon Billings, was he not? A devout Quaker missionary who died in Madagascar in 1877."

"How do you know that?"

"And you were brought up as the ward of Frederick Forrester, chairman of the Friends Foreign Mission Association and friend and follower of Joseph John Gurney, brother of Mrs Elizabeth Fry, the famous prison reformer," the reporter continued.

"I don't see how any of that is relevant to…"

"Oh, but it is relevant, Detective Sergeant. It's *very* relevant."

Billings realised by the reporter's sudden change in tone that he was setting up a trap for him and he was determined not to fall into it. He took a deep breath. "Mr Rook," he said calmly. "The investigation has only just commenced. The suspect's identity has not yet been established, let alone his guilt, and..."

"Let me tell *you* what the problem is, Sergeant."

"There is no problem."

"The problem is *you.*"

"Me?"

"You're a Quaker. You see God in everyone. And in my opinion there should be no room in the police force for bleeding heart sentimentalists like yourself! Because people like these, Detective Sergeant, people like the Wild Man of Sutton Courtenay are *not* human beings! They're monsters and need to be treated as such. It's my job as a reporter to scrutinize our police detectives and make sure they do their jobs right. You've already made a pig's ear of the Whitechapel Ripper case, which is a disgrace, so I'm here to make sure that, unlike the Ripper, the Wild Man of Sutton Courtenay *does* get his just desserts. So imagine my concern, Detective Sergeant Billings, at hearing just now that you've taken *pity* on that monster!" A short pause followed the rant. And then a broad smile appeared on the reporter's face.

Damn it! thought Billings. The blooming bugger has caught me! He could see another damning article about the Metropolitan Police appearing in next week's paper.

When Billings entered the office, he saw Clarkson sitting at his desk with his feet on the table, reading a paper. The Illustrated Police News, of all things. "Morning Billings," he said cheerfully.

Billings mumbled a grumpy reply, walked past him to his desk, sat down and put his head in his hands. He could already feel the blood pound in his head and his left hand was starting to tremble. It was only half past eight in the morning.

"Jacobs wants to see you," Clarkson continued. "Probably wants to brief you about the Lord Palmer case. How's that going, by the way?"

Billings didn't answer. He just got up and walked to his boss' office. Just eight more hours till my next dose, was all that he could think about. Just eight more hours.

Chief Inspector Jacobs was sitting at his desk, his back turned towards the door, staring out of the window. He was frowning and massaging his temples.

Billings stopped in the doorway and cleared his throat. "You wanted to see me, sir?"

Jacobs turned and looked at him absentmindedly. There was a brief pause before he spoke. "Ah Billings, yes. Sit down, sit down."

Billings grabbed a chair and sat down before him.

"So…" Jacobs started ruffling through a pile of files on his desk. Then he stopped and frowned. He seemed to be distracted by something and appeared to have difficulty collecting his thoughts. There was a whole mess of paperwork spread out on his desk. Amongst the various reports and receipts, Billings spotted a letter from the bailiff. It was addressed to Jacobs personally and it looked like a repossession warning. Could this be the reason for his distraction, he thought.

"The Wild Man of Sutton Courtenay," Jacobs said, pulling himself together and grabbing a file from the stack. "I believe you talked to this… um…" He opened the file and looked through the Berkshire CID's report. "Brendan Lochrane."

"Well, I went to see him in his cell on Friday, but I didn't speak with him. He doesn't talk. He has no tongue."

"So I've read. I thought Clarkson was on duty last Friday."

"We swapped shifts. He was tired."

"Oh yes, that's right. The Russian counterfeiters. Well, as if we didn't already have enough on our plates, our superintendent has now also handed us this." He closed the file and slammed his palm on it. "The murder of Lord Palmer. So what are your thoughts?"

"Thoughts, sir?"

"Well, come, come. You saw that man on Friday. What is the next move?"

"Well, I suppose the first thing we must do is to obtain a positive identification of the suspect."

"I thought he matched the description in the police gazette perfectly."

"Not quite, sir. The Berkshire Constabulary described him as being around six foot three. The suspect I saw is considerably shorter."

"So you want somebody to identify him in person?"

"I think that would be best."

"Like who?"

"Well, I thought perhaps Lord Palmer's wife?"

"Ah yes, Lady Palmer. Well, the thing is, Billings, Lady Palmer has made it quite clear to the Superintendent that she does not wish to set eyes on that vulgar man again. 'Vulgar man' were her words."

"But surely, if she's a witness in a murder investigation..."

"I don't much like aristocrats." Jacobs turned back towards the window. "Do you?"

"What?"

"Like aristocrats?"

"I can't say I've ever met any."

"They're decadent. They're like children who've never grown up."

"I wouldn't know anything about it, sir."

"Well, take it from me, Billings. People who've never known money problems become decadent and spoilt." There was a certain bitterness in his tone. "But crimes involving aristocrats are always passed on to the Yard, because these are people with influence and connections. We must always treat them with delicacy. After all, they run the country and the very existence of the CID lies in their hands. We're still on shaky ground, Billings."

Billings knew exactly what his boss was referring to. It had been thirteen years since the Turf Fraud Scandal, but the Metropolitan Police Force was still struggling to live it down. And the lack of progress they were making on the Whitechapel Ripper case was not aiding their cause.

Jacobs turned back to face the detective. "If Lady Palmer says she doesn't wish to set eyes on that vulgar man again, then we must take that seriously. Perhaps we could show her a photograph instead."

"It is hard to tell a man's size from a photograph. It is the suspect's size that is disputed here."

"We could have him photographed next to you. How tall are you, Billings?"

"With all due respect sir, a ruffled, bearded tramp will look very much like any other in a photograph."

"Not without a tongue, he doesn't."

"Isn't it possible, sir, that there are other beggars out there without a tongue?"

"Possible, Billings, but not very plausible."

"But possible, though?"

There was a short pause. "Oh, I suppose you're right, Billings. It looks like we shall have to inconvenience her ladyship after all." This was followed by a mischievous smile. "Lady Palmer is currently staying with her daughter in London. We could send someone to pick her up. But I warn you, Billings, we must tread carefully here. "

"I shall be respectful with her, sir, as I always am with everyone."

It was a little after two o'clock in the afternoon when Lady Palmer came storming into the room. "Never in all my days... well, which of you is Chief Inspector Jacobs?" She was accompanied by a small, wiry fellow with long ginger hair sticking out of a top hat.

It wasn't customary for civilians to enter the

office unaccompanied by a constable, so Jacobs and Billings were taken aback by their sudden entrance.

"Lady Palmer." Jacobs got up to shake her hand. "I am so sorry about you husband's death."

"Why are you sorry? Did *you* do it?"

"No, I only meant..."

"I know what you meant! And I didn't come here for your sympathy or your condolences. Now, will you please tell me why I was whisked down the stairs by one of your officers and shoved into a cab?"

"Mother, you were neither whisked nor shoved," said the ginger haired man who had a joyful smirk on his face and was apparently relishing the spectacle that was about to unfold.

Jacobs walked towards one of the desks and pulled out a seat. "Lady Palmer, please, will you sit down."

She gave him an angry look before obliging him. She removed her hat, pulled up her bustle and perched herself on the end of the chair. "You may at least offer me a cup of tea!" she demanded.

"Of course. Um... Billings!" Jacobs snapped his fingers at his colleague.

Billings looked up from his desk and pretended to be oblivious. "Sir?" (What was he, the tea boy all of a sudden!)

"Tea for Lady Palmer and uh…"

"Etherbridge," the ginger haired man said. "Arthur Etherbridge. I'm married to Lady Palmer's daughter."

"I shall tell Jack," Billings mumbled and left the room. When he re-entered the office a few minutes later with the tea tray, Lady Palmer was still complaining.

"Questions! Questions! You do nothing but ask questions! I know nothing about that vulgar man. I just want to know when he will be hanged."

"We haven't quite established whether the man we arrested last Saturday really *is* Brendan Lochrane," Jacobs responded. "Or that he is the man who attacked Lord Palmer."

Lady Palmer looked as though she was about to rise up from her seat and fling her hat at him, when Billings intervened and offered her a cup of tea.

"You said Brendan Lochrane was in the employ of your husband," Jacobs continued.

"I said no such thing!"

"Didn't you? I thought…" He flicked through some pages on his lap. "Oh, it was a certain Mr Green. Mr Green told the Berkshire Constabulary…"

"Green is the gardener, Mr Jacobs!" said Etherbridge, laughing. He was standing behind

Lady Palmer. "You had better not start mistaking Lady Palmer for the gardener."

Jacobs ignored Etherbridge's joke and continued questioning Lady Palmer. "In what capacity was Brendan Lochrane employed?"

"Capacity?"

"What did he do?"

"Nothing. He did absolutely nothing."

"Well... then why did Lord Palmer pay him?"

"Brendan Lochrane was what Lord Palmer called an *ornamental hermit*," Etherbridge chipped in. "It was all the fashion a hundred years ago. The idea was to employ someone who would live in the grotto which one of Lord Palmer's ancestors had built on the estate."

"A grotto?"

"A grotto, yes. They constructed it in the woods behind the rock garden. Next to the folly of the old Norman wall which was built around the same time."

"And what was this ornamental hermit supposed to do?"

"Well, he was to do what all hermits do. Fast and pray and atone for our sins. He was supposed to be a spiritual presence on the estate. He was to wear a long white robe, grow his hair and his beard and live on meagre rations of bread, water and lentil soup. He was to add a beautiful aesthetic to the environment. After all, nothing can give more delight to the eye than the spectacle of an aged person with a long grey beard doddering about amongst the discomforts and pleasures of nature. It's a common practice in India. Fakirs and holy men and such. They're held in very high esteem over there."

"Well, it's all very fine and well in India, but we're in England!" added Lady Palmer. "And in England we wear clothes. In England we wash. In England we work for the people on whose land we are permitted to live. I think it's obscene. I haven't set foot in our garden since he moved in. And we have such a lovely garden, Inspector."

"I think, however, that Lord Palmer might have been a bit more discriminating in his choice of hermit," continued Etherbridge. "The hermit was supposed to exhibit wisdom and have an air of sagacity about him. Brendan Lochrane was just far too grumpy and malodorous for that."

Jacobs ignored Etherbridge again and continued questioning Lady Palmer. "Why do you think Lord Palmer was attacked by this man?"

"Why? Well, because he was mad, that's why. He's a lunatic. A raving lunatic."

"Could there perhaps have been a dispute? Over

payment maybe? How much *was* he paid?"

"I do not know how much he was paid. I did not get involved in my husband's ridiculous eccentricities. I wanted absolutely nothing to do with that vulgar man. I told him not to allow that filthy person onto our grounds. And now he's dead. Well, he got what he asked for, as far as I'm concerned."

"You should ask Green about his wages," added Etherbridge. "Green dealt with that sort of thing."

"The gardener?"

"He lived in the garden. He fell under the providence of the gardener."

"Would you recognize him if you saw him again?" Jacobs asked Lady Palmer.

"Of course I would. How couldn't I? He is the most revolting piece of humanity you could ever dread to meet."

"Lady Palmer, we would like you to go down to the holding cells and identify the suspect."

"You want me to do what? Absolutely not!"

"I assure you, you shall be perfectly safe. The suspect is behind bars and Detective Sergeant Billings shall be with you."

"May I remind you, Inspector Jacobs, who is the victim here and who is the criminal."

"We have no criminal yet, Lady Palmer. Not

until he is positively identified by you and found guilty by the courts."

Again Lady Palmer gasped with indignation at being spoken to in such an impertinent manner. Billings was quick to defuse the situation by offering his arm to her and aiding her off her chair. "Don't worry, Lady Palmer," he said. "You shall be in safe hands."

Billings led his two visitors down the dark, hollow cellar. Jack and PC Dwight were standing at the cellar's entrance, rigid against the wall like the Queen's guards, looking on with amusement as Lady Palmer and Etherbridge followed Billings timidly down the steps.

"Why are you leading me into these dungeons, Sergeant Billings?" cried Lady Palmer. Her voice was trembling and her eyes darted around anxiously from wall to wall.

"This is where we have our cells, Lady Palmer."

"It's dark in here. Arthur! Where are you, Arthur?"

"I'm here, mother. Hold my hand." Etherbridge grabbed his mother in law's hand and gazed around him with fascination – and a fair degree of trepidation – at the empty iron bar cells and the moss-covered stone walls which were streaking with rain water.

"Where are you taking us, Sergeant?" Lady Palmer continued. "I do not like it here!"

"It's just at the end of the hall."

"I can't breathe! Arthur, I can't breathe! There's no air!"

"Please, Lady Palmer. It's that cell over there." Billings pointed to the last cell, where Brendan was sitting motionlessly on the cold brick floor, his back towards his visitors, his head hanging low.

"There's somebody in there!" cried Lady Palmer and she suddenly stopped in her tracks, causing Etherbridge to bump into her.

"That's the man we're asking you to identify."

"No! I will not do it! I will not take one more step into the dungeon! Get me out of here!"

"Please, Lady Palmer. Just have one look at that man so you can tell us..."

"No! I want to get out! I want to get out now! Arthur! Get me out of here! Arthur!"

Lady Palmer turned around, pushed past Etherbridge, stormed out of the cellar and marched back upstairs to bombard Jacobs with rants and complaints. Never in her life had she been treated with such contempt. How dare the police subject her to such horrors and indignity. *She* was the victim in all this, didn't he know. She came to the police expecting kindness and compassion and instead she was left in the hands of a lowly upstart (meaning Billings) who took her down to the dungeons to face the very man who murdered her husband and tormented her life. It was tactless and cruel and a deliberate attempt to humiliate her. She had a good mind to write to the Viscount Llandaff, who was a personal acquaintance of hers, and have both Billings and Jacobs sacked.

Etherbridge, who had followed her up the stairs and had quietly been listening to her wails of indignation with a barely concealed smirk, reassured Jacobs shortly before they stepped into their cab that Lady Palmer would soon calm down. Her sudden outbursts, for which she was well known, were always short lived and the whole incident would be forgotten about by the time they got back home.

Jacobs, however, was shaken and would not take any more chances. Lady Palmer was not to be bothered by the police again. The case was to be wrapped up as quickly as possible. After all, Lochrane's guilt was undisputed. All that was needed was for someone to identify him as being the Wild Man and that should prove sufficient for him to be hanged. He would arrange for a photographer to take his picture that very afternoon and Clarkson and Billings were to travel to Sutton House the following morning with the photograph, speak to the gardener and get this whole ugly affair over and done with.

CHAPTER FOUR

Extracts from Sebastian Forrester's diary

Tuesday November 4th, 1879

What follows is an illustration of why I am convinced that I can not learn anything useful in this wretched place!

Mr Crickshaw posed an interesting question today: "A poor man, wretched with ill health, lame and defeated, widowed, homeless and struggling to feed his children, asks you why God continues to make him suffer and never ceases to torment him. How would you reply?"

He wanted us to contemplate this question and then to withdraw into the library and scour the scriptures for an answer (he said 'scriptures', not 'bible'). We were given a full hour to research our answers. We were then summoned back into the lecture room and, one by one, we got up and shared our findings with the class. Most of the students turned to the book of Job and uttered all sorts of nonsense about 'testing faith' and 'unwavering obedience', but not I. When it came to my turn, I stood up, held my little book proudly in my hands (the one I'd found in the library, shoved behind the Greek Grammar Volumes) and read out the following:

"They said of Amma Sarah that for thirteen years she was fiercely attacked by the demon of lust. She never prayed that the battle should leave her, but she used to say only: 'Lord, give me strength'."

Crickshaw fell silent for a few moments and stared at me confused, while the other students frantically paged through their bibles to find the corresponding passage. "It's all about the struggle," I explained. "She doesn't ask for it to end. She just asks for strength to confront it."

Crickshaw was unimpressed and asked me what book I was holding.

"Sayings of the Desert Fathers," I replied.

He asked me where I had found it.

I told him in the library.

"Impossible!" he said. "Wycliffe Hall does not hold copies of that book."

I told him that Wycliffe Hall must at least hold one copy of that book, because I did find it in the library (I was not trying to be impertinent, but my answer made some of the other students chuckle, which further infuriated Crickshaw).

"You were meant to find the answers in the bible," he said.

"Why?" I asked (again, I was not trying to be impertinent, but the other students thought I was deliberately trying to be obtuse and laughed again).

Crickshaw went red with indignation and exclaimed that at Wycliffe Hall we were trained to look at facts! Attested historical and theological facts!

"But this is a fact", I replied. "Amma Sarah was a fifth century nun who dwelt in a cell by the Nile for sixty years and battled all manners of temptations and desires."

Crickshaw then argued that that book was not part of the official Christian canon.

"Does it have to be?" I asked him

"Yes, Mr Forrester, it absolutely has to be!" he replied. And when I asked him why, he held the bible in the air and slammed his palm against it. "Because this is our manual!" he said. "This is our law! This and nothing else! 'Sola Scriptura', Mr Forrester! You'll have heard that phrase before, no doubt? Only these scriptures contain all the knowledge necessary for salvation and holiness. Wycliffe Hall was established to combat the professional ignorance of the majority of

well-meaning but uneducated missionaries working abroad and it is our duty to promote doctrinal truth and vital godliness to any future evangelists." He told me I was to refrain from studying anything else while I stayed at Wycliffe Hall.

I nodded and sat back down, but secretly I slipped the little book into my coat pocket and snuggled it back to my room.

Saturday December 13th, 1879

I found a wonderful wooden Spanish crucifix at a small curiosity shop in St Aldate's today. Nineteen inches tall and wholly impressive, it depicts Christ only a few breaths away from his release, the nails tearing at the skin of his hands; his protruding ribs streaked with whipping scars; his face wrinkled in agony; the blood from his forehead trickling down into his eyes, stinging them and making them water; the red swollen lash marks on his curved back. It is beautiful. It moved me profoundly when I found it standing on the ground, shoved behind a mahogany umbrella stand, covered in cobwebs, lost and discarded. I bought it then and there for seven and six and rushed back to my room immediately to hang it on the wall.

Monday December 15th, 1879

Crickshaw called me into his office after lecture today and asked me to remove the crucifix from my wall.

He said that it was scaring the maid and she was refusing to enter the room. I told him that, in that case, I would clean the room myself, and furthermore, that I did not want other people to enter it without my permission.

Crickshaw stared at me with that wrinkled old frown. "It is not your room, Mr Forrester," he said sternly. "It is the college's room. And why should you not want anyone to enter it? There are no secrets in this house."

I told him that if the sight of Christ's suffering was so frightening to that maid, then she had no business working at Wycliffe Hall.

Crickshaw raised his eyebrows. "You are not going to get very far in Madagascar with that attitude," he said. Then he went on to question why I bought that crucifix in the first place. Weren't Quakers normally opposed to any form of idolatry?

I told him we had no rules on the matter.

"Well, Quakers might not have any rules, Mr Forrester, but Wycliffe Hall does!" he replied. Then he gave me his usual lecture about Wycliffe Hall being primarily an Anglican institution and that an exception had been made by accepting me, a Quaker, due to my father's financial contributions to the school. "But we

must draw the line at allowing Catholic iconography from decorating these walls," he concluded. "That crucifix must go!"

I walked up to the wall quietly and obediently took down the crucifix. I might not agree with the teachings of this place, but I do not want to be expelled. Not yet. Not until I'm ready.

Crickshaw's expression softened after that. "Perhaps if you explain it to her," he said. He was referring to Janie, the maid who had taken objection to the crucifix. "Rather than turning your back on her because she takes offence to your icon, you should show her what Christ's suffering means to you. Show her how Christ's sacrifice has redeemed us. Every emotion is a door for God to enter through, Mr Forrester, and it is your job to facilitate that entrance. We must remain forever alert to this and we must grab every opportunity of bringing the Evangelium to the people."

Sunday March 11th, 1880

Last night was cold and clear and if the clouds hadn't started rolling in this morning, our picnic would've been a great success. But as it was, the sky did darken and, although it did stay dry, the frost on the grass hadn't been given the chance to evaporate. The ground remained moist all day and Janie refused to sit down, *even though I'd brought a blanket. Instead she kept walking up and down the tow path or throwing stones into the river or just generally loitering about being a pest.*

"I thought today were meant to be our day," she kept complaining. "You ain't said a word to me all day."

I argued that we had conversed thoroughly for the whole hour it took us to get to the river, but she said she didn't want to hear about all that 'morbid Jesus stuff'. She wanted to hear me talk sweet to her.

"Well, you should have said something," I said, but she looked at me offended and told me she couldn't get a word in. I told her that I wanted to read my book now, so could she please be quiet for an hour or so and allow me to concentrate?

"And what I am meant to do during that time?" she asked.

I suggested she go for a walk.

"But I don't want to go for a walk. I want to fool around with you."

I said we could fool around later.

"But I want to fool around with you now. We only get one day in the week together. Why can't we fool around all day?"

I told her that I wanted to read my book now and begged her once again to go and leave me alone.

"I thought you weren't meant to study on the

Sabbath," she said.

I told her I was not studying but at that point she lunged herself at me and tried to wrestle the book out of my hands. I simply pushed her off me, turned my back towards her and continued reading. She puller her knees up to her breast and remained sitting next to me on the wet ground, sulking. "Your arse is getting wet!" she said. (I adore the way she says 'arse', with that country accent of hers. Pronouncing the 'r' so clearly.)

"My arse is not getting wet," I said, mimicking her accent.

"It is, look." And then she started sliding her hand under my bottom. "You're all wet down there." She put her other hand on my crotch and started feeling around. "You're gonna need me to dry you up, so you are."

I grabbed her hands from underneath me and cast them aside. "Not now, Janie." I said. "We'll fool around later, but right now I have to read."

"But you read all week." She jumped to her feet and started brushing down her dress. "You've got to give your eyes a rest, Sebastian, or you'll go blind."

I tried explaining to her that I read different books during the week. Books I didn't care about. Books that didn't teach me anything. 'Sayings' was the only book that I could learn something from and all I was asking from her was to give me one hour in the week, just one hour, where I could sit quietly alone and enlighten myself. I begged her gently to go to those fields behind us to see if she could find a dry shed somewhere. I promised her we'd fool around then.

"You're starting to bore me, you know that, Sebastian Forrester?" she said. "If you don't start showing me a bit of attention, I'm going to start looking for a different student to fool around with!"

After she had gone, I remained sitting on the cold ground for well over an hour. The cold air had seeped right through my clothes and I was shivering uncontrollably. My hands were red and sore and my fingers were barely able to turn the pages (and my arse was wet, despite the blanket). And yet I wish I could have remained sitting there all day, quiet and upright, moving only to blink or turn the page, and battle the pain and discomforts my body was subjected to with the aid of my book. Oh, how I would have liked to have been amongst them, in the deserts of Egypt, removed from the world, fighting all the temptations and numbing distractions of this world with abstinence, prayer and pain. These men and women had the strength to turn their backs on the world and all its pressures and dedicate themselves selfishly to disciplining their souls and their bodies so that they could take on the sins of the world and redeem us all through their sweat, blood and tears. But I knew Janie was waiting for me, so I got up, put my book back into my coat pocket, folded the blanket *around my arm and headed for the fields to look for her.*

I found her at the abandoned shed near Iffley lock, squatting on the ground, leaning against the wall.

"Hurry up with that blanket," she called. "I ain't lying down on the cold floor."

I threw the blanket at her, took the leather straps from my trouser pocket and proceeded to remove my coat, jacket and shirt. Her face turned sour as she saw me pull the leather belt from my overcoat. "Oh, we're not doing that again, are we?" she complained.

Throwing the belt at her, I told her to use the buckle side this time. Stripped from the waist up, I entered the shed and tied my hands to the cross beam. I heard Janie shuffle in behind me. "Can't we just lie on the floor and fool around?" she said.

"Afterwards," I told her.

"But I don't want to, Seb. You've still got scars from last time."

"Come on, Just fifty lashes."

"No!"

"Twenty-five, then."

"No!"

"Twenty."

"None!"

"Come on, Janie. We'll fool around afterwards."

"But why?"

"I told you why."

"But I don't understand."

"No pleasure without pain, Janie. Now, come on."

Janie gave me twenty lashes. They weren't very hard, but the belt buckle broke my skin after the fifth one and each consecutive lash landed on the open wound, hitting the raw nerve so that I felt the pain right down to my toes. I am unable to recline in my bed now as I write this. The Desert Fathers would use these tortures to beat the demons of lust out of them, but with me they had the opposite effect. The pain just made me randier. Janie and I spent another hour in that shed rolling and frolicking around on the ground so that now the blood of my back has stained her underclothes and she shall have to wash them secretly or burn them, lest her mother should find out. I did it all wrong. There should have been no reward. Pain without pleasure. I must remember that. 'Live as though crucified; in struggle, in lowliness of spirit, in good will and spiritual abstinence, in fasting, in penitence, in weeping.'

CHAPTER FIVE

The Murder at Sutton House

"'Ere, Billings! 'Ow long 'ave we been travellin'?"

Clarkson was staring out the train window. Billings sat opposite him, holding a novel in front of his face. He refused to take his eyes off the book as he mumbled: I don't know."

"We must've been in the train for ages. Are we nearly there yet?"

"I don't know, Clarkson. I'm reading."

Clarkson curled up his lip and tutted. "You're always bloomin' reading when I'm trying to chat to you! Anyone ever tell you you're an unsociable bastard?"

Billings ignored him. He was too engrossed in his book to allow himself to be distracted. He was going through Sebastian's diary and he felt both fascinated and repulsed by what he read. Sebastian was a lazy diarist. He didn't write every day and some days he just summed up with a single word: *'boring'*, *'miserable'* or *'torturous'*. But there were a few entries which surprised and intrigued Billings and which shed light on Sebastian's frame of mind.

Billings was surprised at how little he actually knew about Sebastian. He had always thought of him as a glorious young titan, but there was something very rebellious and conflicted about him. He was full of contradictions and profound passions. Where do such passions come from, Billings wondered. He had never had such passions. He had only ever had anxieties.

Billings closed the book and turned towards the window. Memories of Sebastian flooded his mind. He never had been able to read that boy. Sebastian could be charming and friendly one minute but then, quite unexpectedly, his mood would turn and he'd become cruel and aloof. Billings only ever saw him in-between school terms. Sebastian went to Rugby. The best school in England. But there was no money to send Billings there too. He was forced stay at home – or rather, Mr and Mrs Forrester's home (he could never call that cold Chelsea house his home). Billings didn't go to school at all. Instead Mr and Mrs Forrester took it upon themselves to educate him. Mr Forrester would teach him history and literature, whereas Mrs Forrester would try to improve his writing. And on Sundays, a Quaker school master would stay on at the meeting house to teach French and algebra to whomever wanted to improve their minds. It had been an adequate, albeit patchy education. But it had also been a solitary youth. Billings always wondered whether it was this lack of interaction with other boys which had made him so morose and unsociable.

He always used to look forward to Sebastian's homecoming. That Chelsea house was so hollow and empty without him. He would mark the term end dates on his calendar and count the days. Sebastian was usually restless, grumpy and subdued when he was at home, and he'd take his frustrations out on Billings. He'd say things like: "Didn't they teach you anything out there in the bush, you little numbskull?" or "Look away, ward. I'm not your brother!" But still he'd miss him when he was not there. He'd miss his deep quiet voice, his lovely melancholy eyes or the beautiful sight of his straight strong torso. He suddenly remembered how he'd spent nights sitting alone on his bed with his ear against the wall, secretly listening to Sebastian bathe in the next room, splashing about in the tub, listening to the water trickle down his naked skin and he would feel the blood rush to his head... and to his loins. Yes, he did have strong feelings once. Perhaps he still did. He had just buried them deep inside him. Silenced and pacified them so effectively with morphine and work that he simply forgot about them.

"I don't know 'ow you do it," Clarkson said suddenly.

This shook Billings out of his reverie and he finally turned towards his companion. "Do what?" he asked, putting the diary away in his satchel.

"'Ow can you be on your own all the time?" Clarkson continued. "We've only been away for a couple of hours and I'm already missing the rib. In nine years of marriage I never spent a single night away from her. Never! D'you believe that?"

Billings smiled politely.

"When *you* gonna find yourself a girl?"

"Never." Billings started ruffling through his satchel for Robinson Crusoe. He was not prepared to have this conversation.

"Why do you do it, Billings? Why you on your own all the time?"

"I don't know," he said, grabbing his book and opening it.

"You're not that young anymore, you know? You really ought to start looking around for someone to settle down with. 'Ow old are you now anyway? Forty?"

"Twenty-eight."

"Bloomin' 'eck, really? Hard life, was it?"

Billings ignored him and started reading.

"'Ow come you've always got your conk buried in a book when I try to talk to you?"

There was something about Clarkson's tone that made Billings look up from his book. Clarkson was frowning at him with a hurt expression in his eyes. "Have you got something against me, or what?" he asked.

Damn it! thought Billings. I really must try to be more sociable. "I'm sorry, Clarkson," he said, forcing a smile to his mouth.

"I'm a better copper than you think I am. You got no cause to ignore me."

"I'm not ignoring you. I'm just not used to company, that's all."

"I was born into the police force, I was."

"Were you?"

"My father was the chief inspector of the W Division. You didn't know that, did ya?"

"No."

"Pup of the truncheon, me."

Billings smiled. *'Pup of the truncheon.'* There was a certain rough charm about Clarkson. He wondered why he had never seen it before.

A ruddy-faced young man approached Billings and Clarkson as they stepped off the train. "Inspector Billings?" the man asked.

"Actually, it's detective sergeant," Billings corrected him. He shook the man's hand.

"How do you do. D.S. Ferguson is the name. Are these your bags?" and without waiting for an answer, he grabbed a bag in each arm and marched off towards the exit.

Clarkson looked on alarmed. "'Ere, hang about!" He marched after him.

"The police station is just up the road in Bridge Street," the man called out. "Follow me." He trotted down the platform with the cases, never stopping, never even looking back, his two little legs striding manically beneath him like an upturned beetle. Billings and Clarkson desperately tried to keep up.

"Bloomin' 'eck! Do something about that bloke, will you Billings?" Clarkson huffed, sweat beads trickling down his face. "He's running around like a dog with a banger up its arse!"

Billings had taken a small dose of morphine early that morning. He felt he needed something to help him cope with the long journey and Clarkson's oppressive company. To compensate he deliberately left his ampoules and his syringe at home, even though he knew he would probably not be back before midnight. But now he began to feel nauseated as they chased the local policeman out of the station and regretted that decision.

D.S. Ferguson led his visitors to the police station, where D.I. Northover awaited them.

"Ah, here they are!" the inspector said as Billings and Clarkson stepped into his office. "Our men from the Yard." There was a broad smile on his face as he got up from his desk and walked towards his visitors. He wore a smart suit. His cuff links had been polished and they glistened in the light of the window.

"This is Detective Sergeant Billings," said Ferguson, "and this is Detective Constable Clarkson."

The expression on Northover's face suddenly changed. "A sergeant and a constable?" he asked, raising his eyebrow.

"Yes, sir," replied Billings. "We've brought a photograph of the man we arrested two days ago. We are hoping to obtain a positive identification." He walked towards Northover's desk, rested his satchel on it and proceeded to take out the photograph.

"Are *you* in charge of this investigation, Detective Sergeant Billings?" Northover asked.

"No, sir. The investigation is coordinated by Chief Inspector Jacobs at our end."

"And where is Chief Inspector Jacobs?" Northover looked around him for the missing man.

"He's in London, sir."

"In London?"

"Yes, sir. He sent me and Clarkson to speak to you."

"Too busy, I suppose, to come down himself?"

Billings suddenly became aware of the disappointment in the Inspector's tone. "We always are at Scotland Yard, sir."

"You always are at Scotland Yard," DI Northover repeated bitterly. "Well, we have been very busy ourselves, haven't we, Ferguson? I'm sure cold-blooded murders are commonplace in London and you deal with them as a matter of routine, which must be why Scotland Yard deemed it adequate to send a 'sergeant' and a 'constable' to assist us." He uttered the words 'sergeant' and 'constable' with barely concealed disdain. "But we haven't had a calamity like this since the riot at St Marks Abbey in 1183 and we have been working tirelessly day and night to apprehend the culprit. Isn't that right, Ferguson?"

"That's right, sir."

"Ferguson will take you to Sutton House later so you can meet Bertie Green. In the meantime, here is the file on our progress so far." He picked a file up from his desk and held it out to Ferguson. "Ferguson will take you through it."

Ferguson looked at his boss, confused. "You want *me* to brief them, sir?"

"You brief them, Ferguson." He pushed the file into the sergeant's hands. "I have other things to attend to." And he walked out of the office, clearly feeling himself to be above having to a brief a 'sergeant' and a 'constable'. Even if they were from Scotland Yard.

"Well," said Ferguson, a little flustered at the turn of events.

"Was it something we said?" Clarkson asked with a bemused expression on his face.

Ferguson ignored the comment and opened the file. "So… the facts." He leafed through the report. "Lord Palmer's body was found on the 21st of October at around eight in the morning by Bertie Green, the gardener of Sutton House. The body was lying face down in the earth with an axe sticking out of the shoulder blades. Green was in the outhouse when the murder occurred and had heard Lord Palmer cry out for him, but he was in no position to rush to his aid." He read from the file. "*'It were a sit down visit,'* according to Green, *'me breeches were wrapped around me ankles and I was halfway through completing my purpose. With all the will in the world, I were in no position to jump up and rush to his lordship's help.'*" Ferguson paused and smiled as he read the quote. Billings and Clarkson laughed along with him.

"Why was Lord Palmer calling out for him?" Billings asked.

Fergusson cast his eyes back on the file and continued reading. "*'Green, bring me my shotgun. I have a gypsy parasite here.'* That's what the gardener heard Lord Palmer cry out."

"Gypsy parasite?" Billings asked.

"That's what the gardener said. When he finally concluded his business in the outhouse, he rushed to the woods and found Lord Palmer lying dead on the ground in the manner I just described. It turns out that Lord Palmer was on his way to the horse fair in Abingdon and had decided to take a short cut through the woods. According to Lady Palmer, he was looking to buy a new horse and had put three five-pound bank notes in the inside pocket of his coat. The bank notes were not there when he was found. Also missing was a gold cameo ring with a picture of a Greek warrior and a gold watch engraved with two date palms."

"So what makes you think it was Brendan Lochrane who killed him?" Billings asked.

"Well, Lord Palmer's body was found just outside Lochrane's grotto, it was Lochrane's hatchet which was used in the attack and the man himself disappeared shortly afterwards. As far as we're concerned that's enough to make him a suspect."

"What about the gypsy parasite?"

"Well, that threw us too at first. There were some gypsies here at the time, who'd come down to the horse fair from Somerset to sell a horse. There were four of them. They camped in a field on the south bank of the Thames. We interviewed each one of them, but they all had an alibi in Isiah Frodsham who owns the field and who confirmed that they never left it. You'll find the report of the interviews in this file. According to Green, Lord Palmer called everyone a gypsy. He used the word as an insult and was in the habit of yelling 'gypsy' at anyone who displeased him. This is also confirmed by Lady Palmer. Nobody else was spotted on the terrain at the time of the murder. That makes Lochrane our only suspect. Now, I believe you have a picture of him."

"We do."

"Well, then I suggest we make our way to Sutton Courtenay so you can speak to Green yourself. I have three bicycles parked outside. I take it you both ride?"

Ferguson led his two visitors over the Thames Bridge, past some dew-covered hay fields towards Sutton House, just outside the pretty village of Sutton Courtenay.

"It'll only take twenty minutes if we pedal fast," he called to the others, who were struggling to keep up.

"Mate, what's the bloomin' rush?" cried Clarkson, but Ferguson ignored him and sped off.

As they entered the village, Ferguson pointed towards a charming 17th century farmhouse, surrounded by 100 acres of land, most of which was wooded.

"That's it, over there," he said and he turned into the drive.

Billings and Clarkson followed him. As they approached the house, Billings saw Bertie Green waiting for them at the garden gate. He was leaning against the wall, his arms crossed over his chest, chewing on a reed. He was around sixty years old, with a red, weather-beaten face and thin grey hair sticking out from beneath his cap.

There was a patch of frost on the drive and as the policemen turned into it, Clarkson slipped and fell over.

Ferguson and Billings quickly jumped off their bicycles and rushed to Clarkson's aid, but Bertie Green didn't move a muscle. He remained leaning against the wall, looking at the visitors.

"That be them then, be it?" he asked. "Detectives from London?"

"This is Detective Sergeant Billings," said Fergusson. "And this is... um..."

"Clarkson." the constable replied, dusting himself off and picking his bicycle up from the ground. "Detective Constable Clarkson."

"Found our Brendan, then did 'ee?" Green asked.

Billings replied. "Well, we found a man that fits his description, but whether it's Brendan Lochrane, that's what we're here to find out. I wonder if you could..." He ruffled in his satchel for the photograph and held it out to the gardener. "Could you please take a look at this."

Green glanced quickly at the picture without taking it from Billings. "Oh, arr. That be him, alright."

"Are you sure? Look again, please. Take your time."

"That be him, Sergeant." He hadn't bothered to

take another look. "That be our Brendan. Made it all the way to London, then, did he? How did he get there? I thought you fellas had all the roads blocked."

"We assume he must've taken the river," Fergusson replied.

Billings was still holding the photograph in his hand. "How tall would you say Brendan Lochrane was?" he asked the gardener.

"He'd be 'bout five foot seven, I'd think."

"Not six foot three?"

"Oh no, not six foot."

"Because the local police described him as being six foot three."

"Local police?" He looked at Ferguson. "Is that 'ee, Tomas?"

"The height on the description was an estimate based on Lady Palmer's accounts," said Ferguson.

"But he weren't six foot, Tomas."

"Lady Palmer described him as being tall and imposing."

"He were imposing, alright, but he weren't six foot, Tomas."

"Well, that's it, then, ain't it?" said Clarkson. "We can go back 'ome now, can't we?" And without waiting for an answer, he grabbed his bicycle and started climbing on it.

Billings hesitated. "Would you object if I took a stroll around the grounds?" he asked Green.

Clarkson pulled a face like a sulking child. "Oh Billings, come on! There's no need for that. Let's go back to Abingdon. Have ourselves a couple of drinks, before we go back 'ome."

"You go on ahead. I just want to have a look around on my own."

Clarkson dropped the bicycle angrily on the ground. "I'll wait for you here," he yelled. "But hurry up. My knee needs attending to."

The lawn of Sutton House bordered the woods. A small brook separated the genteel garden from the dark forest beyond it. Billings and Green crossed a small bridge onto a path which led them to Brendan's grotto, hidden amongst the trees. It wasn't a real cave. Rather, it was a small, windowless stone hut built against a mound, under the roots of a tall birch. Grass grew over the roof, making it look more like a badger's den than a cave.

"This is it, Sergeant," said Green, stopping at the grotto's entrance. "This be our Brendan's home."

The grotto was dark and damp. As Billings approached the entrance to peer inside it, a large moth (or was it a bat?) fluttered out of the cave and made him jump.

Green laughed. "This cave's always been popular with animals," he said. He picked up a lantern from inside the cave and lit it. As the cave became illuminated, Billings could make out a wooden bed tucked in a corner and a brazier beside it. Animal hides were scattered on the dust floor. A small copper pot was used for heating water.

"Not a very jolly home, is it, Sergeant?" Green said.

Billings looked around him at the pitiful surroundings. "How did Brendan get to be employed by Lord Palmer?"

"Well, he just replied to the advertisement Lord Palmer placed in the Abingdon Herald."

"For what position?"

"Lord Palmer were looking for a hermit to live in these woods. Arr, that's right. You heard correctly, a hermit. Apparently this whole area which lies between Boars Hill and the river Thames were holy once. All to do with a certain St Aebbe, some northern princess who introduced Christianity to the Saxons. Lord Palmer told me all about her. A shrine were built to her on Boars Hill, or perhaps it were Cumnor Hill. Anyway it were some hill north of here, and they called it Aebbeduna – that's Aebbe's Hill in the old Saxon language – which is where the name Abingdon comes from. Hermits would come to live on the hill in medieval times, and I guess Lord Palmer thought it'd be funny to recreate that. People with money have different kinds of interests than us ordinary folks."

"Yes. They do."

"I recognized Brendan when he showed up for the interview. I'd seen him in these woods before. Came here to poach, I think. We get a lot of poachers around here. I even shot at him once or twice."

"Shot at Brendan?"

"Oh, not to hit him. Just to chase him away. Anyway, I never said nothing about it to Lord Palmer. Poor man meant no harm, he were only doing what he had to survive."

"How much did Lord Palmer offer him?"

"Three shillings a week for a whole year. For that Brendan was offered shelter and a robe to clothe himself with, and sandals for his feet. And he'd have water and bread, and perhaps a few other things to make soup with, but no meat. And he gave him a staff, coz a hermit must have a staff, and he told him not to shave or cut his hair or his fingernails. And if he completed his twelvemonth there'd be a hundred pound bonus."

"Where did Brendan come from?"

"Scotland, I think."

"Why do you think Scotland?"

"Well, there were a woman up in Scotland he'd write to. I used to post his letters for him."

"A woman?"

"Arr, a woman. Lorna Lochrane. He'd address the letters care of to the post office in Whithorn, Wigtownshire. He only wrote to her a couple of times. He weren't allowed to write, of course, but I smuggled in some paper and some ink after he'd signalled me for them."

Billings took his notepad and pencil out of his satchel and started making notes. His hand trembled as he did so.

Green saw this. "Is it too cold for 'ee here, Sergeant?" he asked.

"No, no, it's nothing, I..."

"Come on in. I got something here that'll warm you up."

Green crouched down and entered the grotto. Billings hesitated and looked at the numerous cobwebs which clung to the corners of the doorway and the dead moths trapped in them.

"Come on in," Green said. He pulled the bed away from the stone wall. Behind the bed there was a small hole in the wall and Green pulled out a dusty old bottle and two tin cups. "Gin," he said, proudly holding the bottle up in one hand and the cups in the other. "Sit down and I'll pour 'ee a cup."

Billings entered reluctantly and sat down on the filthy bed.

"I got it for him," Green said, pouring the drinks. "Smuggled it in for him. He weren't allowed no liquor, of course, but he looked so downright miserable, the poor bugger, I thought he needed something to lighten his spirit. And this stuff warms you up like nothing else can. He liked his gin, so he did. He went through four bottles a week. Here 'ee goes." He handed Billings his cup. "Put that down yer. Cheers!" He downed his gin in one go then refilled his cup.

"Did you spend many nights in here chatting and drinking with Brendan?"

"How could I have chatted with him? He had no tongue."

"Of course, I don't know why I...."

"I'd have done it, though. If I could. I'd have sat here with the poor feller and I'd have chatted with him all night. He were a sensitive feller. Even if he did look like a wild man in them dirty rags and that dirty, tangled hair. Although he did smell. I don't know whether 'ee's noticed that?"

"Yes, I have."

"He had a real problem with his odour. And it weren't that he didn't wash. He washed regularly. I saw him do it. Washed himself and washed his clothes. But the smell remained and it were very hard to be close to be him. So I never did speak to him. Why, he'd already been living here for six weeks before I noticed that he had no tongue. Six weeks, can 'ee imagine? I used to bring him his bread, see, and he'd take it from me and then he'd chew on it, and chew and chew, like a bloomin' cow. It were a peculiar way of eating, but I never thought nothing of it until one day he nearly choked. He were coughing and gagging and I ran into the shed and slapped him on his back and then he opened his mouth and tried putting his fingers down his throat to get to the little morsel, and that's when I saw it. I were shocked. 'You have no tongue!' I cried. Then he looked at me angrily and turned away and refused to look at me again for days. I never did discover what happened to his tongue. Does 'ee know, Sergeant?"

"No, I don't."

"Oh, he were a sensitive soul, all right. All he wanted was to be left in peace, but in the beginning, Lord Palmer would invite the locals to his estate, so they could look at the hermit. They came from all over the place. Abingdon, Appleford,

Culham, even Didcot. All came down to stare at the 'Wild Man' as they called him. Lord Palmer would make Brendan get out of the shed every week and walk up to the garden in his robe and staff so the people could see him. They'd gawk at him. And laugh at him. And shout obscenities at him. And sometimes they'd even throw rotting food at him. It were a real freak show. There weren't nothing holy or dignified about it."

"Do you think that is why he attacked Lord Palmer? Because of the humiliation?"

"Oh, that only lasted for the first few weeks. The novelty wore off pretty soon and the people stopped coming. Brendan were left on his own for most of the time after that. Especially as Lord Palmer started spending more time in London. Probably on account of her ladyship being frightened and disgusted by Brendan. Brendan went about his business then. Chopping blocks for the house or collecting tinder for himself. Are we done with this?" He held up the gin bottle. Billings nodded. He placed the cork back on the bottle and replaced it in the hole. But then suddenly he stopped. "I don't suppose there's much point in hiding this now, is there? He's not coming back, is he?"

"No, I suppose he isn't."

"You got him holed up in a prison cell now, have you?"

"He's in a holding cell."

"Waiting to be hanged?"

"If he's found guilty."

"Why do you say if? Does 'ee think he's not?"

"Do *you*?"

"Well, I don't know who else could have killed his lordship. It were his axe. "

"Couldn't somebody else have taken his axe and attacked Lord Palmer with it?"

"Like who?

"Well... somebody who intended to rob him. I understand there was some money missing. And a ring and a watch."

"Oh arr. He'd been robbed, alright."

"Well, then perhaps somebody else took the axe. You did say you get a lot of poachers around here."

"Arr, that we do, but we ain't had any lately."

"So then, in theory, Lord Palmer could have been killed by someone else."

"That's what 'ee said before, Sergeant. But I asked 'ee by who?"

"Who was staying in the house on the day of the murder?"

"Just the Lord, the Lady and the servants. Oh and Mr Percy had been staying at the house for a couple of days, but he left the night before the killing."

"Who is Mr Percy?"

"He were some young scholar from Oxford who'd come to study the hermit. He came here often to talk to Lord Palmer. His lordship were very interested in history, as I mentioned, and liked having Mr Percy around."

"Did you mention Mr Percy to the local police?"

"No reason to. Why? Does 'ee think Mr Percy killed Lord Palmer?"

"Do you?"

"Mr Percy left the night before the killing. I told 'ee that already."

"What time did he leave?"

"Eleven, twelve, something like that. Lord Palmer were killed at eight in the morning. You don't think Mr Percy would linger in these woods all that time, does 'ee? Just to kill Lord Palmer for fifteen pounds, a watch and a gold ring?"

Billings frowned. It didn't sound plausible, but yet, the scholar intrigued him.

"If my calculations are correct," Billings asked, "Brendan had been living on the estate for eleven months when the murder occurred?"

"Arr, that's right. He came here in January, left in November."

"So he was only one month away from claiming his reward, when Lord Palmer died?"

"That's right."

"It doesn't seem reasonable then, does it, that he should kill Lord Palmer for a watch and a ring, if he was only one month away from getting a hundred pounds?"

"No, it don't, Sergeant. It don't seem reasonable at all. But then it never is reasonable, is it? When one man murders another? I think 'ee'll find it's a lack of reasoning that causes such a thing to happen in the first place."

Billings and Clarkson were back on the train to London. It was only three o'clock, but Billings was already feeling unwell. The trembling had started. He had to sit on his hands or keep them in his pocket so as not to expose his condition to Clarkson. Reading Robinson Crusoe was out of the question, he wouldn't have been able to hold up his book. All he could do to avoid Clarkson's incessant chatter was to feign sleep (real sleep was impossible with a pounding heart and recurring nausea). He sat sideways on the bench, leaning against the window with his legs curled up and his hat tipped over his eyes.

But this did not deter Clarkson. He was

completely oblivious to Billings's state of mind and chatted continuously. First about his wife's cooking and the meal that lay waiting for him when he got home; then about how he preferred the dirty, crowded metropolis to the scary open spaces of the countryside; and finally about how he would write his report in pencil when he got back to the office and rewrite it in ink the following morning, as he was more likely to make spelling mistakes when he was tired.

Billings didn't listen. He spent the whole journey calculating how long it would be before he would feel that warm flush of calmness rush through his veins again. It would take another four hours before they arrived in London. It would take another forty-five minutes to get from the station to Scotland Yard. Then there'd be another two hours of debriefing and writing reports before he'd finally be able to go back home. He wouldn't be there before midnight. Oh, how he regretted leaving his morphine at home.

It was seven o'clock when they finally got off the train in London and they made their way to Scotland Yard on foot. Billings made sure to keep a couple of steps behind Clarkson, who still had no notion of the agony he was going through. He clenched his fists tightly inside his coat pocket to disguise the trembling, but the cramps in his stomach were harder to disguise. He had to grind his teeth each time his guts knotted up and he could feel sweat beads trickling down his head.

He was lucky the streets were so dark, but what was he to say when they entered the gaslit office and his current state of malaise was revealed? He was desperately trying to think of an excuse. Could he say it was food poisoning and blame the meal they'd had at the Railway Inn? What did Clarkson eat? Did Clarkson have the same as him? Billings had had stew, but what could he say was in that stew that explained his symptoms?

When they entered the building, Billings rushed to the lavatory while Clarkson ascended the stairs.

"'Ere, where you going?" Clarkson called. "Jacobs is waiting for a debrief."

"I need to spend a penny. You start without me."

He went into the lavatory, splashed some water on his face and looked at himself in the mirror. His face was pale and there were dark rings under his eyes. He was feeling nauseous again, but not nauseous enough to throw up. He wondered whether he should slip into a cubicle, stick a finger down his throat and get all it over and done with. But no, that wouldn't do. The noise would give him away. He took a deep breath, wiped the sweat off his forehead, straightened his collar and tucked in his shirt. Two more hours, he kept thinking to himself. Just two more hours.

He approached the telegrapher before going upstairs.

"I need you to send a telegram to the Wigtownshire Constabulary," he said, fumbling through his satchel for his notebook. At that moment the cramps started again, more severe this time, and he almost doubled over with pain.

"Are you all right, Sergeant?" the telegrapher asked, getting up from his stool and signalling to one of the constables for help.

"I'm fine, I'm fine." Billings took the notebook out of his satchel and ripped off the page with the name he had jotted on it. "Lorna Lochrane in Whithorn. Tell them to find her and ask her to tell them all about Brendan."

"What shall I say it's pertaining to?"

"Tell them it's to do with the Lord Palmer case. It seems the Wild Man has a wife." He took another deep breath, wiped his face with his sleeve, re-tucked his shirt into his trousers and made his way upstairs.

As he arrived at the he saw Clarkson and Jacobs sitting at their desks, looking at him. "It was all for nothing," Clarkson said.

"What do you mean?"

"He confessed. Do you believe it? While we were out there in the sticks, the bloomin' bugger confessed!"

"He confessed?"

"I talked to him while you were gone," Jacobs said. "I asked him if he killed Lord Palmer, and he nodded a clear and undeniable 'yes'."

"It can't be!" Billings broke out in sweat again. "It must've been a nervous tick."

"It was a nod, Billings. I asked him twice, and twice he nodded. Are you alright? You don't look at all well, old man."

Billings felt the sweat trickling down his face. "I'm alright," he said, wiping his forehead with his sleeve. "Where is he now? I want to talk to him."

"He's been transferred to Newgate Prison. Are you sure you're all right? You look ill."

"I'm not ill. I must talk to him, sir. Tomorrow. He is not guilty. There must've been a misunderstanding."

"There was no misunderstanding, Billings. The case is closed."

"But it can't be. He's innocent."

"How do you know?"

"I have an instinct. He can't have done it."

"Then why did he confess?"

"To put an end to it all. Please sir, you must let me speak to him. A grave injustice is about to be done."

"Do sit down, old man. You're clearly not well. Get him some water, will you, Clarkson?"

Billings sat down and put his head between his knees. The shaking had become uncontrollable and his heart was pounding in his chest.

Jacobs squatted down before him and looked him in the eyes. "What's the matter, Billings?" he asked.

"It's nothing, sir. Just something I ate."

"What on earth did you eat?"

"Fish stew. The fish must've gone bad. Please, sir. Lochrane is innocent. He had nothing to gain by killing Lord Palmer. In fact he had everything to lose. He was only one month away from completing his contract and receiving his reward."

Jacobs stood back up and returned to his desk. "The case is closed, Billings." There was a tone of irritation in his voice. "There are no other suspects and he confessed. We already have our hands full with the Whitechapel murders. We are already under constant scrutiny from the press and we don't want that. Which brings me to another point." He looked at Billings again, sitting on the chair, soaked in sweat and shaking like a jellyfish.

"But perhaps that can wait until tomorrow."

"What is it?" Billings asked.

"There's an article about you in The Illustrated Police News."

"About me?"

"A despicable article by a certain Jeremiah Rook. He really seems to have it in for you."

"Why?"

"Apparently you told him you felt sympathy for Lochrane. He has spun the whole thing to show that the CID is too soft and filled with bleeding heart do-gooders who sympathize with criminals. It's all tosh, of course, and I shall certainly write a complaint to the editor. These kind of personal attacks on individual members of the police force are reprehensible and completely unacceptable. But in your case he does have a point. You're a good detective, Billings, but you do have a tendency to take things to heart. Lochrane being a case in point."

Clarkson re-entered the office with a glass of water and handed it to Billings.

"We had better get you a cab to take you back home," said Jacobs. "Get yourself to bed and take the day off tomorrow. Don't come back until you're better."

"What about my report?" Billings asked.

"Clarkson will write it."

"But Clarkson didn't speak to Bertie Green."

"Clarkson will write it!" Jacobs repeated sternly.

CHAPTER SIX

The Mysterious Scholar

It was seven o' clock in the morning. Billings got out of bed, splashed some water on his face, got dressed and headed out of the house. He'd taken the day off, as Jacobs suggested. That blasted tendency of his to take things to heart had reared its ugly head again. He'd been tossing and turning all night, pondering and speculating about Lochrane's confession. Why did Lochrane's plight affect him so? It was the thought of him sitting alone in that cold, damp cave which had impressed him. All his romantic notions of nature and solitude which the tales of Robinson Crusoe had implanted in him had vanished. It was a harsh, lonely life which Lochrane had led – and was still leading – having swapped a cold stone cave for a cold brick cell. All he could think of was that lost and desperate look in Lochrane's eyes. There was a gentleness hidden there behind that rough, weather-beaten face and the dirty beard. A beautiful and melancholy look which somehow felt familiar. Were there echoes there of his own loneliness? Could *he* end up like that if he let his addiction and moodiness get out of control? Was Lochrane a cautionary tale?

Billings stepped out of the house, crossed Chelsea Bridge and made his way towards Hyde Park. Even at this hour, the city was bustling with cabs and omnibuses and commuters and costermongers. He kept thinking about the case. He couldn't let it go. It didn't make any sense. Why would Lochrane subject himself to months of hardship and humiliation then snap only one month before completing his contract and receiving his reward? He couldn't help but think that the Berkshire Constabulary hadn't been thorough enough in their investigation. If only he'd had more time to go through their reports. He remained unconvinced by D.S. Ferguson's explanation as to why Lord Palmer had called his assailant a gypsy parasite. The gypsies had only been interviewed once. Anyone with sufficient money could buy themselves an alibi. And what about Mr Percy?

Nobody had mentioned him to the Berkshire Constabulary so they had no chance to investigate any possible links. There was something about this mysterious scholar which intrigued him. A young man from Oxford studying hermits. Could he know anything about Sebastian Forrester? Could these two cases be linked?

The Etherbridges lived in a smart leafy square in Mayfair. Billings was met by suspicious glances as he entered the square. Nannies pushing perambulators in the park, housemaids dusting carpets at the windows, gardeners sweeping fallen leaves from the doorsteps, all of them glared with distrust and curiosity as he made his way towards the Etherbridge house. But he ignored them. He climbed the steps and rang the bell.

The door was opened by the housekeeper. She scanned Billings up and down before speaking. "Yes?"

"My name is Detective Sergeant John Billings from the Metropolitan Police. I'd like to speak to Lady Palmer."

"Lady Palmer is not receiving visitors."

"I'm afraid I must insist."

"Insist what you like, sonny, but I am under

strict instructions not to disturb her."

Billings was taken aback by the woman's rudeness. Had she not understood him correctly? "I'm *Detective Sergeant* Billings," he repeated, "from the Metropolitan Police. I need to speak to Lady Palmer about the investigation into her husband's death."

"Yes, I heard you the first time. And as I understand it, Lady Palmer has spoken to the police already. Several times, in fact. I am sure that Lady Palmer can not possibly have anything more to say on the topic."

The housekeeper was about the close the door on Billings, but he blocked it with his foot.

"I don't really need your permission to enter, miss… um…"

"Don't you 'miss' me, mister! My name is Hynge. *Mrs* Hynge. And I will not let you in without a search warrant."

Billings frowned. He hated the way popular publications like The Illustrated Police News had given the public inaccurate information about police procedure.

"I do not need a search warrant, Mrs Hynge. I only want to speak to Lady Palmer. She is legally obliged to cooperate. If you will not fetch her for me I shall go in and fetch her myself."

The housekeeper sighed and hesitated. "Very well, then." She opened the door to let Billings in. "I shall fetch Mr Etherbridge for you, but that's all I can do. It's more than my job's worth to disturb her ladyship!"

Billings took off his hat, entered the house and sat down in the hall while the housekeeper disappeared into the drawing room. He looked around the grand, spacious hallway; the Doric columns which flanked the doorway; the large white marble tiles on the floor; the potted palm by the staircase. He then looked at his hat on his lap with the moth-eaten crown and the frizzled brim, and at the cuffs on his black jacket which were frayed and covered in black boot polish. He frowned. He was suddenly reminded of Mr Forrester's Chelsea home in which he grew up and where he was made to feel equally out of place.

"Ah, it's you!" Etherbridge suddenly appeared from the drawing room. He walked towards Billings with that mocking grin of his. "You're the chap who led us into the dungeons."

Billings got up and bowed his head. "I am sorry to bother you again, Mr Etherbridge, but I'd like to speak to Lady Palmer."

"Have you come to apologise?"

"Apologise?"

"For the ordeal you put her through last time."

"No, I have not. I have come to ask her some more questions."

"Questions? Oh dear, oh dear. That *will* be troublesome. Lady Palmer is awfully tired of answering questions. Perhaps if you tell her you've come to apologise. She might let you in then."

"She will have to let me in whether she wants to or not, Mr Etherbridge."

"Yes, yes, of course, my dear chap. But you do want Lady Palmer to cooperate, don't you? If you barge in against her will, she will simply clam up. I know how to handle her, Mr Billings. Say you've come to apologise, then slip your questions into the conversation afterwards. Trust me. That's the way to get results."

Billings hesitated. Was Etherbridge mocking him? "Very well. Tell Lady Palmer that I've come to apologise."

"Good man!" Etherbridge patted Billings on the back and rushed excitedly towards the drawing room. "Wait here," he said, before disappearing.

He reappeared a few seconds later with a broad grin on his face. "Lady Palmer will see you now, Mr Billings." This was followed by a wink .

Lady Palmer sat in a red velvet armchair at the end of the drawing room. A newspaper rested on her lap, but she wasn't reading it. Instead she looked straight at Billings through her pince-nez. "So you've come to apologise?" she said.

"I have."

Etherbridge smiled and nodded at him encouragingly.

"I have already received a written apology from your boss," Lady Palmer continued. "A second apology seems entirely superfluous and a complete waste of time. I hope the Metropolitan Police has better things to do with its time than to go around apologising to people!" She put her pince-nez on the table beside her and continued reading the paper.

Billings looked at Etherbridge. Etherbridge shrugged and smiled apologetically.

"Won't you sit down, Mr Billings," he said, pointing at the sofa opposite Lady Palmer. "Tell us about your investigation?"

"Investigation?" Lady Palmer picked up her pince-nez again and looked at Billings. "What is there to investigate? I though the vulgar man had been caught. When will he be hanged, that's what I want to know."

"He won't be hanged until he is found guilty by the court, mother," Etherbridge explained. "And that won't happen until the police have assembled sufficient facts to prove his guilt. Mr Billings is currently in the process of assembling these facts, isn't that right, Mr Billings?"

"That is right."

"Perhaps, mother, we may be able to assist Mr Billings. I believe Mr Billings has some more questions he wishes to ask you." He looked at Billings and winked again.

Lady Palmer was still staring at him through her pince-nez. "Do you have more questions you want to ask me, Mr Billings?"

"I do, Lady Palmer. I wish to ask you about a certain Mr Percy."

"Clement Percy? What has he to do with anything?"

"I believe he was staying at the house the night before Lord Palmer was killed."

"And what if he was? It is not forbidden, is it? To entertain Mr Percy?"

"Who precisely is Mr Percy?" Billings asked.

"Mr Percy is a scholar, isn't that right, mother?" Etherbridge responded with a smile. "He's an expert on asceticism."

"Mr Percy is a very nice and charming young man," Lady Palmer answered. "Why are you inquiring about him?"

"We need to establish the movements of

everyone who was in the house around the time of Lord Palmer's death. We have yours, we have the servants', but the Berkshire CID's report makes no mention of Mr Percy."

"And why should Mr Percy be mentioned? You can't possibly believe he has anything to do with this ghastly business?"

"Mother, the police need to prove that it wasn't him. They need to prove that nobody other than the vulgar man could have killed Lord Palmer. That is why he is inquiring about Mr Percy. Isn't that right, Mr Billings?"

"That is right."

"Well, you can take my word for it, Mr Billings." Lady Palmer put her pince-nez down on the table and resumed reading her newspaper. "Mr Percy is a deeply religious and highly moralistic man. He cannot possibly be connected with my husband's death."

"What was Lord Palmer's connection to Mr Percy?"

"Mr Percy came to Sutton House to look at the hermit," said Etherbridge. "That's where he met Lord Palmer. They struck up a conversation and Lord Palmer became fascinated by Mr Percy's knowledge of ascetics. He invited him back to the house several times so that he could teach him more about the history of asceticism."

"He was a very knowledgeable young man," Lady Palmer added. "And he told us such fascinating stories. What is the name of that man, Arthur, who sat on a pillar for thirty-seven years?"

"Simeon Stylites," Etherbridge replied.

Lady Palmer clapped her hands with delight. "That's the one. Simeon Stylites. Can you imagine it, Mr Billings? At the time of the Romans, this man climbed up a tall pillar, built a small platform on it and remained there for thirty-seven years. Thirty-seven years! Can you believe it? He never came down. Parcels of food were winched up to him daily. And he was visited every day by dozens of pilgrims and spectators. Isn't that wonderful? Such idiotic things people do in the name of religion!"

"Mr Percy wanted to write a book about the history of ascetics and was looking for a patron," Etherbridge continued. "Lord Palmer and Mr Percy discussed a possible patronage for a while, but the relationship soured over a disagreement about Lochrane."

"What kind of disagreement?" Billings asked.

"Mr Percy agreed with me that Lochrane was a vulgar man," Lady Palmer replied.

"Mr Percy considered the whole custom of employing an ornamental hermit to be vulgar and farcical," Etherbridge added. "He said that offering a financial reward for someone to complete a year of seclusion was entirely contrary to the idea of monasticism and that Lord Palmer's experiment was nothing more than a freak show. Lord Palmer took great offence to that."

"The pompous old fool!" Lady Palmer interrupted.

"He sent Mr Percy away there and then. And that was the last you ever saw of him, isn't it, Mother?"

"Oh, it was terrible, Mr Billings," Lady Palmer continued. "They were shouting at each other. Mr Percy accused my husband of wasting his time, of leading him on, of taking advantage of his vast knowledge with false promises of a patronage. He was so very angry, Mr Billings."

"Where did he go to?" Billings asked.

"Well, back to his home I assume."

"Where is his home?"

"Percy Street in St Clement's," Lady Palmer answered with a smile. "Isn't that funny? Clement Percy lived in Percy Street in St Clement's. He told us that he was looking for rooms in Oxford and when he stumbled upon that address he decided to stay."

"He said it was providence," Etherbridge added.

"Isn't that amusing, Mr Billings?" Lady Palmer asked.

Billings was not amused, but smiled back politely. He didn't believe the story about Mr Percy finding an address with his name. Rather, he suspected that Mr Percy wasn't Mr Percy at all and that he had used the address as a pseudonym.

"Where had Mr Percy acquired all his knowledge about asceticism?" he asked.

"He studied divinities in Oxford," Etherbridge answered. "That is to say, he started studying divinities, but stopped after an argument with his parents from whom he became estranged. He was largely self-taught after that."

"Do you know where he studied?"

"I'm afraid I don't. Do you, Mother?"

"No."

"Could it have been Wycliffe Hall?" Billings guessed.

"I really don't know."

Billings took the 9.52 to Oxford. It was a long shot, but he had nothing else to do that day and the coincidence he had stumbled upon was too significant to ignore. He had never heard of asceticism until he started reading Sebastian's diary. What were the chances of encountering two young men with the same fascination? Could Clement Percy and Sebastian Forrester be one and the same? And if so, was Sebastian somehow connected with Lord Palmer's death? It seemed unlikely, and yet...

He felt a pang of jealousy and resentment as he saw the towers and spires of Oxford approaching through the train window. What a decadent luxury it was to spend all one's time and money studying such an obscure subject. He remembered the comment Bertie Green had made in Sutton House. *"People with money have different interests than us ordinary folks."* What would he have studied if he'd been given the same opportunities as Sebastian, Billings wondered. What career would he have pursued if he wasn't forced to join the police force ten years ago in a desperate attempt to leave the Forresters' oppressive home?

He was still pondering these thoughts when he alighted at Oxford Station and made his way to the parish of St Clement's. He saw a group of jovial students walking towards him as he passed Magdalene College. He noted how handsome they all were and how they all strode towards him with that air of confidence and entitlement that only the privileged possessed. They reminded him of Sebastian. Glorious young titans, the lot of them.

He suddenly felt a mixture of awe and infatuation as he watched them approach. The students glanced at him then laughed. Were they laughing at him, Billings wondered. Even now he felt short, pale and scrawny when he compared himself to these titans. He was conscious of his moth-eaten hat and his coatsleeves stained with boot polish. He lowered his head as they approached and shuffled past them. Why did he always feel so inferior amongst the rich? He was one of the youngest detectives in Scotland Yard, for goodness' sake! An extraordinary achievement after only ten years of service. When would he finally recover from his childhood trauma?

As he walked on towards Magdalene Bridge, he suddenly saw a familiar man leaning against the railings. He was young and thin and wore a long grey overcoat and derby hat. He was smoking a cigarette and looking straight at him.

"Good morning Mr Billings," he said as Billings walked past him. "Fancy bumping into you here."

Billings nodded back politely and walked on, wondering all the time who the man was. It was only after he had crossed the bridge that he remembered. It was Jeremiah Rook, the journalist who had written that scathing article about him. What was he doing in Oxford?

On the other side of Magdalene Bridge lay the parish of St Clement's. Oxford students did not venture here. The people who walked here walked hunched, with their heads down and their eyes averted. This is where the poor people lived; the college porters, the university waiters, the gardeners, the cooks.

Billings continued down Iffley Road towards Percy Street, which was lined on both sides by dilapidated terraced cottages. Clement Percy lodged at number 8. He had learned this from a char woman he stopped in the street. Number 8 was one of the houses she cleaned. But she didn't clean Mr Percy's room. "Mr Percy only pays for lodgings and not for service," she told him. Billings walked on towards the cottage and rang the bell.

The door was opened by a thin, middle-aged woman with a big nose. Her hands were covered in flour and she was wiping them on her apron. "Yes?" she said.

"My name is Detective Sergeant John Billings from the Metropolitan Police. I am looking for Mr Percy."

"Metropolitan Police, eh? It's about time you fellas got involved."

Billings was confused by this comment and didn't reply.

"I don't know how many times I've spoken to the Oxford Police," the woman continued, "and each time they've given me the same reply. 'This is not a police matter, Mrs Warburton,' they keep saying, 'Mr Percy is a grown man and England is a free country. He has the right to disappear.' 'But not when he still owes me a crown in rent!' I keep telling them. Anyway, I see they've finally passed the case on to Scotland Yard."

Billings was quick to take advantage of the misunderstanding. "Um... yes. That's right. May I come in and ask you some questions?"

"I can show you his room if you like." The woman stepped aside to let Billings in. "All his belongings are still in it. I changed the lock, of course. I won't have him slip into the house in the middle of the night and retrieve his belongings while I am still asleep. Oh no, I've learned my lesson the hard way. These impoverished scholars will stop at nothing to avoid paying their bills. He can have his belongings after he's paid me. This is his room, Mr Billings."

She took a key from her apron pocket and unlocked the door to a small room on the ground floor, smearing flour and dough on the doorknob.

It was a dark, narrow room, furnished only with a bed, a desk and a chair. There was a dank smell as they entered and Mrs Warburton quickly rushed to open the window. Billings glanced around the room and scanned through the lodger's belongings. There were several piles of books stacked on the floor and littered across the desk and the bed. One particular book instantly grabbed his attention. A large expanded edition of 'Sayings of The Desert Fathers'.

"When did Mr Percy disappear?" he asked.

Mrs Warburton was still standing by the window, fanning fresh air into the room. "I last saw him on the 21st of October. That's one day before the rent was due. He rushed into his room, after having been away for a week, and started throwing some clothes into a bag. He was about to leave again when I grabbed him by the arm and reminded him about the rent. He had a habit of paying late. 'Yes, yes,' he kept saying as he pulled himself away from me. Well, 'yes, yes' turned out to be 'no, no', coz I ain't seen him since, the sly little fox!"

One day before Lord Palmer was killed, thought Billings. "How long has he been boarding with you?" he asked.

"Sixteen months."

"Is Clement Percy his real name?"

"What do you mean?"

"He lives on Percy Street in St Clement's. Don't you think that's rather a coincidence?"

Mrs Warburton looked confused. "I never thought of that. 'Ere, he's not a wanted criminal, is he? I knew there was something shifty about that man. Never had a penny for the rent, yet managed to get himself enough money to buy all them books. Brought a new book home with him nearly every day. I bet they're all stolen."

"What do you know about Mr Percy?"

"Very little."

"Did he ever receive any mail?"

"Never."

"Did he have any friends come to visit? Or family?"

"No one. And he didn't talk much, either. He were a queer fellow, Mr Billings. He'd go out at the strangest hours and not come back for several days. Then he'd come back into the house cold and pale and shivering and his clothes all dirty and soiled and he'd go back into his room without no explanation. No, not even a 'hello' or a 'good morning' or 'good afternoon.' Nothing. He'd just lock himself up in his room with his books and stay in there for days. I don't even think he ate anything. Well, I hope not, anyway. Lodgers aren't allowed food in the room. We've got a dining room for that. On account of vermin, you see?"

"So Mr Percy had a habit of disappearing."

"He did, Mr Billings, but he's never disappeared when the rent was due before. Well, I'll tell you something, Mr Billings. When you do find him and after he has paid me that crown he owes me, I'll kick him out, so I will. I won't have such queer fellows in my house. No, sir! Not anymore! Enough is enough."

Billings got off the train in Paddington and instead of going back home the long way round, he took a shortcut through Praed Street. He normally avoided walking down Praed Street. There was a certain shop there which he had sworn to himself he'd never enter again. But he'd been feeling tired and melancholy all day. His visit to Oxford had triggered memories of Sebastian and had filled him with a mixture of lust, regret and resentment. A couple of days ago he had received notification from the shop's owner that new stock had arrived and, his resolve having been weakened, he convinced himself that there'd be no harm in taking a look.

"Ah, Doctor Smith," the shopkeeper said as Billings walked tentatively into the dimly lit shop. "How are you? So nice to see you again."

"I am well, thank you." Billings was tense and his hands were trembling. He clenched his fist behind his back and gritted his teeth. He regretted entering the shop. Why had he done it? "I believe you have a new series in," he asked the shopkeeper.

"I do indeed, I do indeed. I have it right here."

The shopkeeper crouched down and took a large brown paper envelope from beneath the counter. He was a short corpulent man with dark, oily skin. Of Arab descent, perhaps. Or maybe Greek. He called himself Al Bull, but Billings knew that that wasn't his real name. He smiled sleazily, almost mockingly, as he pulled a series of cabinet cards out of the envelope and displayed them one by one on the counter. They were albumen photographs of young, nude men, practising various sports in a forest meadow. There was one of a naked discus thrower looking like a Greek statue. There was one of two men wrestling naked by a river, and one of a naked man leaning against a tree holding a javelin. Billings could feel the blood rush to his face as he looked at the photographs.

"They're from a German sports camp," the shopkeeper said. "They have the young men exercise in the nude, in keeping with the custom of the Greek Olympics."

Billings looked away, desperate to conceal his blushing. "These will do. Thank you," he said, swallowing.

"I thought they would." The shopkeeper smiled as he collected the pictures and pushed them back into the envelope. "Are the anatomical classes going well, Doctor Smith?"

"Very well, thank you."

"I'm sure these photographs will be of great benefit to your students."

"I'm sure they will. How much are they, please?"

"Seven and sixpence, please."

Billings ruffled in his pockets for the money.

"I also have a series of photographs from the South Seas," the shopkeeper continued, "of very young boys in provocative poses. Would that perhaps be of interest to your anatomy students?"

"No, thank you. Just these will do." Billings lay the money on the counter and picked up the envelope. He tried sticking it into the inside pocket of his great coat, but it wouldn't fit. He folded the envelope and tried again, but still it was too big.

The shopkeeper watched with an amused glint in his eye as a flustered Billings continued to struggle with the envelope. "You'll damage the pictures like that," he said.

Billings didn't reply and tried one more fold and

finally succeeded in putting the envelope away.

"Is it just muscle structures your students are interested in?" the shopkeeper asked . "Or do they like young, lithe physiques as well? Because if so, I have some pictures in the back room which might interest you."

"No, thank you, Mr Bull. I'm in a hurry."

"Oh, it won't take long, Doctor Smith. My assistant Charlie will gladly show you. You haven't met Charlie yet, have you? He is a very pleasant young man. I am sure you'll like him – Charlie!"

A young man pulled open the black curtains which divided the shop from the storage room and moved to stand next to the shopkeeper behind the counter . He had a gleeful and cocksure expression in his hazel-green eyes. His thick, dark blond hair was ragged and uncombed (it was so thick, it was practically uncombable). His shirt was only half-tucked into his trousers and the top buttons were undone, revealing pale flesh and a few curly chest hairs. Billings, who had been desperate to turn his back on the shopkeeper and rush out of the shop, raised his head to look at him and was instantly infatuated. Everything about the young man displayed confidence and carelessness, the exact qualities Billings never possessed, and he was fascinated.

"Charlie, this is Doctor Smith," the shopkeeper said. "Doctor Smith is an expert in anatomy. Doctor Smith, this is Charlie," he now pointed to his assistant, "who, as you can see, has a very lovely anatomy."

He laughed. And Charlie laughed along with him. But Billings was not amused and looked away embarrassed.

"Go on, Doctor Smith," the shopkeeper continued. "Let Charlie show you what he's got. It won't take long, but I'm sure it'll be to your satisfaction. Ain't that right, Charlie?"

"That's right, Mr Bull," Charlie answered with that nasal Cockney twang which Billings always found so ugly, but which now sounded so lovely coming from Charlie's lips.

There is an intricate link between delusion and depravity, Billings thought afterwards. The one always precedes the other. He'd had a deluded notion that it was better to love and lose than never to love at all; that a man needed to be touched and held regularly in order to function properly; that all men were entitled to some carnal satisfaction, regardless of their preference or inclination. These deluded notions had passed through his mind shortly before committing the act of depravity which was to follow.

He followed Charlie into the back room. The room was packed with crates and boxes. Billings stood in the middle of the room rigidly, pale and nervous, while Charlie closed the black curtain and turned around to face him.

"Well then, Doctor Smith," he said, looking at Billings with that cheeky smile. "What do you want to do?"

"Do?" Billings was trembling and sweating. "I thought you were going to show me some more pictures?"

"Pictures?" he laughed. "What do you wanna see pictures for, if you can have the real thing? It's a bob for a rub, a shilling and sixpence for a bagpipe, and a half crown if you want the full story. But we'd have to do that somewhere more discreet. Mr Bull has a room with a bed available upstairs which you can rent for a shilling. So what will it be?"

"I… um…"

"You're in a hurry, ain't ya? So I'll give you a bagpipe. It won't take long. You got the money on ya?"

Billings rummaged in his pocket and took out some coins to show Charlie.

"You can pay Mr Bull on your way out. Now, come and stand by the light." Charlie walked towards the wall opposite the window and turned the key on the gas lamp.

Billings remained standing where he stood, looking unsure of himself.

Charlie frowned. "Well, come on then."

"I… um… I think I'd rather look at the pictures," Billings said.

Charlie laughed. "Will you stop going on about the pictures. Can't you see I'm offering you the real thing? Now come here."

Billings approached him reluctantly. Charlie grabbed the lapels of Billings's greatcoat and pulled him towards him, then proceeded to cover his face and neck with kisses. Billings felt his heart pound as Charlie's hands reached into his greatcoat and grabbed hold of his chest. He closed his eyes and clenched his fists. Charlie proceeded to slide his hand down towards his crotch. Goosebumps rose all over his body and shudders rushed through him like electric current when Charlie knelt down before him and started unbuttoning his trousers. He took a deep breath and flung his head back when suddenly, through his closed eyelids, he saw a flash of light which woke him from his erotic trance.

"What was that?" he said alarmed and pushed Charlie's fumbling fingers away from his trouser buttons.

Charlie looked up. "What?"

"There was a flash of light."

"I didn't see nothing."

Billings's heart was still pounding, but this time with alarm, rather than titillation. "There was a light," he said. He rushed towards the window and opened the shutter. "I clearly saw a light."

"It was probably lightning," said Charlie, who was still on his knees by the gas lamp.

"It can't have been lightning. It's not raining."

Billings stuck his head out of the window and looked up and down the narrow alleyway which led from the shop's back entrance to Praed Street. There was nothing there other than a few empty crates which had been stacked against the wall.

"It must've been dry lightning, Doctor Smith. Nothing to worry about. Now, come over here and let me finish giving you your bagpipe. I ain't even started yet."

Billings turned to look back at Charlie, kneeling on the cold brick floor. The gaslight flooded his head and Billings could see the dirt on the back of his neck and his shirt collar. He also saw black specks crawling through his unruly hair. Was it lice? Charlie suddenly didn't look so appealing anymore. That cheeky, cocksure smile was replaced by a bored and impatient frown and Billings felt dirty and sleazy. The thought of that dirty boy's hands all over him suddenly made his whole body itch. How could he have allowed himself to sink to this?

"I had better go," he said, buttoning up his trousers and tucking in his shirt.

"Ain't you gonna let me finish giving you your bagpipe?"

"I'm sorry. I have to go."

"You are still gonna pay, me ain't ya?"

Billings dug into his pocket and took out some coins. "I have two shillings," he said and held out the coins to Charlie.

"You gotta pay Mr Bull at the counter."

"Why don't you take them off me?"

"I don't know, Doctor Smith. I ain't supposed to. You gotta pay Mr Bull at the counter."

Billings approached him, grabbed his hand and placed the two shillings in it. "Keep the money for yourself," he said closing Charlie's fingers over the coins. "I'll tell Mr Bull that I changed my mind and that nothing happened. Which is the truth." He then turned his back on Charlie, cut through the black drapes and walked back into the shop.

"Finished already?" the shopkeeper asked.

Billings didn't answer. He just rushed passed him and out of the shop.

As Billings crossed the corner into Edgware Road, he bumped into a man carrying a heavy black leather case over his shoulder and knocked the man's hat off his head.

"Oh, I do apologise," Billings said.

The man crouched down to pick up his hat, but when he lifted his head and looked at Billings, a broad smile appeared on his face. "You again!" he said.

It was Jeremiah Rook.

"What a coincidence!"

Billings looked at him suspiciously. Was it really a coincidence that he should bump into the reporter twice on the same day. And in two different towns?

"You should watch where you're going, Mr Billings," the reporter continued. "You nearly made me drop my equipment."

Billings looked at the leather case hanging from the reporter's shoulder and wondered what it contained.

"'Ere, you're not shadowing me, are ya?" the reporter asked with a cheeky smile.

"I might ask you the same question?" Billings replied tersely.

"Why would I shadow *you*? Have you been doing something you shouldn't have?" There was a mocking glint in the reporter's eyes as he asked this and Billings's attention was again drawn to the suspicious case on the reporter's shoulder.

"I expect it's just a coincidence, then," Billings concluded. "We must've taken the same train back from Oxford and we must both be on our way home."

"I expect that must be the case."

"Well, good day to you then, Mr Rook." Billings tipped his hat at him.

"Good day to you, Mr Billings."

When he got back home, Billings rushed straight to his room. He took the envelope with the cabinet cards out of his pocket, grabbed a box of matches from the windowsill, crouched down before the fireplace and set fire to it and its contents. Watching the cindered remains disappearing down the roster, he decided he'd take a generous dose of morphine that night. He was determined to sleep soundly. He'd sleep so soundly that, when he'd wake up the following morning, it would be as if this whole day had never occurred. As if the day had just been a bad dream. Like one of those morphine-induced nightmares he sometimes had. He hadn't given in to temptation. He hadn't soiled his consciousness. He hadn't plotted to maltreat another fellow human being. He hadn't risked jeopardizing his career. It had all been a bad dream, that's all. A bad, disturbing dream, the likes of which he'd had many times before.

CHAPTER SEVEN

Mr Forrester's Confession

It was Sunday. Billings stood outside the Forrester's house, waiting to be let in. He had rung the bell twice already. Finally the maid opened the door. She looked tired and haggard. Billings could hear some commotion in the drawing room. Mr Forrester was shouting angrily and knocking things over and his wife was trying to shush him in a gentle, but exasperated tone.

"Mr and Mrs Forrester are not receiving guests at the moment," said the maid before Billings had the chance to introduce himself.

"Will you tell Mrs Forrester that it's John Billings," he said. "She'll want to see *me*."

"I'm sorry, sir, but I've been given instructions not to..."

"*Detective Sergeant* John Billings," he interrupted. "From the Metropolitan Police."

That always did the trick. After a reluctant pause, the maid stepped aside and let him in.

Billings walked up to the drawing room. The door was open and he could see Mr Forrester sitting up in his bed, pale and unshaven. His hair was dishevelled and there was an intense, almost bewildered look in his eyes. His wife stood beside him. A lock of her hair hung loose over her pale face.

Mr Forrester caught sight of Billings standing in the doorway and his face lit up instantly. "John!" he called out.

His wife turned around to face him. "You've come at a bad time," she said, brushing her hair away with her hand.

The room was a mess. Sheets, blankets and pillows were scattered over and around the bed; a silver spoon lay abandoned on the floor next to the shattered remains of a discarded soup bowl; a chair had been thrown over and lay tumbled on its side.

"Come in," Mr Forrester said. "Come sit beside me." He tapped the seat of the chair beside his bed. "How is your investigation going? Have you found anything out yet?"

Billings approached the bed and sat down. "I'm

afraid I haven't, sir."

"But did you study Sebastian's letters?"

"Yes."

"And?"

Mr and Mrs Forrester stared at him with wide, expecting eyes.

"Are they both his?" Mrs Forrester asked. "Is he still alive?"

"It's too early to tell yet, Mrs Forrester," Billings replied. "Now, I was hoping to speak to Mr Forrester."

"What about?"

"There are some questions I want to ask him."

"Can't you ask me?"

"I'd rather ask him."

"But what's it about?"

"For God's sake, woman!" Mr Forrester cried suddenly. "Don't you see the boy wants to talk to me on his own! Just get out of the room, will you!"

Mrs Forrester hesitated and looked at Billings, offended.

"Please, Mrs Forrester," Billings said, smiling gently. "If you want me to find Sebastian, then you must let me go about it my own way. There are things a son tells his father that he doesn't tell his mother and vice versa. I shall, at times, need to speak to both of you separately. But right now I need to speak to Mr Forrester."

"Very well," she said. She looked disappointed. "I'll be back in a while with Nancy to clean up the mess." She left the room.

"Well, what do you want from me?" Mr Forrester asked.

"I want to talk to you about Sebastian's disappearance. I want you to tell me why he ran away from university?"

"I don't know. Nobody knows."

"Was there some sort of argument between you?"

"Argument?"

"Some sort of estrangement?"

"Why are you asking me that?"

"In his letter Sebastian made certain allusions to a disagreement. *'Papa will know what I mean. He won't understand or agree, but he'll know.'* Why did he write that?"

"He was being enigmatic."

"But you must have a suspicion."

"I don't."

"Mr Forrester, the only way for me to find out what happened is by retracing Sebastian's steps and seeing where that leads to. I need to know what you know about his elopement. You can be frank, with me, Mr Forrester. I'm here as a friend.

Not a policeman."

There was a short pause.

"Yes. Yes, you're right. You should know everything."

Suddenly Mrs Forrester re-entered the room with the maid, who was carrying a duster and pan. Mr Forrester grabbed a pillow from the bed and hurled it at them.

"Out!" he cried.

The pillow hit the maid on the head and she froze in fear. Mrs Forrester gave her husband an angry look. "Freddy, we just want to clean up the soup you..."

"Out! The both of you!" He grabbed another pillow from the floor and hurled it again, this time hitting his wife.

"All right, all right, we'll clean it later!" Mrs Forrester and the maid shuffled out of the room.

Mr Forrester turned back to face Billings. "There is something I should tell you," he said, panting after his exertion. "Cecilia doesn't know. I don't want her to know, but something did happen. Something horrible did happen, which I..." He stopped and looked away. He swallowed a few times, as if he had something stuck in his throat.

"Shall I get you some water?" Billings rose up from his chair, but Mr Forrester held out his arm and urged him to sit down again.

"No, no, stay here. Stay here, John, and listen to me. I will tell you. But as a friend. As a dear *friend*, do you understand me? Look at me." Mr Forrester stared intently into Billings's eyes. "I will take you up on your offer. I'll talk to you, but as a friend and not a policeman."

Billings nodded quietly. There was clearly going to be a criminal element to Mr Forrester's confession, which he would have to ignore.

Mr Forrester leaned back into his pillows, turned his head away from Billings and, looking up at the ceiling, related the following story:

It was late morning. Ten o'clock. Maybe eleven. I was sitting in my office preparing for my lunchtime meeting when my secretary knocked on the door.

"A telegram has arrived for you, sir," he said, popping his head into the room and waving the envelope at me.

I don't like to be disturbed when I'm doing the books and made no attempt at hiding my annoyance.

"Can you not open it and deal with it yourself?" I said, frowning.

"Do you think I should?" he replied. "It's

addressed to you personally."

We didn't get many telegrams at the bank and when we did they were usually addressed to the director or to one of the brokers, but never to me personally. So I took the envelope from Stevens, walked with it towards the light of the fireside and opened it with a degree of trepidation. Good news always comes to you in the form of a letter. It's only bad news that needs to be rushed through the telegraph posts.

'Leaving Wycliffe Hall to marry. Sorry to disappoint, but can't be avoided. Help in finding employment appreciated. Sebastian.'

I recognized it immediately for what it was – a cry for help. Why would he send a telegram to announce the occasion unless he wanted to be rescued from it? It was obvious what had happened. He'd been ensnared by some callous young girl and needed my assistance in freeing him from his obligations. It's an age old story, John, and one which would undoubtedly end up costing me a lot of money.

My day was perfectly ruined after reading that. I cast the telegram into the fire, sat ill-humoured and distracted though my client's meeting, then rushed off to the post office to let my son know I'd be coming down the following morning to see how we could get this ghastly affair settled.

I found Sebastian sitting on a bench on the platform at Oxford Station, staring at his shoes, looking pale and glum. He didn't lift his head to look at me as I stepped off the train. Even as I approached and called out his name, he stubbornly refused to look me in the eyes.

You know, of course, that I've always had a strained relationship with my son. It's his passiveness which annoyed me. The way he would sit at home, before the fireplace, hour after hour, without stirring. I'd come into the room in the morning and he'd be there, sunk in his chair, staring into the flames. I'd come back again in the evening and he'd still be there, in the same position, not having moved an inch.

"Let him be," Cecilia would say. "He's thinking. He lives in his mind."

Well, thinking is for old people, John. For people whose bodies have failed and who now have a lifetime of regrets to ponder. Sebastian was a young man, at the prime of his life. Never again would his body contain as much energy and potential as it did then and it bothered me that he was wasting it. He had no passion. He had no ambition. He always said he wanted to follow God's will, but it wasn't his idea to train for missionary work, it was mine. He never showed any interest or enthusiasm for going to Africa. I wanted God to move in him. Not just to live in him, but to *move* him. To fill him with purpose. And love. And charity. But it was also meant to be a challenge. One filled with danger. You of all people must know how dangerous life can be in Africa. It was to be an adventure. A memory to treasure and inspire him throughout his life. Something that would serve him in his future career, whatever that might be. All young people want that, don't they? To travel? To see more of the world? To break away from their parents and their childhood lives? He never said he didn't. If he had wanted to do something else, I'd have supported him in that. If he had wanted to join the navy, or go into trade, or follow me into the bank, or emigrate to America even. I'd have gladly supported him in anything, so long as he showed a passion for it. But he never did. He always did just what he was told and was perfectly content to allow other people to lead his life for him.

I must admit that as I sat in the train to Oxford, I did derive a small amount of satisfaction at the thought that he had got a girl in trouble. At least it showed that there was something which could stir his blood enough to get his body into action. But when I got off the train and saw him sitting on that bench, staring at the ground with his shoulders hunched and his hands in his coat pocket, I felt that rage rise in me again and I had to bite my lip to stop me from scolding him.

"Sebastian!" I called.

He finally lifted his head and looked at me, with that dead and melancholy stare of his.

"What have you done now?" I said to him. It was meant to be a light-hearted comment aimed at breaking the ice, but he didn't take it as such, and hung his head again. I sat down beside him and put my hand on his knee. "So what's her name?" I asked.

"Janie Drew," he mumbled, still staring at his shoes. "She's one of the maids at Wycliffe Hall."

"And what do her parents do?"

"Her mother is an innkeeper in Farmoor."

"And her father?"

"He's a navvy. He's in India working on a rail bridge."

"Does she have any siblings?"

"She has four older brothers. They're all abroad."

"All of them?"

"Two of them are with their father in India, one of them is with the South Staffies in Africa and the other one has gone to Australia."

"So she lives alone with her mother in Farmoor?"

"Yes."

"How far along is she?"

"About three months."

"Three months? God help us!" It was much worse than I expected. "And what does her mother make of all this?"

"She's not happy."

"No, I should think not! So what will you do now?"

He shrugged.

"Perhaps she can accompany you to Madagascar?" I offered.

"Her mother won't let her."

"She'll be a married woman, then. She won't need her mother's permission."

"She doesn't want to leave her mother on her own."

"So what will you do, then?"

He shrugged again.

"Well, come on Sebastian, you must have thought about it a little bit." Sebastian's unresponsiveness was annoying me and I was struggling to keep my patience.

"Janie's mother says I could live with them and work at the inn," he said, still looking at his shoes.

"That's nonsense, Sebastian. You can not waste

your life doing menial jobs which are below your station."

"Why not?"

"Because it'll make you bitter and angry, that's why! You'll only end up hating your wife and child for it, trust me. As far as I can see, we've only got three options. Option one: you marry her and she accompanies you to Madagascar. Option two: I provide her with sufficient funds to look after the child and her mother. And option three..." I stopped.

Sebastian raised his head and looked at me with interest. "What's option three?"

"Why don't you arrange a meeting for the four of us? You, me, Janie and her mother. I'll be here for four days."

"Four days?"

"Yes, I told your mother I was going to Birmingham for a meeting about the miners' houses charity I'm setting up. I said I'd be back in the weekend."

"You didn't tell her about me?"

"I'll be staying at the Station Inn. Go back to your college, speak to that girl and arrange a meeting for the four of us tomorrow. We'll discuss the options then."

As Sebastian and I rode into the small village of Farmoor, we saw Mrs Drew standing in the doorway of her inn. She was a large woman with a stern face. Her hair was pulled back tightly and tied into a knot at the back of her head. She was wearing a long white apron which reached down towards her ankles and she had wooden clogs on her bare feet. Her arms were crossed over her breast and she was watching us with a hostile stare. I nodded at her as I disembarked the carriage, but she didn't reciprocate. She just continued to stare at us, frowning.

"Mrs Drew, my name is Frederick Forrester," I said as I walked towards her, holding out my hand.

"You had better come in quickly before anyone sees us," she said. "I have some tea in the lounge." She stepped aside and Sebastian and I shuffled quietly into the house.

As I entered the lounge, I caught my first glimpse of Janie. She was sitting in the corner, looking down and fiddling with the buttons of her blouse. I nodded at her, but she refused to turn her head and acknowledge me. She was a plump girl and, although I could see she was dressed up in her Sunday best, there wasn't the slightest trace of elegance about her. I wondered what Sebastian ever saw in her.

The room was small, but tidy and cozy. There was a large oak dresser against the wall, displaying a collection of ornamental plates and beer mugs. There was a round table in the middle of the room and a large oil lamp with a beautiful ceramic shade hung low over the centre of it. The table had been laid with a damask tablecloth and silk embroidered napkins. A tray with a tea pot and china cups stood waiting for us. It was clear that every effort had been made to display to us that this was a respectable household with high aspirations.

"Sit down, Mr Forrester," said Mrs Drew as she followed us into the room and closed the door behind her. "The punters will start coming in at four and you must both be gone by then. This is a small village and I don't want any tongues wagging. Will the gentlemen have some tea?" And before we got the chance to reply, she started pouring our cups.

Sebastian and I both took our seats at the table. I caught Sebastian glancing over at Janie as he sat down, but she refused to look back at him and remained sunk in her chair like a sack of potatoes, fiddling with her clothes, sour-faced and sulking.

"Well..." said Mrs Drew, sitting down opposite me and sliding the tea cup towards me. "It appears we have a bit of a problem, Mr Forrester."

'A bit of a problem.' Those were the precise words she used. She had a very affected way of speaking and her speech was littered with words which were far above her station. She had clearly spent a great deal of her life studying the speech patterns of the upper classes.

"It needn't be a problem, Mrs Drew, if the youngsters agree to marry. I believe Sebastian has already proposed."

"Oh yes, he has proposed alright! He has proposed to ship my only daughter off to Africa and deprive me of the only family I have left. No sir, I will not allow that!"

"No, I didn't think you would."

"The boy will have to stay here if he marries her. He'll have to stay here and help me with the inn."

"I'm sure there's many a young man who would be delighted at that prospect, but I'm afraid I have higher aspirations for my son."

"My inn not good enough for your boy, is it Mr Forrester?"

"Let us not be sensitive, Mrs Drew. I can see that this is a respectable household and I do not look down my nose at you or your daughter, but I have invested a considerable amount of money on my son's education and future and I do not wish to throw all that away on account of his youthful folly." I looked over at Sebastian at that point and saw him frozen in his seat, looking down at the table, defeated and embarrassed. "You and I both know that marriage is out of the question," I continued, "so let us not waste any more time on that subject and let us get straight down to what this meeting is really all about."

"Oh? And just what is this meeting really all about, Mr Forrester?"

"Money."

"Money?"

"You want money, Mrs Drew, and I'm prepared to make a deal with you. So I suggest we kick off negotiations and start naming our prices."

There was a long silence. Mrs Drew frowned, then took a deep breath, sat up in her seat and looked defiantly at me. "You say you don't look down your nose at me and yet you come into my house and you offer me money?"

I was taken aback and started to stutter. "Well, I... I only meant for the child. It will cost money to bring up a child and I'm prepared to pay my share."

"You say that this is a respectable household and yet you expect my unmarried daughter to bring up your son's bastard?"

Mrs Drew's haughty accusations were irritating me and I'm afraid I lost my patience. "Well, then what the devil do you want, Mrs Drew!"

"I told you what I want, Mr Forrester. I want your son to marry my daughter and help me run the inn!"

"That is out of the question."

"Well, then we're at an impasse, aren't we?"

There was another long pause as Mrs Drew and I both took a deep breath and calmed ourselves down. Sebastian and Janie both remained frozen in their seats, looking passively at the ground as their futures were being decided for them.

"There is one other option open to us," I said eventually.

Mrs Drew suddenly looked up with interest. "Oh? And what may that be?"

"There is some medication."

"Medication?"

"To bring on your daughter's cycle."

"Her cycle?"

I could tell by the tone in her voice that her surprise was fake. She knew exactly what I was talking about and had clearly been waiting all this time for me to introduce the topic.

"There are pills she could take which will cause her to menstruate again," I explained. "I know a pharmacist in London and I'm perfectly willing to..."

"You want to kill the baby. That's right, isn't it? That is what you're suggesting."

"I'm sorry?"

"This is murder you're talking about, Mr Forrester."

"Well, I... I am merely looking at all the options which are available to us, Mrs Drew. Do you have any other suggestions?"

"No, I don't. I don't have any other suggestions. I just think we should call a spade a spade, that's all, so that we know exactly what we're talking about. Killing the baby is our only option, Mr Forrester, and I'm glad you agree."

I looked at her surprised.

"I suggest that you go to London and get me a whole stack of those pills and do so quickly before her tummy starts growing and the whole village finds out what state she's in."

I got some diachylon pills from my pharmacist. Janie was supposed to take two a day for a number of weeks. It would make her ill enough to cause an abortion, but not ill enough to kill her. However, Janie proved too sturdy a girl and, when after a couple of weeks there were still no signs of any ill health, her mother increased her dosage to five pills a day. Janie soon started becoming weaker after that. She became bed-bound and complained about pain in her muscles and her face. At one point she wasn't even able to move her arms. But the baby was still there, and growing. So the dosage had to be increased again.

Sebastian was overwrought. He wrote to me nearly every week, especially during the last stages of Janie's illness, describing in lurid detail the manner in which the poison was affecting her. There was a vindictive tone to his letters. I think he wanted to punish me. To confront me with the consequences of my decision. To make me feel guilty. And I did feel guilty. I was afraid that a doctor might be called in at some point and that our misdeed would be exposed, so I urged Sebastian to prevent that.

Janie miscarried in her fourth month and lost a lot of blood in the process. Considering her already frail condition, this eventually led to her death. The coroner rightly attributed her death and miscarriage to lead poisoning, but believed her to be contaminated by the water from the outdoor tap in Wycliffe Hall's courtyard, which was still connected to the old pipes and wasn't meant for drinking. We were in the clear, but Sebastian was heartbroken.

It had never occurred to me that he might really have been in love with the girl – or perhaps it was the loss of the unborn child he lamented. Either way, he was inconsolable. And he blamed me. His letters became more and more vicious and hostile (I burnt them all, of course. Cecilia still doesn't know anything about this). He refused to take any responsibility for the course of events and went into a depression. In his letters he wrote about running away; about escaping the world and all its horrors; about getting rid of all his possessions so as never to have to lose anything again; about starting over and being reborn.

I wasn't surprised when I heard that he had run away. I even thought it might do him good, which is why I took no measures to recover him. I thought he'd be able to heal himself and that he'd return to Oxford a stronger and more capable man, but it wasn't to be. Sebastian never was a fighter. He never took control of anything. All this talk of doing God's will. It wasn't out of piety or religious conviction. It was just an excuse not to take responsibility for his own life.

CHAPTER EIGHT

The Deptford Jewels

Billings arrived at the office before anyone else. That was the way he had planned it. He climbed the stairs of the empty building and slipped into the filing room. He opened up the 'L' drawer and flicked through the files until he found the document he was searching for.

Lochrane's confession had been typed, probably by Jacobs himself. It was signed at the bottom by the suspect. It was an elegant signature, with large bold curls and a confident dash which underlined the name. This wasn't the signature of a simple and uneducated man, thought Billings.

Lochrane confessed *'by his own free will and without enticement'* that on the 21st of November 1890, *'he did attack Lord Palmer in the woods of his estate with a hatchet, creating deep wounds to the shoulders and the back of the head, thereby causing his death.'* It was an unremarkable confession, which didn't shed any light on the life of the culprit or what might have led him to commit the crime. In short, it did nothing to set Billings's mind at ease. He returned the confession to the filing cabinet and was about to leave the room when suddenly he saw Jacobs coming up the stairs, wearing his greatcoat and carrying his umbrella.

"Good morning, Billings," Jacobs said, then stopped and glanced at him suspiciously. "What are you are doing in the filing room?"

"I... um... I was checking on something for a case I'm working on."

"Really? What case is that?"

"It's... um..."

"That wasn't Brendan Lochrane's file you just put back, was it?"

"I just wanted to read his confession."

"Why?"

"I was curious."

"Curious?"

"Yes, sir."

Jacobs paused and looked him up and down. "We had an eventful day yesterday, Billings."

"Did you, sir?"

"We found the Russian counterfeiters. That is to say, we found their workshop. An abandoned warehouse in Deptford. The Russians managed to escape and took all the money with them, but they did leave behind a stash of stolen jewels."

"Jewels, sir?"

"Yes, a box full of golden rings and diamond brooches and such. It's in the safe now. Clarkson is collating all the reports we've received of jewels stolen in the Metropolitan area. There should be a nice reward for us when we return the jewels to their rightful owners."

"That's good news, sir."

"How are you feeling, by the way?"

"Much better, sir. Thank you."

"Good. Good." Jacobs took off his hat and greatcoat and hung them on the hat stand next to the filing room. "I'd like to see you in my office in ten minutes," he said, then turned away from Billings and continued down the corridor.

"You're a good detective, Billings," said Jacobs. He paced up and down his office as Billings stood in the doorway watching. "You're meticulous, conscientious, responsible. But you do have a weakness." He suddenly stopped pacing and looked Billings straight in the eyes. "And we both know what that is, don't we?"

Billings looked confused.

"You have problems letting go," Jacobs explained. "We are here to deter and prevent, Billings. Deter and prevent. That's our job."

"I know," Billings said.

"It is not our job to set injustices straight – legal, moral or otherwise. We have other people to do that for us. Judges and vicars and philosophers. *They're* our moral crusaders. We're just here to catch criminals."

"I know," Billings repeated.

"What were you doing in the filing room just now?"

"I told you. I was reading through Lochrane's confession."

"Why?"

"Because I'm not convinced he really killed Lord Palmer."

"But he confessed, Billings."

"I know, but..."

"It was *his* axe which was pulled out of Lord Palmer's shoulder blades. Nobody else was spotted in the vicinity. And he confessed. Do you think that that is enough evidence for a judge to convict him?"

"I do, but..."

"Well, then your job is done. You've got the evidence, the case is closed."

Billings didn't know what to say.

"You care for people, Billings, and that's a good and admirable quality to have. But we mustn't let it get out of hand."

"I don't know what you mean."

"I'm talking about Saturday. About you being ill."

"But you told me to take the day off."

"Because you were ill."

"It was the soup, sir. I had some fish soup at the station which..."

"Fish soup, my arse! I've seen your hand tremble more than once, Billings."

Billings was dumbfounded and didn't know where to look.

"I've seen enough opium dens and dope fiends in my time to recognize the signs."

Billings looked horrified.

Jacobs put his hand on the detective's shoulder and smiled. "Don't worry, Billings. We all have our poison – brandy's mine – but the thing is not to let it interfere with your life."

"I just missed a dose on Friday, sir. That's all. It won't happen again."

"Don't misunderstand me, Billings. This is not a

telling-off. You're a good detective. I told you that. And I have great plans for you."

"Plans, sir?"

"Yes. You've got gifts, Billings. Why do you think you've been promoted? There aren't many twenty-eight year old detectives in Scotland Yard."

"I don't know, sir."

"It's because you've been well brought up. Because you speak properly and write eloquently. That's a rarity in the Metropolitan Police. And you're educated. How many languages do you speak, Billings?"

"Some French, some Malagasy."

"There you go. They need people like you in the Special Branch. *That's* your future. Fighting terrorism, protecting foreign dignitaries, international liaisons. In a couple of years time, Billings, I'm sure I can arrange a transfer for you. But you'll need to be in control of yourself."

"I assure you, sir, I am in control."

"Perhaps you should take some more time off."

"Time off? What for?"

"Take a holiday. Enjoy yourself. Get yourself a woman. A woman, mind. Not a wife. Whatever you do, Billings, be sure never to marry. Women can not be trusted with money. They buy everything they see and before you know it, you're financially ruined." He laughed bitterly. Another reference to his current money problems, Billings thought. "But do get yourself a woman, Billings," he continued. "You can do with a good fuck."

Billings was taken aback. "I beg your pardon?"

"No, really Billings, I'm serious. Nothing like a good fuck to release some of that tension. Works much better than whatever opiate you're taking. There's plenty of places you can go to, some of which are perfectly hygienic."

Billings felt the blood rushing to his face and didn't know where to look.

Jacobs laughed. "Don't be embarrassed, Billings. We're both men of the world, aren't we?"

"I'm not embarrassed, sir."

"You should look upon me as a father, Billings. I know you haven't got one, and as a father I tell you to get yourself a woman once in a while."

"Will there be anything else, sir?" Billings was desperately trying to control the rush of blood to his head.

"No, Billings," Jacobs was still laughing. "You can go now. But think about the holiday."

"Yes, sir. I will." And he quickly left the room.

"'Ere, Billings! Have you heard about the jewels?"

Clarkson sat at his desk when Billings came into the room. He was sifting through piles of reports with a broad grin on his face.

"It's a treasure trove, Billings!" he said. "Jacobs says it was my shadowing of the suspect that helped them locate the warehouse. That means I qualify for a percentage of the reward. And it's going to be a big one, believe you me! Look at this." He picked up a report and read it out loud. "'*A twenty pound reward is offered to anyone who helps retrieve a diamond, ruby and pearl locket which was snatched off the collar of Miss Constance Paxton-Wright outside St James Theatre on the evening of February 6, 1890.*' I bet that locket's in there somewhere. Them Russians have been doing nothing but steal our jewellery and make fake roubles."

Suddenly Billings saw an opened copy of The Illustrated Police News lying on his desk. It featured a large drawing of a wild, drooling man with crazed eyes and a long beard attacking a defenceless old gentleman with an axe in a dark wood. The heading read: '*Will the Wild Beast of Sutton Courtenay strike again?*' Beside that article ran a parallel story with the following heading: '*Is There Any Room In The Metropolitan Police Force For A Quaker Detective?*'

"Who put this here?" he asked Clarkson.

"One of the clerks put it there. There's an article about you in it."

Billings opened the paper and read.

Detective Sergeant John Billings is a well scrubbed, clean faced young man with a soft, gentle voice and a tidy, but dull appearance. He wears a black suit, with a black waistcoat and a white shirt buttoned up to the collar, but no neck tie or cravat. This would not be in keeping with his puritan faith. A dash of colour to his attire would be considered extravagant and unnecessary.

He heard some snickering in the corridor. He turned around and saw a couple of clerks in the doorway, looking and laughing at him. They quickly moved on as Billings scowled at them. He continued reading.

Detective Sergeant Billings, you see, is a Quaker. He sees God in everything and everyone and doesn't believe evil exists. This, ladies and gentleman, is the man Scotland Yard has put in charge of the Lord Palmer case. Lord Palmer was murdered in his own woods by a ferocious mad man who hacked him to death with an axe. It is a crime which has shocked the nation and has made us wonder whether anyone is safe in this country. We all know about the succession of murderous atrocities the poor of Whitechapel have had to contend with, but it would seem now that even the aristocracy in the home counties aren't safe in their own houses. Unlike the Ripper, Lord Palmer's murderer is known and has been caught. The diligent PC Henries found the vile, beastly man (who'd been nicknamed 'The Wild Man Of Sutton Courtenay') hiding in the bushes in Battersea Park, no doubt waiting to pounce on his next hapless victim. When I asked DS Billings to give me a description of this ferocious villain, he became quiet, turned to look reflectively at the sky and with a tear welling up in his eye he said: "The man I saw yesterday was meek, tired and docile. He was confused and scared and I felt pity for him." Well, I ask you! I have no doubt that Detective Sergeant John Billings, with his love and sympathy for all humanity, would have made an exemplary tutor or nanny to my children, but what the country needs right now is a police force which is as tough and ruthless as the murderous lunatics it is supposed to catch. It didn't appear to me when I spoke to this lily faced young man, that he really had the strength, wile and cunning to outsmart the very criminals we are paying him to catch. Which made me wonder, dear readers, whether there really is any room in the Metropolitan Police Force for a Quaker detective.

"That's your name in the papers, Billings," said

Clarkson. "How about that then, eh?"

Billings folded the paper and threw it in the waste bin. "What a ridiculous article!"

Clarkson didn't know how to respond and smiled at him with sympathy.

Still fuming, Billings sat down at his desk and tried desperately to control the trembling in his hand which had started up again.

There was a knock on the door and a timid voice gently called out his name.

"Detective Sergeant Billings?"

"What!" Billings turned around and scowled at the door.

Jack was standing in the doorway. "There's a man at the reception desk asking for you."

"For me? Who is it?"

"He says his name is Clement Percy."

As Billings came down the stairs, he saw two men standing at the reception desk. One was a bespectacled young man with a brown jacket and trousers which were a few sizes too short. The other was a frail old man with a long, grey beard which reached down to his navel. A thick woollen cape was draped over his shoulders. They were looking at him as he approached.

"Are you Detective Sergeant Billings?" the young man asked. He looked angry.

"Yes."

"Then will you please explain, Mr Billings, why you have been slandering me all over Oxford!"

Billings was taken aback by the sudden vitriol and paused temporarily. He was half-expecting to bump into Sebastian Forrester after hearing the name Clement Percy, and he was still recovering from the disappointment.

"Slandering you?" he asked, confused.

"I come back from visiting my uncle in Wales yesterday only to find my landlady screaming blue murder at me from the stairwell! She changed the lock to my room and has confiscated my clothes and my books! Now, what in the devil's name have you been telling her about me!"

The young man's face had become bright red with indignation and his hands were trembling with rage.

"There has clearly been a misunderstanding, Mr Percy," said Billings. He placed his hand calmly on the young man's back and tried leading him to one of the offices. "Please, will you accompany me to…"

The young man, however, would not be placated that easily and shook the detective's hand off his back. "There certainly has been a misunderstanding! I read about Lord Palmer's death in The Morning Post and came straight over here to assert my innocence. Lord Palmer and I may have had a disagreement, but I would never resort to committing murder. I am a gentle and peace-loving man and I resent being implicated in this atrocious deed."

Billings became aware of the attention the commotion was attracting. He looked around the reception area and saw various officers, clerks and visitors staring at them. He even noticed that some of clerks from the first floor had been drawn out of their offices and were standing in the stairwell looking down at the spectacle.

"Nobody is accusing you of murder, Mr Percy. Now please, will you just calm down and…"

"We have come all the way from Abergavenny," the young man continued, "at considerable expense to me and my family in order to testify that I was staying with my uncle in Wales from the 21st to the 26th of this month. Isn't that right, *ewythr*?"

The old man nodded and mumbled a few words in an agitated, but incomprehensible manner.

"My uncle doesn't speak any English, but I can translate for him. He agrees that I was with him on the dates which I have just mentioned!"

Suddenly Billings saw Jacobs join the clerks on the stairwell. Damn it! he thought. He didn't want Jacobs to know that he had been continuing the investigation on his day off.

"Is everything all right, Billings?" Jacobs called.

"Everything is fine, Mr Jacobs." He turned back to the young man and his uncle. "Please, Mr Percy. You will cease this commotion at once and follow me to my office. I shall have our boy bring us some tea and we'll discuss the travel expenses somewhere more quiet. Jack…" he turned towards the boy who was standing by the reception. "We shall be in room three. Bring a tray of tea." He put his hands on both of the men's backs and gently, but forcefully, guided them towards the office.

"My uncle lives just outside the hamlet of Clydach," the young man said taking a sip from his cup. He had calmed down and his face had resumed its normal colour. His hostility had ceased the moment Billings offered to refund his train fare. Billings would have to pay it out of his own pocket, of course. The case had been closed and no further expenses had been authorised, but Billings was desperate to remove the man and his uncle from Jacobs's prying eyes and he could think of no other way of doing so than by offering the young man some compensation.

"He has a small stone cottage overlooking the Brecon Beacons," the young man continued. "It's nothing much. Just one room with a bedstead and a shed and a goat, but it is beautifully isolated. There's no one else around for miles and miles. My uncle doesn't like being amongst people, isn't that right, *ewythr*?"

He turned towards his uncle who was sitting next to him. He looked pale and tired. His hands trembled as he held the cup and saucer to his lips. The journey and the commotion had clearly taken their toll on him.

"Are you all right?" Billings asked.

"Oh, he's just tired." The young man took the cup and saucer away from his uncle and put them on the table. "He isn't used to so many people. He has been living alone in the Brecon Beacons for twenty-six years. I'm the only one who ever visits him. He has no other family. He is a true Welshman, Mr Billings. Of the old order."

"Perhaps he should lie down for a while? We have a bed in the surgeon's office."

"No, no. We're lodging around the corner from here. We'll go back to Wales tomorrow. He's seventy-six years old, but he's still strong and healthy, isn't that right, *ewythr*?" He slapped his uncle on the back, jolting him awake. "My uncle is a wise man, Mr Billings. He has had no education. He cannot read or write and he can only speak a few words of English, but he is the wisest man I know. And do you know why?"

He looked at Billings, expecting an answer. Billings shrugged.

"Because he's Welsh, that's why! He is a true Celt and the Celts are the carriers of the ancient wisdom. You didn't know that, did you?"

"No." Billings wasn't really listening. Instead he was looking with concern at the old man nodding off.

"Christianity came to the Celts when it was still pure and beautiful, see? Before it was ruined by the imperial Romans with their rigid hierarchies and their pompous grandeur. Celtic Christianity was a simple, mystical religion. We had no archbishops or cardinals or popes. We had no grand, ornamented churches or cathedrals. We just had peaceful congregations of people who had respect for each other. And we had a love of simplicity, which our saviour had imparted on us."

"I believe you are a scholar, Mr Percy."

"I am self-taught mostly, but yes, you could call me a scholar of religion."

"And I believe you have plans to write a book?"

"Indeed I do, Mr Billings. It's about this very subject I am talking about. About how Christianity has been ruined by the Romans and further vulgarised by barbarians such as the Goths and the Franks and the Saxons. My book is about how the Celts preserved the original, mystical beauty of our Saviour's philosophy and how, in the midst of the Dark Ages, when the wisdom and sophistication of the Romans and Greeks had been completely wiped out in Western Europe, it was Celtic Ireland which had become the centre of knowledge and philosophy."

"Why did you argue with Lord Palmer the day before he died?"

"It was all over that Brendan Lochrane who lived on his estate. That so-called hermit. Lochrane was not a hermit! He was nothing but a wretched vagrant. A drunk. A leech. It sickened me the way Lord Palmer offered him money, as if money could ever be a motivation to a true holy man. And the way Lord Palmer displayed that poor wretch to the public like a performing monkey. It was a slap in the face to me and my uncle. My uncle is a true hermit, see? In the tradition of St Anthony and the Desert Fathers. Not like that bestial, vulgar man Lord Palmer had living on his estate. But Lord

Palmer didn't understand. He was a typical Saxon. He was arrogant, haughty, and bigoted, and like all Saxons he took the beauty and wisdom of an ancient culture and turned it into a mockery. He made it cheap and vulgar and ugly. I told him all that and, of course, he kicked me out of his house. Well, I wanted to be kicked out. I did not want to have anything to do with him and his hideous wealth."

"You did not want his patronage?"

"Patronage? Never! Never would I sell my soul to a Saxon!"

"Lady Palmer told me that you had asked him to be your patron."

"Well, I asked him, yes. In the beginning, when we first met. I thought he had a genuine interest in spirituality and asceticism and we struck up a friendship. But then I realised that his interest was nothing more than morbid curiosity and I walked out on him. That was on the 21st of October and I never saw him since."

Billings turned his attention back to the old man. His eyes were closed and his chin was resting on his chest. He was breathing deeply, almost snoring. "Perhaps you should spend the night here," he offered. "We have a bed in the surgeon's office, as I said, and we can make it quite comfortable."

"No, no. Don't trouble yourself, Mr Billings." The young man turned towards his uncle and shook him awake. "*Ewythr, deffro,*" he said, "we must go back to the boarding house."

The old man's eyes sprang open and he looked around confused.

"I'll ask Jack to get you a cab." Billings got off his chair and headed for the door.

As Billings watched the young man and his uncle accompany Jack out of the building, Jacobs suddenly crept up behind him.

"What was that all about?" he asked.

Billings turned to face his boss. Jacobs looked angry.

"It was nothing, Mr Jacobs."

"It was not nothing. I heard the man shout about the Lord Palmer case."

Damn it! thought Billings. How was he going to get out of this one?

"It's just a false lead. A misunderstanding. It's all been cleared up now."

"I thought I told you to leave that case alone."

"And I have."

"Then why were you wandering around Oxford yesterday, questioning boarding house keepers?"

Billings looked aghast. How did he know about

Oxford?

"I thought you were ill," Jacobs continued.

"I… um… I was doing a personal investigation."

"A personal investigation?"

"I was looking for an acquaintance who disappeared from Oxford ten years ago. Sebastian Forrester. I had reason to believe that perhaps his case was connected with that of Lord Palmer, but it turned out to be a false lead. It was all a misunderstanding, Mr Jacobs, and it's been cleared up now."

A desk clerk suddenly approached the two men, holding a piece of paper in his hands. "A telegram just arrived for you, Detective Sergeant," he said. "It's from the Wigtownshire Constabulary."

Billings reached out for the telegram, but Jacobs snatched it from the clerk's hands before he could get to it.

"Why is the Wigtownshire Constabulary wiring you?"

"It was a lead which I received from Bertie Green," Billings explained.

"Bertie Green?"

"The gardener in Sutton Courtenay."

Jacobs opened the telegram and read it aloud. *"Located Lorna Lochrane on the Isle of Whithorn. Admits to being wife of Brendan Lochrane who went missing over a year ago. Is anxious for more information about husband."*

He looked up from the paper. "I suppose you won't need to follow this up either, will you?" He held the telegram in front of the detectives face and scrunched it up.

"No, sir."

"I suggest you wire the Wigtownshire Constabulary and tell them that Brendan Lochrane has confessed."

"I will, sir."

Jacobs continued to stare at Billings, uncertain of whether or not to believe him.

Billings wondered why Jacobs was so anxious to put this case to rest – it wasn't like him not to investigate a case thoroughly. He put it down to his current financial worries and stared back without batting an eyelid.

There was a short, tense pause.

"You're still not looking well, Billings," Jacobs said.

"Am I not, sir?"

"You're very pale. Why don't you take another few days off?"

"Oh, that won't be necessary, sir. I'm perfectly all right."

"Remember the conversation we had in my

office? You take things too much to heart. It is affecting your health and I don't want to lose you from my team. You're too good a detective." There was an attempt at a smile. "Take some days off and go somewhere peaceful. Away from London. Have you any relatives in the country?"

"No."

"Well, stay at a country inn, then. I hear Cornwall is beautiful at this time of year. Take some days off, Billings. I don't want to see you here again until next Monday." And with that, Jacobs turned his back on Billings and headed for the staircase.

CHAPTER NINE

The Isle of Whithorn

A cruel bitter wind blew in from the Irish Sea as Billings got off the carriage on the Isle of Whithorn. The whitewashed houses which lined the street looked draughty and ramshackle. The pebbled beach was littered with old pieces of fishing nets and discarded floaters, and the boats which stood on it barely looked seaworthy. This was a cold and desolate-looking place. Billings stood in the deserted street and looked forlornly at the coachman making his way back up the causeway to the mainland. Why did he go on this trip? Why couldn't he let go of this infernal case? What was this grip which Lochrane held over him? If Jacobs were ever to find out that he had disobeyed his orders again, he'd be in deep trouble.

Two black-clad women with weather-beaten faces walked towards him carrying empty lobster traps. He approached them to ask the way, but as he came nearer, they fled as fast as they could, mumbling something unpleasant in their incomprehensible accent.

An old white-haired vicar peeked at Billings through the crack of the door of a small white church on the other side of the road.

"Excuse me," Billings said, hurrying towards the church. "I'm looking for the house of Lorna Lochrane."

"She's nae there," the vicar said, clinging tightly to the door as another gust of wind swept down the road. "Who are you?"

"My name is Detective Sergeant John Billings."

"From Wigtown?"

"No, from London. I wish to speak to her about Brendan Lochrane."

"Brendan Lochrane, eh? We had some officers from Wigtown here only a few days ago. You've located him then?"

"Yes."

"Well, why don't ye come in, Sergeant." The vicar opened the door. "It'll be quieter inside and Lorna won't be back till six. Come into the back room, I've got a fire lit in there."

Billings followed the vicar to the room at the back of the church. A fire roared in the fire place causing the room to glow.

"I like to sit in here in-between services," said the vicar as he nestled himself in his chair by the fire and wrapped a blanket around his lap. "Grab yourself a chair, Detective Sergeant, and bring it by the fire."

Billings did as he was told. "Do you know Brendan Lochrane?" he asked.

"Aye, of course I do. How couldn't I? He's been living amongst us for nearly ten years. Will ye share a dram of whisky with me?" The vicar lifted a whisky bottle up from a side table and held it temptingly before the detective.

"No, thank you."

"Go on. It'll warm you up."

The vicar poured a glass and handed it to Billings. He took it reluctantly.

"I heard he was in London," the vicar said. "In jail."

"That's right."

"Killed someone, I heard."

"He's been accused of murdering Lord Palmer."

"Och, dear me." The vicar shook his head and tutted. "That is a shame. But not entirely unexpected."

"Why do you say that?"

"You'll have read all about him, no doubt. About how he came to live among us."

"No, I know nothing about him."

"Oh, but my good man! It's been in the local newspaper. It was quite a sensation at the time."

"I know nothing about it."

"Well, I can show ye." The vicar got up and hurried towards the bookcase. "I should have a clipping somewhere," he said, searching through his books. "A young reporter from Glasgow came here a few years ago and wrote a whole article about it. Ah, here it is." He pulled out a large album and leafed through it. "I collect articles about the Isle. I plan to write a history at some point before I die. This place has a rich history, you know? Birth place of St Ninian. Christener of the Picts. Ah, here we go. This is it."

He handed Billings the opened album. A newspaper article had been cut out and stuck on its pages. The title read: *Brendan - The Mystery of a Stranger Stranded on the Galloway Coast.*

"He was washed up on our shore," the vicar said. "Swept in by the sea."

"Where from?"

"No one knows. He never said. No tongue, you know?" He laughed. "Ye can take it with ye, if you want." And without waiting for a reply, he took the album, ripped out the article and handed it to the detective. "I have other papers. I can make new cuttings."

"Thank you." Billings folded the article and put it in his pocket. "What kind of man was he?"

"What kind of man?"

"You said you weren't surprised that he had killed someone."

"Och, well he was a queer fellow. Not quite right in the head, if ye know what I mean."

"No, I don't."

"Well, he did some peculiar things. Had a habit of torturing himself."

"Torturing himself?"

"Aye. He'd starve himself sometimes, or he'd lash himself, that sort of thing. One time he'd hammered a nail into his hand. No one knows why, but there were traces of the blasphemous about it."

"What do you mean?"

"Well, some of the villagers started reading all sorts of things into it. They saw parallels with the events described in the bible. I had to warn them in a sermon not to confuse mania and delusion with godliness. Brendan was not a sane man and he caused a lot of suffering to Lorna."

"His wife?"

"No, they were never married. Lochrane is not his name. It's hers. We don't know his real surname. But he lived with her. She looked after him. No, he wasn't a pleasant man. And I don't just mean the putrid smell that hung about him. He was peculiar. Difficult. It all had to do with his past, I'm sure. Something very traumatic must have happened to him that has made him want to forget it all and start again. That's what he came here for, in my opinion. To be reborn. Where are you staying? You're not planning to go back to Whithorn tonight, are you? You won't find anyone to take you at night."

"I haven't thought about it."

"Why don't you stay at the Old Anchor Inn? It's just down the road. It's where all the passengers for the Liverpool ferry stay. Have ye yer night clothes with ye?" He looked at the detective's satchel.

"Yes. Thank you."

"Lorna's is the last house on the street. She should be back by seven. Would ye like another sip, Detective Sergeant?" He held up the bottle again.

"No, thank you." Billings got up. "I think I'll book myself into the inn and read that article. You have been very helpful. Thank you very much."

Brendan - The Mystery of a Stranger Stranded on the Galloway Coast.
by Angus McVey

It was a cold winter in February, 1885. The Galloway coast had been battered repeatedly by severe storms for several days and there were no signs of the winds abating. I was on my way to visit my aunt in Liverpool, but no ships would set sail under these conditions and so I became stranded on the Isle. There I sat in the Old Anchor Inn, moping over a mug of ale waiting for the weather to ease, when all of a sudden a panicked crowd of men entered accompanying a heavily bleeding man towards the bar.

"Quickly! Get some bandages and alcohol!" I heard one of them call out. "Brendan's had an accident!"

"Accident, my a---!" another man grumbled angrily.

I saw a young bearded man with a rough, red face in the middle of the panicking crowd. He held up his left hand which was bleeding profusely. His shirt and the upper part of his trousers were stained with blood and there was a track of dark red dots, from the door to the bar, where the blood had dripped on to the floorboards.

"What's he done now?" asked the barmaid – a large bossy woman with a dirty apron and a kerchief on her

head – as she looked at the injured man.

"He's hammered a nail into his hand! Look!" One of the men grabbed the bearded man's hand and held it up for the bar maid to see. She shrieked in horror at the sight of it and nearly fell over backwards. All the punters got up and gathered around the bar to watch the spectacle and I had to crane my neck in order to get a good view. It was just as the man had described. A six-inch nail had been driven right through the palm, the sharp end protruded from the other side.

While everyone around him fussed and panicked, the young wounded man, whose name apparently was Brendan, remained strangely quiet and unfazed. There was a certain serenity to his face amidst all this chaos which intrigued me. Who was Brendan and why did he drive a nail into his hand? It would take another two days before the ship's captain felt safe enough to set sail and during that time, bit by bit, as I conversed with the locals, I learned the curious story and fascinating history of this remarkable man.

Five years ago a fisherman by the name of Paul Lochrane found a currach upturned on the beach of a small bird island known locally as St Ninian's Rock. Currachs are small, leather boats which are still commonly used in the West of Ireland, but which have mostly been replaced by the modern wooden variety in Scotland, so seeing one stranded so awkwardly against the rocks was unusual. But an even greater surprise lay waiting for Paul Lochrane as he approached the boat: a man lay underneath it, cut and bleeding and half-submerged in the water.

Paul lifted the man into his boat, rowed him ashore and took him to his house, where he left him in the charge of his sister while he rushed off to fetch a doctor. It was during the doctor's examination that they were met with yet another surprise. The man had no tongue. It had been completely sliced off, leaving only the frenum lingering lost and useless in his mouth.

Word spreads quickly in a place like this and soon the whole village had gathered outside Paul's house to wonder and speculate about the mysterious shipwrecked stranger and his unusual leather boat. Who was he and what was he doing in these waters? Could it be an Irish fisherman swept to the Scottish shores by the wind and the current? Or was it a convict, escaped from one of the prison hulks anchored off the coast of Belfast? Or perhaps a former Fenian terrorist, fleeing the anger of the comrades he'd exposed, the removal of his tongue being the price he'd had to pay for his betrayal. The villagers have had to wait a long time for their questions to be answered, and they are waiting still, for to this day, five years since his extraordinary rescue, the man has refused to divulge any information about himself other than his name: Brendan.

Two of the three theories, however, have already been discounted. He is not an escaped convict. The local police carried out extensive checks both in Britain and in Ireland and there had been no reports of any fugitives from any of Her Majesty's prisons. Nor could he have been a fisherman swept away from the Irish coast. The West coast fishing community hold their Irish cousins in great esteem and they were adamant that the clumsily constructed currach in which Brendan had been found was the work of an amateur. It had been shoddily patched together and the leather had not been tanned and treated properly, which is why it had already started to disintegrate in the salt water.

So that left only the third option: Brendan must have been a fleeing member of a criminal organisation, and perhaps his fear of his band mates' reprisal was the real reason for his continued silence.

Whatever the reason for Brendan's arrival, the locals welcomed him into their community and took him under their wings. The Isle of Whithorn became Brendan's new home and he even married Paul's sister, Lorna, who had nursed him back to health. But he remained an outsider and repeatedly tested the patience of his adopted community with his peculiar behaviour.

"He's a queer, odd bird," said one of the locals who sat at my table. "This business with the nail's not the first daft thing he's done. He went missing one night,

remember?"

The group around me nodded over their drinks as they recollected.

"We searched all over the place until we found him sitting on top of St Ninian's Rock the next morning. Stark naked, he was. Just sitting there, grabbing his knees to his chest, shivering and clattering his teeth. He'd left his clothes on the beach by the harbour and had swam to the rock in the middle of the night. Why? No one knows."

"And then there was the time he'd locked himself up inside Lorna's coal cellar," another man chipped in. "He'd buried the key and told Lorna to slide food and water under the door once a day. He'd been there for three days before Lorna finally knocked the door down. There's something definitely not right in his brain. "

"It's coz he can't talk," one of the women said with a touch of sympathy in her voice. "That's his way of attracting attention." The men around me burst out laughing, but the woman persisted. "It's true. He's a wean without his tongue. That's how weans behave. He were trying to show us something."

"But he has his wee board and chalk," one of the men argued. "Why does he not write on that?"

"Coz he can't write," another man said.

"Aye, he can. I've seen him do it."

"He can write his own name, that's all. Brendan's an

idiot."

Suddenly the company gasped, as if a great blasphemy had just been uttered.

"*Don't misunderstand me. He's a good lad and all that. At least when he's not drinking or acting stupid. But he's a simpleton. His mother must've dropped him on his head when he were a wean. There's no other explanation.*"

"*I don't agree,*" *the woman said, shaking her head.* "*There's something wise about him.*"

"*Wise?*"

"*The way he sat on that rock. Quiet and still and giving himself over to the wind and the rain and the cold.*"

"*What're ye talking about, ye mad bint!*"

"*Men don't understand. For you the wind and the sea are there to be conquered, but there's something saintly and humbling about giving in to the elements.*"

"*Saintly?*"

"*That were St Ninian's Rock he sat on. That weren't no ordinary rock. That were St Ninian's Rock.*"

I was desperate to meet this intriguing man myself, but despite all my efforts to track him down, Brendan proved to be as elusive as he was enigmatic. After two days the boat was ready to depart and much to my regret, I was forced to leave. I took a different route back home and bypassed the Isle all together. But one day I should like to return. One day I should like to go back to the Isle, make my acquaintance with this mysterious fellow and form my own opinions. Is he a saint or a sinner? A lunatic or an eccentric? A wise man or a fool? One day I should like to find out.

Billings stood outside Lorna's house at the end of Harbour Row. He'd been waiting for fifteen minutes. It was pitch black and bitterly cold. All he could hear were the waves lapping against the rocks on the pier and the wind – that cold, constant wind. He lifted the collar of his greatcoat to shield himself from the cold, when finally he saw her. She approached him carrying a basket of oysters. He stepped out of the doorway and tipped his hat. "Good evening,"

She nodded back quietly, then walked straight past him to unlock her door.

"My name is Detective Sergeant John Billings. From the Metropolitan Police."

"I know who you are."

"I'd like to talk to you about Brendan Lochrane."

The woman opened the door. "You'd better come in." She lit a lamp by the side of the door and entered the house. Billings followed her in. He found her kneeling before the hearth, lighting a fire. He looked around him. It was a small room. There was a bedstead on the far side. A table with two chairs in the middle of the room with a long fishing net spread over it. On the table under the net, there was a shuttle, a gauge and a ball of twine used to repair the net. The basket of oysters was on the floor next to a cupboard with pans, mugs and other cooking utensils dangling from hooks.

"I have some news about Brendan Lochrane," Billings said.

"Aye, I know. He's in prison." She got up and walked towards the cupboard, out of which she took a tin cup and a bottle of gin.

"He's accused of killing Lord Palmer."

"And you're here to clear him?" She poured herself a drink.

"Well, I do have reason to believe he may be innocent. Which is why I wanted to speak to you."

She downed her drink in one go. Then she walked back towards the hearth, pulled a chair from underneath the fishing net, set it before the fire and nestled herself in it, holding the bottle of gin between her legs.

"I'd like to find out more about him," Billings continued. "Where he came from. What kind of man he was."

"The Reverend told me you read the article," she

said.

"I did."

"Well, then you know as much as we know."

"I'd like to ask you some questions about your life with him."

"Why?"

"I'm looking for clues. I'm trying to find out why he would confess to a crime which..."

Suddenly she turned towards Billings and, for the first time since meeting him, looked him in the eyes. "He confessed?"

"Yes, he did."

"Well, that's it then, isn't it? He'll be hanged!"

"Not if we can persuade him to..."

"How am I going to pay the rent now? Those ten shillings he sent every month was all he was ever good for! Well, that didn't last very long, did it? Useless bloody bastard!" She poured herself another drink and downed it, then turned back towards the fire and poured herself a new cup.

Billings was a shaken by her sudden change of mood. "He can still retract his confession," he said. "There's not enough evidence to convict him if he retracts his confession. We would have to reopen the case. But I need more information about him. I need to know just what kind of a man he was."

"He were selfish, that's what he were! Selfish,

lazy and useless!"

"Was he violent towards you?"

"Ten years I looked after him." She got up, grabbed the basket of oysters, took a pan from the cupboard and started cleaning the oysters into it. "Ten years of buying his food, of paying his rent. Never did he bring home so much as a penny. 'You've got to get yourself a job', I told him. 'You can not keep relying on the charity of my brother and the kirk.' We're a proud people in these parts. We're poor, but we're proud." She took out a carrot and some onions and started chopping them up and adding them to the pan. "But what could he do?" she continued. "His hands were too thick and clumsy for the nets and he refused to get back into a boat. There's nothing else in a place like this for a man who can't talk. So he'd sulk. And he'd drink. And if he felt I nagged him too much, he'd throw a tantrum and lock himself up in the coal cellar, or swim out to the Rock or drive a bleeding nail through his bleeding palm! He were a wean. A spoiled little wean!"

"Yet you looked after him for ten years."

"Aye, I did. Well, a woman's got to love someone." She took a plate with a small piece of salted beef on it and started dicing it up and adding it to the pan. "I never had a wean of my own. My first husband drowned and... well, let's just say I have nae got much going for me looks-wise. No man wants a drunk, shrivelled-up old maid. But then my brother came home dragging a strange, wounded man over his shoulder. He were helpless and mysterious and... well, love comes easy to a woman when she's needed. She don't need nae other reason." She picked up a jug and poured water into the pan. Then she took a stoneware bottle of stout, pulled out the cork and emptied the contents into the stew.

"Why do you think he stayed here with you for ten years?" Billings asked.

"Nowhere else to go to, I guess. I never knew what went on in Brendan's head. He did nae share things with me." She took the pan, dragged it towards the fire and hung it on a hook over the flames. Then she sat back down on her chair and poured herself another cup of gin. "We had a little chalk and board for him which we borrowed from the school," she continued, "but he refused to use it. After he recovered he'd mope about the house, drinking loads and looking miserable. There was clearly something ailing him and I wanted to relieve him of it. So I took the board and I'd write on it. I know, it were daft of me, but it were easy to forget in the beginning that he weren't deaf, just dumb. 'I love yer, Brendan,' I wrote. 'I wanna help yer. Tell me how to help yer?' But he'd just laugh, take the board off me, correct my mistakes and walk away."

"The crime he is accused of is a heinous and horrific one," Billings said, wanting to bring things to a close. "He's accused of killing his employer with an axe. Would you say Brendan had a violent streak about him? Was he ever violent towards you?"

"He were only ever violent towards himself."

"Why do you think he did things like that? Lock himself up in the coal cellar or hammer a nail into his palm?"

"I do nae know, but it weren't what some of them think. He did nae see himself as some sort of local Jesus and me as his Mary Magdalene. That's what some of them think, but it is nae true. I think it were frustration. Frustration of not being able to talk, of being dependent on me." She suddenly turned back to face the detective. "Will you be seeing him again?" .

"I intend to when I return to London."

"And will you make him retract his confession?"

"I will try."

"If you succeed, Sergeant, will you ask him to come back to me? I want him back.

CHAPTER TEN

2nd extract from Sebastian Forrester's diary

Wednesday March 17th, 1880

It is the day after Janie's funeral and in the courtyard of Wycliffe Hall workmen are replacing the water pipes. I wish I could've attended the funeral. No one knows of my attachment to Janie. Although I think Crickshaw suspects something. He has commented repeatedly on my being glum and subdued of late and has given me a few sympathetic glances.

No mention was made of Janie's death at this morning's assembly, but there's been a lot of fuss about the possibility of lead poisoning. All students who complain about tiredness and muscle ache have been advised to seek medical attention immediately, and we've been reminded not to drink from the taps in the courtyard. If only they knew about the rotten trick Father and Mrs Drew have played on them. I found out only yesterday that Mrs Drew accepted a generous offer of compensation from Wycliffe Hall for the death of her daughter.

Why am I the only one to be broken up about this? Father has not made any comments about this tragedy in his letters to me. He has ignored all my accusations, my lengthy descriptions of Janie's horrible illness, my remonstrations and regrets, and writes instead of his charities. What the devil do I care about his charities! He still prides himself for being a good Quaker and thinks we've done the decent thing by offering to marry Janie, when anyone else in my position would simply have thrown money at her and have left her to her own devices. But the truth is that what we have done is worse. We have committed the greatest sin of them all. We have committed murder! Am I to be the sole bearer of our preposterous crime? Am I to atone for all three of us? Has the burden of redemption been placed once again on the son?

Monday March 22nd, 1880

Crickshaw called me into his office again. He was not happy with my essay about the epistles. He told me I'd done nothing but rephrase what was already written in the New Testament. There was no deduction, no interpretation. "This is not an essay, Mr Forrester," he told me. "This is an exercise in copying!"

Well, I don't care about the epistles and I told him that. They mean nothing to me. There's nothing in them but rules and regulations and statutes and doctrines. What happened to love? What happened to faith? Human hearts are not governed by rules.

Crickshaw told me that we needed rules to keep us from us straying. Without them how would we know that we had strayed?"

"We'd feel it!" I replied. (I think I may even have shouted.) I told him that when _I_ had done something wrong, I could feel it burning inside me. I could feel it eating me up.

He just smiled back at me with sympathy (I really do believe he must know something of what I'm going through) and said that not everyone was like me. Some of us needed rules.

I sniffed at this. The Desert Fathers didn't have rules, I told him. (He frowned at my mention of the Desert Fathers, but I ignored him and continued ranting.) The Desert Fathers found their own ways to God through prayer and intuition. I told him that that was what I wanted to learn about. I didn't want to read about Romans and Corinthians. I wanted to read about our *own home-grown saints. Like St Cuthbert, who would sneak out of the monastery in the middle of the night, wade into the sea and pray with the rhythm of the waves until the sun came up. Or St Columba who would sail to the remotest islands in his quest for solitude. Or St Brigit, the glorious mother of Kildare, who healed fallen women of their pregnant state. (I nearly broke into tears when I mentioned St Brigit. Where was she when Janie needed her? Crickshaw saw me become upset and put his hand on my shoulder, but I shook it off.) These were people who knew about passion. They knew about instinct. They listened to God with their <u>hearts</u> and not their <u>brains.</u>*

Crickshaw remained calm and replied that all these saints I mentioned were scholars once too. Everything they learned, they learned from the bible. The bible was our primary source, he reiterated. All knowledge stems from there and no other book would do.

Well, I don't care about the bible . 'Sayings' is <u>my</u> bible. 'Sayings' is <u>my</u> primary source. I grabbed the book this evening before turning in, opened it at a random page and this is what I read:

'A brother was leaving the world and, though he gave his goods to the poor, he kept some for his own use. He went to Antony, but when Antony learned what he had done he told him: 'If you want to be a monk, then go to the village, buy some meat, hang it on your naked body

and walk back here.' The brother did as he was told, and as he walked back to the cave, dogs and birds followed him and tore at his body. He came back to Antony and showed him his torn body. Then Antony said, 'Those who renounce the world but want to keep something for themselves are attacked in that way by demons and torn in pieces.''

There are no better words to describe how I feel. My soul, my whole being, has been torn to shreds. Janie's death is the consequence of ignoring God's call. I know what I need to do now and I can not postpone it any longer. Tomorrow I shall leave. I shall go to the wilderness, give myself over completely to the will of God and be reborn as someone else. I will take nothing with me, other than some clothes and the money I need in order to reach my destination. Even my book, my worthy and beloved book, which has taught me much and has given me such consolation through my many trials, I shall leave behind. As Evagrius once said: 'I shall leave behind all, even the word which commands me to leave behind all.'

CHAPTER ELEVEN

In Cumberland

Billings decided to spend some time in the Lake District before returning to London. It took him four hours to travel from Whithorn to Kendal and he spent those hours pondering all he had learned on the Isle. A disturbing notion occurred to him during that journey. Could Sebastian Forrester and Brendan Lochrane be one and the same? There were some parallels in their respective stories and the dates seemed to fit.

He thought back to that day when he visited Lochrane in his cell and tried to summon the image of the man's face to his mind. There was something about Brendan's eyes which looked familiar, he remembered now, and a feeling of dread came over him. Could this glorious, young titan – the hero of his youth, the man he had loved and envied in equal measures, the first object of his waking desires – really have turned into a pathetic old wretch in the space of ten years? This thought was too disturbing to contemplate!

When he alighted at the station in Kendal he made his way to Wildman Street. Mr Forrester had given him the business card of Mr Edmund Pringle, the private detective he had hired ten years ago to find Sebastian.

Pringle had his offices above a tea room which, according to the chatty proprietor, had recently opened to cater for the booming tourist industry and which prided itself in being the only place in the whole of Kendal to sell postcards. Indeed, Billings did see an impressive display of prints and photographs of the Lakes behind the counter when he entered.

Billings climbed the stairs to the first floor and knocked on the door with Pringle's name sign stuck on it. There was no reply, but he could hear someone snoring inside. He knocked again, louder this time. Still there was no reply. The door was unlocked so he opened it slightly and poked his head into the room.

"Mr Pringle?" he called out.

A fat, middle-aged man with large side whiskers

and a balding head lay draped over an armchair. His jaw was open and his eyeglasses rested precariously on his chins.

"Mr Pringle?" Billings repeated.

Pringle jolted awake and looked at Billings with a shocked expression on his face.

"I'm Detective Sergeant Billings from the Metropolitan Police. I'd like to speak to you, if I may."

Pringle remained looking at his visitor, alarmed and confused.

"It's about a case you handled ten years ago."

"A case? Ten years ago?"

"A missing person case. Sebastian Forrester."

Pringle finally sat up and put his eyeglasses back on his face. "Did you say the Metropolitan Police?" He straightened his collar, tucked in his shirt and brushed the hair on the side of his head.

"Yes."

"Scotland Yard?"

"Yes."

"I've never been visited by a Scotland Yard inspector before," he said with a touch of alarm. "What is it precisely you want from me?"

"Do you remember Mr Frederick Forrester?"

"Mr Frederick Forrester? Yes, I seem to remember his name."

"He employed you ten years ago to find his son who went missing in this area."

"Oh, yes. I remember now. A young tourist who came for the lakes. Killed himself, didn't he?"

Billings was taken aback by that blatant remark, even though it was a theory which he had himself once entertained. "Well, it appears he didn't," he said. "Mr and Mrs Forrester have received a letter."

"From him?"

"Or someone claiming to be him. I've re-opened the case and was wondering whether I could discuss it with you."

"Why, certainly! Certainly you may!" He suddenly sounded relieved and enthusiastic. "It is a great honour to be asked to help out someone from Scotland Yard. Come in, please, Mr... um..."

"Billings." He entered the office and pulled up a chair from behind the desk.

"I assure you, I shall do everything in my power to assist you. Now let me get his file." Pringle rushed excitedly towards the filing cabinet. "Mr Forrester was a banker, was he not?" he asked while he searched through his files. "And his son a divinities student?"

"You have a good memory, Mr Pringle."

"Yes. Yes, I do." He giggled like a girl. "I've always had a great memory. The mother used to call me a walking encyclopaedia. Ah, here it is." He pulled out a file and returned to his seat. "Mr Forrester must be quite an important man for the Yard to be involved," he said, sitting back down on the couch.

"This is not an official investigation."

"Oh." Pringle sounded disappointed.

"Mr Forrester is a personal friend of mine. I'm doing this as a favour."

"I see."

"Mr Forrester received a letter from somebody in Oxford claiming to be his son. When he went to Oxford to meet him, he vanished again. I have compared the handwriting from the letter he received with that of letters he had written before and they matched, so I am now working under the supposition that Sebastian Forrester is still alive."

"Quite plausible," Pringle agreed. "After all, no body has been found."

"The last place we know him to have stayed at is the Lakeside Hotel on the banks of Lake Windermere."

"That's right." Pringle looked at the reports on his lap. "That's what it says here."

"What I would like to determine, with your assistance, is what became of him when he left the hotel."

"Well, let us see." Pringle started reading his report. "He checked into the hotel on the 19th of March, 1880. He looked pensive and subdued, according to Mr Tavistock, the hotelier, and according to Mr Forrester that had at the time been his normal disposition. On the morning of the 22nd, Sebastian Forrester told Mr Tavistock that he was going to take a trip on a steamer and would be back late, to which Mr Tavistock replied that there probably weren't any steamers sailing yet as it wasn't quite the season for it, but that he hoped he'd have a nice day anyway and that he'd tell the cook to prepare a cold supper for him for when he returned. Unfortunately Sebastian Forrester didn't return that night, nor indeed any other night. He disappeared, leaving all his clothes and luggage behind him and his bill unpaid."

"Do we know anything of his movements on that day?"

"Yes, indeed we do, Mr Billings. I did make inquiries and it turns out that a steamer did cruise the lake on that day and the captain confirmed Sebastian Forrester was on it. It was easy for the captain to recognize him, because he only had three passengers on that particular trip: Sebastian Forrester, a mother and her daughter. The mother and daughter were local people. She sold flowers to tourists while her daughter was left on the bank to stare with awe and wonder at the steamers which cruised the lake. It had apparently been a long cherished desire of the little girl to sail on one of those boats herself, and upon hearing this, Sebastian Forrester treated the girl and her mother to a trip. I don't know if any of this is significant, but it seems to have moved the old Mr Forrester when I told him about it so I made a note of it in my records." Pringle looked up proudly. "I pay attention to this sort of thing, you see? In a case like this, when a young man deserts his family, there are often personal histories which one doesn't like to pry into, but which can reveal a lot, so I always like to record people's reactions when I report my findings."

"Do you know where he got off?" Billings asked.

"Yes, I do. According to the captain he got off in Ambleside, at the north end of the lake. The mother and daughter remained on the boat and returned to Bowness. The captain asked him whether he wanted to be picked up again later in the day, but he said no, which the captain thought peculiar as Mr Forrester wasn't carrying any bags or even wearing a coat. I have two more pages in this report, would you like me to carry on?"

"Please do."

"You can see that I have been thorough." Pringle smiled proudly as he turned the page. "He was spotted walking down Bog Lane by the minister of Brathay Church, who spoke to him briefly and said he looked glum and distracted. Bog Lane goes right through the fells all the way to Coniston Water, but I'm afraid this is where the trail ends. There were no further identifications of Sebastian by any of the other people I spoke to."

"So what do you think became of him?"

"Well, Bog Lane is a long road. It was a little past three when he got off at Ambleside and it starts getting dark at around half past five in March. Where would he have slept? Remember, he had no coat and wasn't carrying anything to keep him warm. There is an inn quite far down the road, the Drunken Duck, which lies in Barngates, but he wasn't spotted there either. The Drunken Duck is a tavern for local farmers and farmhands and a young gentleman like that would most certainly have stood out. So my conclusion is that he must've left the road altogether and either headed into the woods or returned to the lakeside."

"Why would he head into the woods?"

"I don't know. Perhaps he didn't wish to be seen by anyone."

"Why would he wish not to be seen?"

"Well, presumably he was up to no good, Mr Billings, otherwise why would he run away?"

"At Scotland Yard we are taught not to presume, Mr Pringle. And anyway, he *was* seen, wasn't he? By the minister of Brathay Church, according to your own report."

"We searched the woods extensively," Pringle continued, ignoring the detective's retort. "I hired a number of men to comb the area but we found no evidence of his presence."

"I'm still not clear, Mr Pringle, why you felt you had to search the woods."

"Well, we had to start the search somewhere."

"It must've been quite an expensive operation, combing the woods."

"Mr Forrester told me no expense was to be spared in finding his son."

"Do you have *any* justification for spending such a large amount of Mr Forrester's money?"

It had become clear to Billings that Pringle had indeed been milking the Forresters, as Mrs Forrester suspected.

"I was working on a particular theory, Mr Billings," Pringle replied defensively.

"And what theory would that be?"

"I've already explained that several witnesses have confirmed that he looked distraught and that his father agreed that he was. My theory is that he came to the Lake District suffering from melancholia."

"And you believed he committed suicide?"

"Yes, I did."

"And hanged himself from a tree?"

"Possibly. Or otherwise he returned to the lake and drowned himself."

"So you dragged part of the lake?"

"Indeed I did."

"Another expensive operation, no doubt."

"It is a lengthy and labour-intensive process, Mr Billings. It does not come cheap." Pringle had gone red and was shuffling uncomfortably in his seat. "Excuse me, Mr Billings." He rose from his seat and poured himself a glass of water.

There was a short pause in the interview and Billings took a few short breaths to collect himself. "Where does Bog Lane lead to?" he asked after Pringle had re-taken his seat.

"It leads to the village of Brantwood on the bank of Coniston Water, which is about seven and a half miles from Ambleside."

"He could've walked that in one night."

"Without being seen?"

"Didn't you say it was already dark?"

"Well, yes, but..."

"It seems to me he walked through the night all the way to Brantwood. Did you make any inquiries there?"

"No, I did not." Pringle was starting to look flushed again. "There is no reason to believe Sebastian Forrester went to Brantwood. He'd have checked out of the hotel and taken his belongings with him, if that had been his intention."

"Perhaps it was a decision he made on the spur of the moment. Did you explore any other avenues?"

"Mr Forrester and I agreed to end the investigation after we dragged the lake."

I'm not surprised, after the expense he had already incurred! thought Billings, but remained silent.

"I did keep an eye out for any noteworthy stories which appeared in any of the local newspapers," Pringle said. "I receive all the local papers and regularly cut out articles which might be of interest to me and stick them into my scrapbook. I could show you if you like." Without waiting for an answer he got up and pulled his scrapbook out of the bookshelf.

"There was one story which appeared in the Whitehaven News which interested me at the time, but I had already closed the investigation and

Whitehaven lies too far outside the area in which I was looking, so I didn't follow it up. Here's the article." He handed Billings the opened scrapbook. "I'm not sure why this intrigues me. Perhaps it's just my instinct, but I do find that when two unusual occurrences happen in the same period of time, even if they seem completely unrelated, they're usually connected."

Gentleman's Clothing Found In St Bees Field

A pile of gentleman's clothing was found in the middle of a field in the small Copeland village of St Bees. The items were discovered by Jedediah Tooke, a local shepherd, as he grazed his flock in a meadow by the Pow Beck stream. "They looked like high quality clothing to me," said Mr Tooke. "Shirt, striped trousers, waistcoat. And smart too, not the kind of donkey jackets us wears around these parts." The clothes, which included a pair of shoes and long cotton drawers, had been left neatly folded in the middle of the field. "He took everything off except his hat," said Mr Tooke. "Can't think why anyone would want to undress here. The stream is hardly deep enough to swim in." The items of clothing are currently being held by the police and the villagers have been advised to direct any naked man wearing nothing but a hat to the local police station, where his clothes will gladly be returned to him.

"I don't suppose you know what Sebastian Forrester was wearing at the time?" Billings asked.

"That's a detail I didn't think to ask."

Shame, Billings thought, but it didn't surprise him.

After his interview, Billings returned to the Lakeside Hotel and took his nightly dose of morphine. Feeling both light-headed and clear-minded at the same time, he peered at a tourist map of the counties of Cumberland, Westmoreland and Lancashire and traced the path Sebastian might have walked. Although he thought Pringle to be a most disagreeable character, he did feel that he had the right instincts. Something also drew him to make a connection between Sebastian's disappearance and the discovery of the abandoned gentleman's clothing. Looking at the map, he saw that Bog Lane led to an old Roman path known as Hardknott Pass, which crossed the wild, empty fells right towards the coast. The village of St Bees, where the clothes were found, lay to the south of Whitehaven, at the edge of the Lake District, only forty-three miles from Ambleside. It seemed perfectly feasible to him that Sebastian might have walked it.

The following morning Billings got up early,

headed into town and bought himself a piece of warm cotton-combination underwear, a blanket, a pannikin and some rope. He rolled up his blanket and strapped it to his satchel with the rope. Then he tied the pannikin to his belt. Thus packed, he took a steamer across the lake to Ambleside and, ignoring the curious looks from passers-by, he headed down Bog Lane towards the coast.

It was clear and sunny when he started his walk at a little past two, but a couple of hours later, the sun started to set and a band of bitterly cold air slowly descended upon him. He took his blanket from the satchel and threw it over his head, blocking out the breeze and trapping his body heat. It was just his face which got cold now. The bitter air stung his cheeks and his forehead, dried his lips and frosted his eyes. But he took the discomfort and paced on determinedly, stopping only occasionally to boil some water and make himself some tea, or take a few bites of the loaf he had brought with him.

He was conscious of being a peculiar sight with his satchel strapped to his back and his blanket over his head, but there was no one there to witness it. He was all alone in this beautiful, desolate land. Like Robinson Crusoe. All he could see around him were the dark blue peaks jutting out from the ground in the distance and the black and grey shades of grass, shrubs and rocks, all illuminated by the moon's eerie light. The night was quiet. There were no sounds other than that of the light breeze and his own footsteps, crushing the ground beneath with a beat and rhythm which soothed him.

He walked for hours. From two o'clock in the afternoon till four o'clock the following day, ignoring the pain in his thighs and calves, the blisters on his feet and his dry, cracking lips. He was in another realm during that walk, removed for a few hours from this physical world, from the heavy loads which kept him grounded, from his pondering, cumbersome self. Was he meditating? Could this be what Sebastian had strived for in his diaries?

When the sun rose the following morning, he had left the behind the moors and mountains and found himself wandering through meadows and farmlands, following a path along a stream which he later found out was called Pow Beck (the very stream at the banks of which the clothes were found). At around four o'clock, he finally caught a glimpse of the village of St Bees lying in the horizon. His loaf had been fully eaten by then and his tea completely drunk. He was shattered and hungry and his body no longer had the energy to keep him warm.

As he followed the path towards the village, he suddenly saw a small chapel on a hill. Next to it stood a small priory. On the same hill next to the priory, there was another building. It was a strange cone-shaped structure, made of flat stones which had been piled on top of each other without the use of mortar, and which looked like a giant bee hive. He kept gazing at it, wondering what it was, when suddenly he heard someone calling him.

"Good afternoon."

One of the monks had stepped out of the priory and stood in the doorway, peering at him. He was a big man, in his fifties, with a rough, tanned face engraved with laughter lines and a thick band of greying hair above his ears.

"Good afternoon," Billings replied, surprised by the monk's sudden appearance. "I come from Windermere. I've been walking all night. I'm on my way to Whitehaven, but I was wondering if I could shelter here for the night. I'm cold and hungry and..."

"We have just sat down for supper," the monk said, in a quiet voice with a thick French accent. "You are welcome to join us."

"Thank you." Billings rushed towards the door,

relieved. "My name is Billings, by the way. John Billings."

"How do you do. I'm Brother Martin."

Billings followed the monk towards the dining room, where four other monks were sitting quietly at a long table. He nodded at them politely, but none of them reciprocated. He sat down among them while Brother Martin served him soup. The monks didn't speak or look at each other during the meal. They were all in their forties or fifties, except for the one sitting at the head of the table. He was probably in his seventies and Billings assumed that he was the prior. The prior was the noisiest eater. He was unable to eat his soup without letting half the contents of his spoon trickle down his mouth and drip back into the bowl. Suddenly, as Billings was staring at him, the prior lifted his eyes and gave him a fierce, scowling look, like that of a disapproving school master. Billings quickly looked away, hung his head and ate his soup in silence.

After supper, Brother Martin led Billings to his cell.

"The Priory of The Holy Virgin was built in 1846 by four Cistercian monks who crossed the channel from France, intent on rebuilding monasteries which had once existed on ground proclaimed holy by the early Christian Celts," the monk explained. "I came over from Nantes four years ago. This will be your cell."

Brother Martin opened the door to a small, bare room, furnished only with a bed, a desk and a large crucifix on the whitewashed wall.

"We rise every morning at ten to four," he continued, "and we retire at eight. You are welcome to join us during our meals, which, as you have seen, are done in silence. And, of course, you are welcome at community mass, but for the rest of the time we will ask you to keep yourself to yourself."

"Thank you."

"You are welcome to stay with us for as long as you like. We continue the tradition of receiving guests with reverence and kindness, but without letting this impair the monastic quiet. I remind you that this is a silent order and I would appreciate it if you would refrain from speaking needlessly to anyone before eight o'clock tomorrow evening."

"Thank you, but I shall continue towards Whitehaven first thing tomorrow morning. How much should I pay you for your hospitality?"

"We do not charge our guests for their stay, but we are grateful for any offerings you may choose to convey."

"I shall certainly leave something before I go."

"I wish you good night, Mr Billings. May God be with you."

"May God be with you too."

Billings walked into his room, put his satchel on the bed and took out the wallet with his morphine ampoules. He looked out the window as he prepared his syringe. The strange cone-like building next to the house was clearly visible from his room. Billings could see a small opening on one side of the cone through which a man could enter and another small opening at the top which looked like a ventilation hole. The building was surrounded by a low, round wall made of the same un-mortared flat stones. He wondered about the building's purpose, when suddenly he saw a light being lit inside the structure. He squinted his eyes and peered closer. A man emerged from the building holding a lamp in his hand. He was dressed differently to the other monks. He wore a brown woollen tunic and cape. He looked dirty and bewildered. His head was completely shaved except for a band of hair which crossed his scalp from ear to ear. The man walked out of the building towards the edge of the stone wall, placed the lamp on the ground, then pulled up his tunic and squatted down. He remained there for a while, looking around him, oblivious to his audience, then pulled a handful of grass blades out of the ground, wiped his backside, picked up the lamp and returned to his bee hive.

Who on earth was that? thought Billings, looking at his syringe and wondering for a fraction of a second whether or not he had already injected.

When Billings woke up the following morning, he could hear the monks outside working in the orchard. He picked his watch up from the floor and checked the time. It was ten minutes past eight. The walk must have tired him out more than he had anticipated, he thought. He got up and gathered his belongings into his satchel.

His limbs were sore and stiff as he walked into the orchard to say his goodbyes. The chapel bell started ringing just as he approached the orchard, summoning the monks to mass.

"Lauds," Brother Martin whispered to him as he walked past him to the chapel.

Billings felt it would be disrespectful to leave during prayers, so he waited outside the chapel for the monks to re-appear. He waited for nearly an hour, listening to the mumbled prayers and tuneless chants. When Lauds was over, the monks re-emerged from the chapel and made their way silently back to the orchard where they picked up their tools, except for Brother Martin who went towards the detective.

"You're leaving us, then?" he said.

"Yes, I am."

"Are you a Catholic, Mr Billings?"

"I am a Quaker."

Brother Martin raised his eyebrows. "Ah, how interesting. So you do not believe in the church?"

"No, I don't."

"The Pope would call you a heretic." He said this with a smile.

Billings smiled back. "I suppose he would."

"In a way, we are quite similar."

"Are we?"

"Like you, we try to find our own individual connection with God. At least we have that much in common."

Billings dug into his pockets for some coins. "I'd like to thank you for your hospitality."

He gave the monk a couple of shillings. Brother Martin nodded gratefully, took the coins and put them in a pocket of his scapular.

Billings turned to leave when a thought suddenly occurred to him. "That stone building next to the priory?" he asked.

"Ah. The Celtic cell."

"What is it?"

"It is what I said. A Celtic cell. It's what medieval Irish monks used to live in."

"I saw someone come out of it last night."

"That would be Brother Pelagius. Our hermit."

"Hermit?" Billings was intrigued by the sudden occurrence of that word.

"This priory was built on the foundations of a Celtic monastery, which was dedicated to St Bega – after whom the village of St Bees is named – but which was destroyed during the dissolution of the monasteries under Henry the Eighth. St Bega was an Irish princess who was promised in marriage to a Viking prince, but valuing her virginity, had fled across the Irish Sea to the Lancashire coast where she led a life of exemplary piety. We are particularly interested in Celtic Christianity at this priory and we like to emulate the life of the early Irish monks."

"Why?"

"The early Celtic monks were quite different to us. You'll have seen Brother Pelagius's habit is different to ours, as is his tonsure. There was never anything like this in France. Or indeed anywhere else in Europe. Ireland was the only country in Western Europe not to have been Romanised. It was the Romans who spread Christianity in Europe, as you know, and even after the decline of the Roman Empire, Roman influence still lingered throughout Europe. But not in Ireland. Ireland remained isolated and free of any Roman influence, so when Christianity arrived there it grew and evolved in a very special manner. There is a particular book which was very influential in Ireland at the time. 'Sayings of The Desert Fathers'."

Billings's heart leapt at the mention of that title. He instantly reached for his satchel and pulled out the book.

"Ah, you have it. How wonderful!" The monk took the book out of his hands and leafed through it. "The Vatican feared this book at first, because it took power away from them. They didn't want people to find their own connection with God. *They* wanted to be the bridge to heaven. That's why we call the Pope the pontiff. But the Irish were free from Roman influence and that included the Vatican. And they took this book to heart. But they adapted it to suit their own surroundings. There were no deserts in Ireland, but there were islands, and bogs, and other inhospitable locations, so the Irish set up monasteries there. They took to the seas in their small leather boats and went to wherever

God's winds blew them. It is fascinating, Mr Billings. Truly fascinating. But tell me, why is it you carry this book around with you?"

"It belonged to a friend of mine who went missing. I am a detective. I'm investigating his disappearance. Have you been at this priory long?"

"Four years."

If Sebastian had ever stayed at this priory, Billings thought, it would have been ten years ago. "Do you get many visitors?" he asked.

"Not many. You're the first since I've been here."

Suddenly they were interrupted by the prior, who marched angrily towards them from the orchard. "What's all this talking!"

Brother Martin pulled a face like a chastened school boy. "Our guest was only asking how many visitors we've had."

The prior turned towards Billings. "Why are you asking so many question? Are you a reporter?"

"A reporter?"

"Mr Billings is a detective," Brother Martin explained. "He's looking for a man who went missing ten years ago."

The prior stared at Billings with a fierce and intense look on his face. "This is a silent order, Mr Billings! And we do not concern ourselves with the past. We stay in the present. Forever in the present!" He turned his back on the two men and returned to the orchard.

"Scotland Yard, eh?"

The desk sergeant looked cynically at Billings through his eyeglasses, holding the detective's identification badge in his hands. They were standing at the reception desk in Whitehaven police station. Billings had asked the desk sergeant if he could speak to the chief superintendent, but the desk sergeant was being awkward.

"The badge looks genuine enough," he said, still twisting and turning the badge in his hands.

"That's because it is genuine." Billings was struggling to keep his patience. "Now, please will you let me see the superintendent."

"The superintendent's not here, Mr Billings. He's down at the harbour, working on a case."

"When will he back?"

"That's hard to say. There's never any way of telling how long these things are going to take, is there? You should've sent us notice. You can't expect our superintendent to be at your beck and call, Mr Billings. Even if you are from Scotland Yard."

Billings ignored the hostility in the sergeant's

tone. "Is there someone else I can talk to?"

"Well, that depends on what it is you want to talk about, Mr Billings."

"I am working on a missing persons case and I need to take a look at your records."

The desk sergeant raised his eyebrows "Take a look at our records? We can't allow just anyone to come in and browse through our records, Mr Billings. This isn't a public library."

"I'm not just anyone," Billings replied tetchily.

"No. You're Detective Sergeant Billings from Scotland Yard." The desk sergeant said his name in a mocking, sing-songy way. "Who is this missing person you're looking for?"

"His name is Sebastian Forrester."

"He must be a very important man if Scotland Yard is involved."

"This is not an official investigation," Billings said reluctantly.

"Not an official investigation?"

"This is a private investigation. I'm doing a favour for a friend."

"So you're not from Scotland Yard?"

"I *am* from Scotland Yard. I'm on my annual leave."

The sergeant noticed Billings's agitation and a small smile appeared in the corner of his mouth. "I see."

"Now, may I please speak to someone about this."

"What precisely is it you wish to speak to someone about, Mr Billings?"

"I need some information about some clothes which were found by the Pow Beck stream."

"You're not a reporter, are you?"

Why was everyone asking him whether he was a reporter, thought Billings.

"You are aware that it is against the law to impersonate a police officer?"

"I am not a reporter, Sergeant. I am a genuine police detective. You have my badge in your hands."

"You haven't re-opened the case of the mutilated monks, have you?"

"The what?"

"The great scandal at the Priory of The Holy Virgin nine years ago? Where the clothes were found?"

"Yes," Billings said, quick as a flash. "I have re-opened that case."

"Everything there is to know about that case has already been printed in the papers. There's nothing new to report."

"May I please speak to someone superior."

"I shall have to check with the boss. This may take a while."

"Please take your time."

"Scotland Yard, eh?"

Inspector Blunt was munching a beef and oyster pie. Billings sat opposite him, watching the corpulent inspector eat his luncheon while PC Goodthwaite was in the adjacent filing room, searching through the cabinets for the report.

"Yes," Billings replied.

"And you say this is a private case?"

"Yes."

"Is that allowed?"

"I'm doing it in my own time and I'm not being paid for it."

Billings found it hard to look Blunt in the face. The inspector kept speaking with his mouth full.

"I'm surprised you haven't heard of the St Bees scandal before," the inspector said. A bit of onion fell out of his mouth and landed on his chin. "It was big news over here. Perhaps it wasn't reported on down south. I don't suppose you lot care much about what goes on up here."

"It's not that. I just don't read the papers regularly."

The inspector raised his eyebrows in surprise.

"You don't read the papers?"

"Not unless it's relevant to a case I'm working on. I find them depressing."

"How ever did you get to work for Scotland Yard with that attitude?"

Billings ignored the tone of disapproval.

The inspector turned back towards his colleague in the filing room. "How you getting on back there, Goodthwaite?"

"It might help if I knew the precise date, sir," the constable replied.

"1881 or 1882 thereabouts."

"Perhaps you could fill me in while the constable searches for the report," Billings proposed.

"Perhaps I could." The inspector swallowed the last bit of his pie and wiped his hands on his lap. "Basically what happened, Mr Billings, is that a doctor from St Bees was called out to the priory in order to attend to two monks who'd been injured. When the doctor arrived he found the two monks lying ill and feverish in their beds, and after further inspection he saw that their tongues has been sliced off."

"Their tongues?" Billings's heart leapt at the revelation.

"That's right, their tongues. The doctor said the prior had told him that the monks had sliced off their own tongues two days before, and that the Prior had tried dealing with the injury himself, but that he was unable to avoid the monks' mouths from becoming infected and had no choice but to call for the doctor."

"Why did they slice off their tongues?"

"Well, the Prior was very cagey about that, which is why the doctor informed the police and why an inquiry was launched, which even involved the Bishop of Liverpool having to come over to Whitehaven to testify."

"What was the outcome of the inquiry?"

"The outcome was that the monks had inflicted their own injuries in an attempt to take their vows of silence to an extreme, and that the prior was entirely ignorant of this decision and was therefore not to be blamed. The two monks weren't official members of the order and lived separately from the priory, in some sort of stone hut."

"A Celtic cell."

"A Celtic cell, that's right. Well, these two monks, or novices, lived together, you see, in this Celtic cell. One of them was called Pelagius. And the other one..."

"Brendan?" Billings guessed.

"That's right, Brendan. So you *have* read about this, Mr Billings. Well, something very peculiar was going on between those two monks in that cell. Something very peculiar indeed, if you know what I mean." He laughed and winked at the detective, but Billings had stopped paying attention. He was too shocked by the turn of events.

"You know what these Catholic clergy are like, Mr Billings," the inspector continued. "Dirty little buggers, the lot of them!" He laughed again. "What do *you* think, Goodthwaite?"

"Sir?"

"Are you a Catholic?"

"Church of England, sir."

"Good lad!" The inspector turned back towards Billings. "Well, they were expelled, of course. One of them returned several years later and is still there. As for the other, well, he came here to Whitehaven. He was taken in by a tanner, a notorious character by the name of Barnabas Crooke."

"Taken in? Do you mean employed?"

"Well, if you can call it that. Crooke just placed Brendan on the pavement in the middle of King Street – just round the corner from here in fact – where he'd sit all day, with his cap on the floor, begging. He made a very pitiful impression, did Brendan. His eyes, you know? There was something deeply melancholic about them. And the way he'd sit, perfectly still on that cold stone floor, in all kinds of weather, shivering sometimes, and pale and wet. He attracted a lot of pity and attention and made a fair amount of money in the process, which Crooke then took off him in exchange for food and a bed."

"Where is this Barnabas Crooke? Could I speak to him?"

"He's gone, I'm afraid. He landed in the house of correction in Peter Street a couple of years ago after an attempted burglary, but disappeared with his son after he was released. Well, good riddance, as far as I'm concerned. They were crooks by name as well as by nature!"

"So what happened to Brendan?"

"I don't know, Mr Billings. He wasn't seen again after Crooke got arrested. You got that report yet, Goodthwaite?"

"I think I have, sir."

The constable appeared from the filing room and walked towards the desk with two reports in his hand. The inspector took the report off the constable and gave it to Billings.

"There you go, Mr Billings. There's the report about the clothes, and there's the confession Brendan wrote for us when we pulled him into the station. That should tell you all you need to know.

CHAPTER TWELVE

Statement taken from Brother Brendan (real name unknown) June 3rd, 1881

I joined the priory in March 1880. You needn't know anything about my life before that. Except that it wasn't much of a life. In fact it was no life at all. It was a period of gestation, a womb in which I grew and developed. My real life started on that cold spring day in 1880 when, after wandering aimlessly through the hills and lakes of Cumberland, I stumbled quite unexpectedly upon the sight of a priory, standing before me on a hill just outside the village of St Bees. The sun broke through the clouds at that moment and when a beam of light illuminated the chapel, I knew immediately what I had to do. Without a moment's hesitation, I took off all my clothes and walked towards the priory, naked like a newborn babe, freed from all my possessions and my previous incarnation.

There were five men living in the priory at the time. The four French founders and a young local man called John Morgan Quick, who'd joined as a novice two years previously. They were having breakfast when I knocked on the door and were shocked when I stumbled into the house cold, naked and bleeding. (I had to walk through a bramble bush and up a pebbled path to get to the door, so my feet and shins were cut and covered in blood.)

"Who are you? What happened to you?" one of the monks said, alarmed and embarrassed, not knowing where to look.

"I've been driven here by God," I said.

"Why are you undressed? Where are you clothes?"

"I have no clothes."

"What is your name?"

"I have no name."

"Where do you come from?"

"Nowhere. I have no history."

"This is not an asylum! We are not a charity!" he cried. "This is a Christian retreat for men who seek to be closer to God. You should go to the police station or the poorhouse if you are in any trouble."

I assured them I was not looking for asylum. I told them that I'd received a calling from God and that the Lord had led me here.

"Please will you put your clothes back on and send us

a letter! This is not the way to approach a house of God."

I repeated that I had no clothes. I had given up everything as God had commanded me to. I told them that I was only doing what God had asked of me and that if they refused to let me in, I'd sleep on their doorstep until they changed their minds. If they refused to feed me, I'd simply starve outside their gates. They had no choice in the matter. God had decided.

They gave in after that. They quickly grabbed a spare tunic from a chest and wrapped it around me. Then they fed me some soup and, after some further questioning, they reluctantly agreed to take me on as a novice.

We rose every morning at three-thirty for vigils and silent prayer. Breakfast was at six-thirty followed by lauds at seven. Mass was at eight. We worked from nine to noon (we had an apple orchard and we made cider. We also kept bees and cows). Sext was at twelve-fifteen, our midday meal at twelve-thirty then we went back to work until five-thirty. Vespers was at six and Compline at seven-thirty. We retired at eight.

Before Lauds and Compline, when the brothers retired into their cells to read and study, John Morgan and I were put to clean the house. John Morgan was a simple young lad whose parents had moved to Liverpool from Ireland. He'd had a brain fever at the age of five which left him weak in mind and body. He must've been only sixteen or seventeen when his parents dumped him at the priory. The poor lad was forced to live alone amongst these dour middle-aged Frenchmen (some of whom didn't even speak any English) for two whole years, so when I moved in, he was naturally very happy to have the company of someone his own age.

He followed me everywhere and talked incessantly. He talked as we scrubbed the floors or emptied and rinsed the pisspots; he talked while we picked the apples or pruned the trees; he talked while we milked or grazed the cows. He talked about everything, what he felt, what he thought, what he saw, what he did. All he hadn't been able to say in the last two years he now unleashed on me. It drove me to despair. This was supposed to be a silent order and this simpleton's incessant chatter was restricting my ability to meditate and commune with God.

I begged the brothers to grant me refuge from our resident imbecile by allowing me to study with them for a couple of hours every day. But they refused. The books which had been imported from the mother abbey in Dijon were fragile and valuable and were not to be touched by a novice. These were not the famous canons to which I had already been exposed in my previous life. These were obscurer texts which were written long ago by people living on the fringes of Christendom. I told them that the daily routine at the priory was too boring and monotonous for me and that I longed desperately for the world of knowledge which lay hidden from me in the library. But the brothers argued that enduring and cherishing this monotony would bring me closer to God. I disagreed. I told them that it was only the body which needed to be punished and exhausted. The mind needed to be enlightened or it would starve. And if the mind starved, then so did the soul. After five months of pleading, the brothers finally gave in.

Suddenly a whole new world opened up to me. The brothers had been particularly interested in Celtic Christianity (which is why they'd come to Britain in the first place) and their library was filled with books about the Celtic saints. I read all about St Patrick, the enslaved shepherd boy who broke free from his shackles and converted the High Kings of Ireland; and St Kevin who lived in a cave, slept on a bed of rock and prayed for hours submerged to his chin in the icy waters of Glendalough; and the most fascinating saint of them all, St Brendan, who took to the sea in a small leather boat and ventured into the unknown looking for the Isle of the Blessed, making it all the way to America. The priory held a copy of the Navigatio, the book which details his epic journey, and I read it over and over again. The Irish monks had a great tradition of sailing into the unknown. Like the Desert Fathers of Egypt, they saw the sea as their watery desert and they would give themselves over completely to its winds and its currents. It was a tradition which stemmed from the old pagan custom of tying criminals up, putting them in a boat and setting them adrift to be left to the mercy of the gods. What a way to atone!

The lives of the Irish monks moved me profoundly and I desperately tried to emulate them. Soon I had made myself a new tunic from rough, untreated sheep's wool, shaved my head in the style of the Irish tonsure and called myself Brendan. (John Morgan, of course, did the same and he took the name Pelagius, after the Romano British ascetic whose real name was probably Morgan – a name I chose for him.) I then begged the brothers to allow me to construct a Celtic cell on their grounds so that I could live in it in solitude and expose my body to the elements, but they started growing tired of my unorthodox ways and told me I was being difficult and contrary and that I should learn some humility and stop romanticizing the past.

I objected to being called a romantic. I was only looking for hardship. It's in suffering that we find God. Away from the distractions which bring us pleasure and comfort. Our life in the priory was not hard. This was a feeble, watered down version of what the Desert Fathers had endured. Where was the hardship in getting up every morning at three o'clock, when most of us were already in bed at eight? Where was the hardship in not talking all day, when we could speak all we wanted after

Compline? This was a comfortable life we were leading. We were wallowing in comfort and vanity.

But they didn't understand. Why did I feel the need to torture myself, they asked. What was I trying to prove to them? They said I was treating suffering as a sport, as a test of endurance, as a spectacle and a freak show. Real suffering doesn't come in one intense sweep. It is a slow, creeping thing which gradually engulfs you and traps you for the rest of your life. It is unwise to continuously subject your body to pain and discomfort. Our bodies need to be kept strong and healthy, because real hardship affects your soul and you need a strong body to cope with it.

I ignored them. While they were in their rooms napping, or at the table getting drunk on cider, John Morgan and I were wandering the hills and valleys, looking for flat stones with which to construct our cell. Soon we had built a strong and sturdy bee hive and we had moved in. The brothers tolerated our presence and even brought us food. Despite their many protestations, they were clearly glad to be rid of us and probably also a little curious at our experiment.

But the experiment failed. It was supposed to be a life of basic simplicity; of not eating or wearing more than was necessary to keep the body alive; of enduring pain and discomfort with serenity; of suffering in stillness. But all this was impossible with John Morgan. I simply could not make him understand what we were trying to achieve. No matter how many times I tried to explain it to him, how many times I reprimanded him, or how I endeavoured to ignore him, John Morgan could not stop from talking. It wasn't just in his nature to be chatty, there was something wrong with him neurologically. He kept on babbling, repeating the same old nonsense, not caring whether or not he was being listened to. There was no desire to express anything. It was as if his mouth had been wired to his brain and moved with every thought or perception which occurred in his mind. Even in his sleep, I could see his mouth move and hear him mutter nonsense.

He did try, though. He was so in awe of me and so keen to please me, that he hated being told off. He was able to stay quiet for a few minutes after I'd reprimanded him, but then he'd forget himself and he'd start talking again. I wondered whether perhaps it was this condition which led his parents to dispose of him at the priory. The brothers had coped with him by ignoring him and allowing him to wander around the grounds like a babbling maniac, but I could not ignore him. Yet neither did I want to get rid of him. It was easy enough for me to endure the extremes of weather, I had trained my body well enough for that in my previous life, but John Morgan's noise and presence were part of the elements which I had chosen to subject myself to and I needed to *find a way of appreciating and cherishing them. In this, though, I failed.*

Rather than thinking of myself, of considering John Morgan's noise a problem that I had to learn to deal with, I started thinking that this was a problem for him too, that he must surely be tired of his own talking, that his jaw must surely need a rest. The notion of cutting off his tongue was a frivolous one at first, one borne out of anger and frustration. But as time progressed, that idea seemed to carry greater weight. Silence would bring John Morgan closer to God, as it would me. If I cut my own tongue out first, John Morgan would inevitably follow my example. I could live without a tongue. I had no need for taste or speech. It would be a commitment to God. A sacrifice.

And so it happened. One morning I took the shears we used in the orchard, stuck out my tongue, lay it on the lower blade, and after counting to five, squeezed my right fist slowly and carefully until I held the dead, bleeding flab of meat in the fingers of my left hand. The pain was excruciating, it struck every nerve in my face and it made my stomach turn. But I had meditated beforehand and I took the pain, as I had taught myself to do, cherishing every stinging beat. Then, with a mouth filled with blood, I handed the shears to John Morgan, who had been sitting before me, watching the act with silent awe. (Yes, he was silent then. It hadn't occurred to me before, but I remember it now.) John Morgan took the shears from me and without hesitation, stuck out his tongue and lay it on the blade. I suspect now that John Morgan wasn't aware of how much the act would hurt. I'd become good at not showing my pain and perhaps I should've warned him, because as soon as he started cutting, he cried out like a slaughtered pig and, with his tongue only half cut, he dropped the shears on the ground, got up and ran out of the cell holding his hands to his mouth, the blood seeping through his fingers and staining his tunic. It was John Morgan's agonized squealing which alerted the brothers.

I don't really need to tell you what happened next. The brothers made a botched attempt at stitching John Morgan's tongue back up and gave us alcohol to rinse our mouths with, but they were unable to fight off infection. They called for a doctor after a few days and the doctor alerted the police. And so here I am now, in this police station, writing my statement. I am mute and homeless and my infected frenum has caused a vile odour to emanate from my mouth, which continues to repulse other people. But I have no regrets. I did what I did for God, knowing that it would cause me a lifetime of suffering. This has been my commitment, my sacrifice. I shall continue to live my life as though crucified; in struggle, in lowliness of spirit, in good will and spiritual abstinence, in fasting, in penitence, in weeping.

CHAPTER THIRTEEN

Bashun

Billings stood outside the Forresters' home, waiting for the door to be opened. He had arrived back in London late the previous night and hadn't had much sleep. The painful revelations of the preceding days had once again deprived him of his rest. He was about to break out into a yawn when the maid finally opened the door.

"Good morning, Nancy," he said, stifling his yawn. "Is Mrs Forrester in?"

The maid looked even more haggard than he did. She beckoned him in without responding and led him towards the drawing room. Billings looked around the hallway as he followed her. A basket with dirty sheets stood in the middle of the floor next to a pair of empty bed pans; a cabinet against the wall was stacked full with medicine bottles; a dinner tray with a half-eaten bowl of gruel on it lay on the ground just outside the drawing room door. Mr Forrester's illness had clearly taken its toll on the household.

Nancy knocked on the drawing room door then popped her head in to announce the visitor.

"It's the detective, ma'am."

Billings peeped over the maid's shoulder. Mr Forrester sleeping in his bed. His wife sat beside him, with some needlework resting on her lap.

"Oh John, you're back!"

Mrs Forrester said, putting the needlework on the floor and getting up from her chair. She looked thin and dishevelled. She rushed towards him, wrapped her arms around his neck and kissed him on the cheek.

"Did you find anything out?"

"I have some news." He broke away from her embrace and turned towards Mr Forrester. He was thin as a skeleton, his eyes were closed and his jaw dropped open. For a minute Billings thought he was dead, but then suddenly he saw Mr Forrester's hand jerk and a weak groan escape his lips.

Mrs Forrester caught him looking. "He's deteriorating rapidly. Keeps slipping in and out of consciousness. It won't be long now. What is your news?"

"Perhaps you should sit down."

"Sit down?" Her face went pale. "Why? Is it bad news?"

"Sit down, Mrs Forrester, and I'll tell you."

She staggered backwards, feeling behind her until she found her chair, refusing to take her eyes off Billings for a moment.

"I have a list of items I'd like to read out to you." Billings took a piece of paper from the inner pocket of his jacket. "Please tell me if you recognize any of these items of clothing." He held the note before him and began reading out loud. "A pair of striped woollen trousers with five black buttons; a white cotton shirt with a stand collar; a plain, light brown waistcoat with satin lining and velvet collar; a pair of black leather ankle boots with round toe; a pair of white cotton drawers labelled with the following letters – B.A.S.H.U.N..."

"Bashun!" Mrs Forrester suddenly called out.

"Do you recognize it?"

"That was Sebastian's nickname. When he was little he couldn't pronounce his own name. Bashun was all he could come up with. The servants have labelled his clothes with that name ever since."

"These clothes were found discarded in a field just outside of Whitehaven."

"Whitehaven? But what does it mean? Do you think that he..." She fell silent and started breathing heavily.

"I think he's still alive, Mrs Forrester," Billings said quickly, hoping to reassure her. "And I think I know where he might be."

As they stepped out of the cab, Billings observed how Mrs Forrester seemed to be completely unfazed by the revelation. He was afraid that she'd be overcome with fear and shame at the prospect of seeing her son in prison, but she wasn't. She wasn't deterred by the sight of the heavy iron doors which led into Newgate Prison. She wasn't shaken by the jangling keys on the chain of the guard who led them to Sebastian's cell, or by the clanging echo of their footsteps over the metal corridor. She kept her head held high all the time they were in prison, staring straight ahead of her, doing her best to block away all distractions. There was no look of fear or shame in her eyes. There was just an icy determination to be reunited with her son.

The prison guard stopped at one of the cells and unlocked the door. Billings wasn't as calm as Mrs Forrester seemed to be. He felt butterflies in his stomach. He was still disturbed by the notion that Lochrane and Sebastian were one and the same, and secretly hoped to have been mistaken.

"I think I should go in alone at first," he whispered to Mrs Forrester. "I have to prepare him. He doesn't know we're here."

Mrs Forrester understood and nodded her consent.

A strong smell hit Billings's nostrils as he entered. It was that same putrid smell which he encountered when he visited Lochrane in the holding cell. The prisoner stood at the end of the room, his back towards the door. He was basking in the light of the sun shining through the high barred window. He wore a grey uniform, which was a few sizes too big for him. His trousers slowly slipped from his waist, but he didn't seem to have the energy or care to pull them back up. His prison cap lay on the bed. His head had been completely shaved.

He hadn't moved since Billings entered the cell and seemed to be completely unaware of his visitor. He didn't even react when the door was slammed shut and the lock turned. Billings wondered if he was deaf.

"Brendan?" he said softly.

The prisoner ignored him.

"Sebastian?" Billings tried.

Suddenly the prisoner's ears pricked up and he

turned towards the door. His beard had been shaven off, which completely altered his appearance and made his eyes stand out. Billings recognized him immediately. It really was Sebastian. His face was jaded and craggy, his skin tanned and beaten by the weather, but his eyes – those blue, penetrating, melancholy eyes – remained the same. How could he not have recognized him before? His heart pounded in his chest as Sebastian continued to look at him, curious and confused.

"It's John," he said quietly. "John Billings."

Sebastian still didn't show signs of recognition.

"Gideon Billings's son. Don't you remember? Your parents looked after me for a few years." Still no reaction. "You used to call me 'ward'. 'Numbskull'."

It was of no use. Sebastian clearly didn't know who he was. He lost all interest in his visitor and turned back to face the wall. Billings wondered whether he was suffering from amnesia.

"I'm a police detective now. I've come to help you," he continued. "I don't believe you killed Lord Palmer. You were only one month away from claiming your reward. You had nothing to gain from his death, but you had everything to lose. Nor is there any real evidence against you, except for your own confession."

Sebastian's back was still turned towards the door and there were no signs that he'd heard anything Billings had said.

"I don't know why you signed that confession," Billings persevered. "Perhaps you were confused, or you thought that there was no hope, but you can still retract it. It won't count as evidence if you do."

It was hopeless. His words just seemed to bounce off the prisoner's back. And yet he had reacted when he called out his name.

"Sebastian?" he called again. "Bashun?" he tried. Still nothing. Then a thought suddenly occurred to him. "Your mother is here," he added.

Finally a reaction. Sebastian straightened his back.

"She's standing outside. She's longing to see you."

Sebastian turned back towards the door. There was a pained and expectant look in his eyes now.

Could it be that he just doesn't remember *me*? Billings wondered, but he quickly collected himself. "She doesn't want to see you hanged," he said. "But that is what will happen if you don't retract your confession." He took a notepad and pencil out of his satchel. "You can write your story down on this. Write down exactly what happened, explain that your confession was made at a time of confusion and despair, but that it was false. Then give the letter to the guard and ask him to give it to the magistrate."

He reached the notepad to him, but Sebastian gave no indication that he was going to take it.

"Your mother will employ a lawyer, but it is crucial that you retract your confession within the next few days before the trial date is set."

Sebastian looked past him at the door. He wasn't listening. He just wanted to see his mother.

"I'll leave this here." Billings put the notepad and the pencil on the bed, then went towards the door and knocked on it. "Will you let her in please, officer."

As the cell door opened slowly, Sebastian tilted his head sideways to get a better view.

Mrs Forrester entered slowly and stopped just one step away from the door. The door slammed shut and made her jump.

Sebastian eyed his mother up and down. He looked with interest at her grey hair; her wrinkled, gloveless hands; her black dress and woollen shawl.

Mrs Forrester stared back, but her façade soon cracked. All the tension of the last few hours, the last few years, was finally released. She put her hands to her face and stood shuddering and sobbing, desperately trying to suppress the sounds of her wails.

Then, quite unexpectedly, Sebastian went towards her, wrapped his arms around her, lay his head on her shoulder and sobbed along with her.

Billings knocked on the door and asked the guard to let him out. He waited outside the cell, watching the prison guard pace up and down the corridor, jingling the keys on his chain. He heard a lot of sobs inside the cell, but there was no talking.

After only three minutes, the guard suddenly stopped pacing, walked towards the cell and opened the door.

"I'm gonna have to ask you to leave now, ma'am. Please will you let go of the prisoner."

Mrs Forrester and Sebastian reluctantly let go of one another and dried their eyes.

"I will arrange a lawyer for you, my dear," Mrs Forrester said as she exited the cell. "We'll get you out of here, my darling. We'll do everything we can. We'll have you back home soon so you can see your father before he..." She stopped herself just in time. Sebastian was still drying his eyes on his sleeve and didn't appear to have registered the gaffe.

"Hey, look who's back! 'Ow were the lakes?"

Clarkson looked up from his desk when Billings entered the office. His table top was stacked with paperwork. "I've been going through these bloomin' reports all week, Billings. I'm all beady-eyed." He rubbed his eyes with his hands. "But I tell you what, it'll be worth it. I took all the reports which offered a reward for the retrieval of stolen jewels then tried to match them with the stash we found in Deptford. There's gonna be an 'andsome reward at the end of this. Jacobs says we might get up to ten pounds all together. Out of which twelve shillings will go to me. Think of that, Billings! Will come in handy for Christmas, eh? I could get myself a nice big goose out of that."

Billings smiled and made his way to his desk.

"Now I just need to match the remaining jewels. It's bloody tedious work, Billings. Especially as some of them don't seem to have been reported stolen. Take a look at these, for instance." He picked up a report and read out loud. "'A leather pouch containing a gold cameo ring with a picture of a Greek warrior and a gold pocket watch engraved with two date palms.' Sound pretty fancy to me. Why would you not report these?"

The description of the items rang a bell in

Billings's mind, but he couldn't place them.

"'Ere, Billings, what are you doing for Christmas? You should come over."

Billings smiled politely and brushed the notion away with his hand.

"No really, you should. There'll be enough goose to go round. They've got a big one at this goose farm in Clapham Common. A big brute of a beast. I've named him Mr Boogledug. I'm gonna tell the chap to reserve him for me."

"I don't want to inconvenience your wife."

"It's no inconvenience. She'll love to meet you. So, that's settled then. You're spending Christmas with us."

Clarkson turned back to his report and Billings smiled politely, hoping Clarkson would forget about the invitation closer to the time.

"Oh, by the way. Jacobs wants to see you," Clarkson added. "He's in a foul mood today."

Jacobs was pacing about restlessly in his office. Billings stopped in the doorway and tapped gently against the door.

"You wanted to see me, sir?"

Jacobs stopped and turned to face him. There was an angry look on his face. "Had a nice time in the Lake District, did you?"

There was a hostile tone to his question, but Billings wasn't sure whether it was intentional, so he ignored it. "Thank you, yes."

"Relaxing, was it?"

"Yes, sir. It was."

"Good! Good!" Jacobs walked towards his desk, which was once again cluttered with bills and invoices, and picked up a letter. "I just received this from the magistrate." He held the letter up and looked angrily at Billings.

"What is it?"

"You know perfectly well what this is, Billings. Lochrane has retracted his confession!"

Billings wasn't sure why this would anger Jacobs, but it seemed tactless to smile, so he tried to conceal his satisfaction.

"I believe you've had a hand in this?" Jacobs asked.

"I visited him in Newgate yesterday and I gave him some advice." Billings looked at the letter in Jacobs's hand. It was a long letter. Five or six pages, tightly packed with Sebastian's elegant writing. He was desperate to find out what it contained. "May I see the letter?"

"No, you may not!" Immediately, Jacobs locked the letter up in his desk drawer. "Why did you talk him into retracting his confession?"

"I am convinced he's innocent, sir."

"And what evidence do you have to support this?"

"None yet, sir, but I'm sure if we look hard enough, we can..."

"He's an acquaintance of yours, it seems."

"Yes, sir. His real name is Sebastian Forrester and he's the son of a family friend. I hadn't seen him in over ten years, but when I was in Whitehaven, I..."

"Ah yes, Whitehaven," Jacobs interrupted. "I've heard about your adventures in Whitehaven."

Billings looked confused.

"The Whitehaven police contacted us to verify that you were a Scotland Yard detective. It seems this little trip to the Lake District wasn't as relaxing as you made it out to be, was it, Billings?"

"I... um..." Billings was taken aback by Jacobs's anger and started stuttering. "I was working on a personal case."

"A personal case?"

"Mr Forrester asked me to help him locate his son who went missing ten years ago."

"So you went behind my back?"

"I had no reason to tell you, sir. I didn't know at the time that the cases were connected. I only recently found out that Sebastian Forrester and Brendan Lochrane were one and the same."

Jacobs stared at him, wondering whether or not he was telling the truth.

Could this be the reason for his anger? Billings wondered. That he had not confided in him? "I assure you, sir. I had no reason at the time to suspect a connection."

"The trial was set for Friday, but it has been postponed," Jacobs said. "We've been given two more days to come up with the evidence or he'll be released. We do not have time for this nonsense, Billings! The case was closed and now you've gone and..." Jacobs threw the magistrate's letter back on his desk and sat down.

"Maybe if I go back to Abingdon and look through the evidence with the Berkshire Constabulary. The gardener did mention that they had a lot of poachers, so perhaps..."

"I've already sent Inspector Flynt."

"Inspector Flynt? But wouldn't it make more sense to send me?"

"You're off the case, Billings. You're personally involved."

"But..." This came as a veritable shock and Billings was dumbfounded.

"I'm sending you to Norfolk."

"Norfolk?"

"The Prince of Wales is holding a Christmas

reception at Sandringham House. I'm transferring you to the Security Service."

"Security Service?"

"It's only temporary. They need more people. But if you play your cards right, there'll be a promotion in it for you. This is Special Branch, Billings. This is where you belong."

"But I'd far rather..."

"This isn't a proposition, Billings. This is an order. Your train leaves this evening at five, so you'd better get back home and start packing your bags."

"'Ere, why you back so early?" asked Mrs Appleby as Billings entered the house.

Billings frowned. "I'm off to Norfolk," he mumbled. He took off his coat and hat and hung them on the hatstand. "I've just came to pack my bags."

He was hoping he'd be able to slip in and out of his room quietly without being barraged by his landlady. But that was not to be.

"Norfolk? What's in Norfolk?" Mrs Appleby asked. "They don't half make you travel about, don't they? First it was Berkshire, now it's Norfolk. By the by, a parcel arrived for you this morning."

She picked up a brown envelope from the hall table and held it out to him. "It was shoved through the letter box at around ten o'clock. I was having my tea in the parlour when I heard a noise in the hallway. 'That can't be the postman,' I thought to myself. 'He's already been.' So I rushed out and saw that envelope lying on the doormat. No stamps, no postage mark, just your name."

Billings stared at the brown envelope and was instantly reminded of his shameful visit to Mr Bull's shop several days ago. The envelope had the same tint and was of the same size. Surely Al Bull couldn't have been so careless as to send new photographs directly to his house?

"'Ere, you've gone all pale!" said Mrs Appleby. "I hope it's not to do with work. I don't want any police matters taking place in my house."

Billings took the envelope off his landlady and felt its weight. A feeling of dread rose within him as sordid memories flashed through his head: Al Bull's mocking grin as he struggled to hide the envelope in his breast pocket; the musty smell of the shop's back room; Charlie's dirty fingernails as his hands fumbled all over his body.

"Thank you," he said abruptly, then ran up the stairs with the envelope.

"What, you're gonna open it in your room, are

ya?" Mrs Appleby called after him, disappointed. "I hope it ain't nothing serious?"

Billings rushed into his room and locked the door behind him. He plunged down onto his bed and held the envelope before him. His heart pounded as he stared at it. He remembered now that there had been a flash of light outside the window when he was with Charlie. He had a horrible premonition. This can't be true, he thought. Please God, let this not be true.

With trembling fingers he unsealed the envelope. It contained three cabinet cards. He pulled out the first. It was exactly what he dreaded. The picture was of him, standing clearly in the light of the gas lamp with Charlie's arms flung around his neck, and his mouth kissing him on his face. The second one had Charlie on his knees before him, running his hands down his torso. The third one clearly showed Charlie's hands undoing his trouser buttons. The pictures were well lit and the ecstatic expression on Billings's face, with his head flung back, his eyes wide shut and his mouth half-open, left no doubt as to what kind of activity was taking place.

If there were three pictures, there must have also been three flashes, he thought. He could only remember one flash. Had he really been so consumed by desire that he hadn't noticed? It surprised him that he had such passion in him.

He dropped the pictures on to the bed and shook the envelope. A small piece of paper slipped out from within it and floated down on to the floor. There was something written on it. He picked it up and read it.

LAY OFF, OR ELSE…

What does it mean, he wondered. He looked back into the envelope to see if there was anything else, but it was empty. There was no demand for payment. No calling card. No sign of who had sent this to him or why. Then it suddenly occurred to him. Jeremiah Rook! The reporter who had written that peculiar article about him in The Illustrated Police News. He had bumped into him in Oxford and again later on Edgware Road. He was carrying some kind of mysterious equipment around his shoulder. It must have been a camera! Had Jeremiah Rook been shadowing him? Had this whole scene been carefully orchestrated in order to entrap him? If so, by who? And why? Did this have to do with the Lord Palmer case? Was this an attempt to scare him off the investigation?

He picked the cabinet cards off the ground and

shoved them back into the envelope. Then hid the parcel under his jacket, ran out of the room and down the stairs. Ignoring Mrs Appleby's concerned questions, he rushed out the door and took a cab towards Paddington. He only had three hours before his train would leave for Norfolk and he hadn't packed his bags yet, but this couldn't wait. He had to know what was going on.

As Billings approached Praed Street from Paddington Station, he could see Al Bull's shop in the distance. It was shut up. Wooden boards covered the windows and a padlocked chain was wrapped around the door handle.

He's fled, thought Billings. That blessed Arab has fled. His heart sank.

He walked towards the shop. The little window by the back entrance - the one through which the photograph had been taken - had also been boarded up. He tried pushing open the back door, but it was locked. Billings hung his head and put his hands to his face. What the devil was he to do now?

Suddenly he heard a noise inside the shop. Something or someone was shuffling inside the building. He looked around for something he could use to prise open the board on the window. He found some shards of a discarded roof tile on the ground, one of which seemed the right shape for his purpose. He picked it up and climbed onto an upturned barrel conveniently located beneath the window (the same barrel, no doubt, on which Jeremiah Rook had stood with his apparatus when he took the photograph). He stuck the shard underneath the board and prised open a gap big enough for him to look through. The shop was dark. He heard more shuffling noises coming from the shop's front room. Could it be rats, he wondered. Suddenly he saw a light inside the shop and large shadows were cast on the floor. Billings now saw that the room had been stripped bare. The shop's contents had been packed into crates piled up against the wall. Al Bull had not fled yet, but he was intending to.

Billings moved his head closer to the window. "Mr Bull, is that you?"

The shuffling stopped and the light was extinguished.

"Mr Bull, I know you're in there. Let me in. I have you speak to you."

It would've been foolhardy for the shop's occupier to continue to pretend that the building was empty. The candle was re-lit and Al Bull came into view, holding the lantern over his head.

"Doctor Smith, is that you?" The shop owner saw Billings peeping at him through the small window and laughed. "What are you doing Doctor Smith? I thought you were a burglar."

"Open the back door, Mr Bull. I have to speak to you."

"I'm closing down, Doctor Smith. I'm moving to Birmingham."

"Open up."

Al Bull opened the back door. Billings climbed down from the barrel and approached him.

"Would you care to explain the meaning of this." He took the envelope out of his coat pocket and showed him.

"That has nothing to do with me, Dr Smith."

"You know what it is, then?"

There was a pause. What a blunder. Al Bull had spoken too soon.

"No, I don't know what it is," he said a little flustered, "but whatever it is, it has nothing to do with me."

"You set me up, didn't you?"

"I don't know what you mean."

"You know perfectly well what I mean!" Billings slammed the envelope against the door, causing Al Bull to cower back. "Who asked you to do this?"

"I have nothing to say to you, Doctor Smith." The

shopkeeper retreated back into his shop and grabbed the door, ready to shut it, but Billings stuck his foot in the opening just in time to block it.

"Tell me who put you up to this, you blessed little Arab!"

"Leave my shop now." Al Bull continued to push the door shut, "or I will cry out for the police!"

"I *am* the blessed police!"

The shopkeeper was stumped and gave up trying to close the door. "Ah, so that is why!" His eyes lit up and a strange little smile appeared on his face.

"That is why what?"

"I wondered why the foreign gentleman was so interested in you. I thought perhaps you were a judge or a councilor, but you're far too young and shabbily dressed for that. But you're a policeman." He laughed. "Oh boy, oh boy! Are you in trouble!"

"Who are you talking about? What foreign gentleman?"

"I don't know who he is." Al Bull took a cigarette out of his shirt pocket, put it in his mouth and lit it with the candle. "Really, I don't. I just know that he came into my shop a few days ago and offered me three hundred pounds for my client list. I've been offered money for it before, but never as much as that. And I was desperate to leave this shithole and start a respectable shop in Birmingham. So I sold it to him. Then he came back the next day and offered me a further hundred pounds if I arranged for you to visit me. He had picked your name out of the list. I didn't ask why. Why would I?"

"And what about Charlie?"

"Oh, Charlie has been working for me off and on. But I didn't put him up to anything. What you did with him, you did out of your own free will. I played no part in that. I have broken no laws."

"You're a pornographer."

"Excuse me, Doctor Smith, but I am not a pornographer! I am a dealer in artistic photographs."

"You are a blackmailer."

"It weren't me who blackmailed you, Doctor Smith."

"Did you know there was a photographer outside?"

"Of course."

"Then you were party to a deliberate act of blackmail. And that is a crime, Mr Bull."

"And so is sodomy!"

There was a pause. Al Bull was right. Technically no sodomy had been committed, but the pictures were compromising nevertheless. His reputation and career were at stake.

"What did the man look like?" Billings asked.

"Look like? I don't know. Tall. Dark."

"Where was he from?"

"I've no idea."

"Arab?"

"No, he was definitely not an Arab. Russian maybe."

"Russian?"

"Possibly. I don't know. Now please, Doctor Smith. I've told you all I know and it's three o'clock. I'm supposed to vacate the premises by four and I'm not yet packed."

CHAPTER FOURTEEN

Sandringham House

"There will be eighty-four guests in total," said Chief Inspector Wright.

Billings was sitting in a private room at the White Swan in the village of Dersingham, listening to the briefing of the following day's activities. There were sixteen officers in the room. Eight Yard men who had travelled with Billings from London and eight local officers from the Norfolk Constabulary.

"The guest list includes the Prince's sister, Her Imperial Majesty the Empress Frederick; the ambassadors of France, Spain and Denmark; our foreign secretary the Marquess of Salisbury; the governor of The Imperial East Africa Company, and many other notables."

"Will the Queen be there?" The question came from an eager young Norfolk constable, who was sitting in the front row taking careful notes.

"No, the Queen is in Osborne House."

"Always bloomin' is," mumbled Sergeant Cooper who was sitting next to Billings. This caused a ripple of chuckles amongst the men.

CI Wright was not amused and turned towards the sergeant. "What was that, Mr Cooper?"

"Nothing, sir."

"The Queen is in mourning, Mr Cooper, as I'm sure you are aware. She has retired from public life."

"She's been in mourning for twenty-nine bloomin' years! Ain't it 'bout time she came out of it?" This was followed by more laughter.

Sergeant Cooper was a fellow Yard man who'd been loaned to the Security Service. A stout, middle-aged man with a bushy moustache who'd been whining and complaining all the way from London about having to protect the 'toffs and swells at their little do'. CI Wright ignored him and continued with his briefing.

"There are thirty-two servants resident at Sandringham House, but most of the guests will also bring their own, which means that there will be over two hundred people present at the reception tomorrow. And there's only sixteen of us, so we must remain alert at all times. There have been no threats and we have no reason to suspect any trouble, but at a gathering like this we must always anticipate intrusions from the usual opportunists who hope to gain notoriety by harming the Prince of Wales or a member of his family. By the usual opportunists, I mean people such as Fenians or anarchists or..."

"Disgruntled mistresses!" Sergeant Cooper again, causing another ripple of laughter from the men.

CI Wright ignored him and continued with his briefing, but Billings was annoyed by the constant interruptions and turned to scowl at Cooper.

Cooper had been particularly raucous on the train to Norfolk. He'd taken a pair of dice with him and had started playing with some of the other officers, laughing and shouting and annoying the other passengers in the process. Billings had asked him to keep it down (mostly because he was trying to read Robinson Crusoe and couldn't concentrate) but this didn't go down well and Cooper had lashed out at him. Cooper had called him dour and boring and had nicknamed him *'Little Miss Proper-Drawers'*. Billings hadn't replied to this and simply got up and walked off to a quieter carriage. But as he did so he heard Cooper whisper to the others: "That's the one from the newspaper article. You know, the Quaker," and they all burst out laughing again.

"I hope you're not frowning at me, Miss Proper-Drawers?" Cooper whispered.

Billings didn't answer and turned back to the briefing. From the corner of his eye he saw Cooper make an obscene gesture to his cronies, who then laughed.

The real reason for Billings's agitation had nothing to do with Cooper. He was still preoccupied with the fate of Sebastian and Mrs Forrester. He had managed to send Mrs Forrester a telegram before he departed to Norfolk, explaining that he'd been taken off the case. He told her not to worry because as far as he was concerned there simply wasn't enough evidence to convict Sebastian. But he was not convinced of this himself. He regretted not having done more to investigate the case when he was in Sutton Courtenay. His goal at the time had only been to obtain a positive identification, so he hadn't even looked at any other evidence the Berkshire Constabulary might have assembled. And now it was too late.

He was also concerned about Jacobs. Why was Jacobs so upset to find out Sebastian had retracted his confession? It occurred to Billings now how unusual and irregular the way Jacobs had extracted the confession from Brendan was. Why couldn't he have waited for Billings to return? He assumed the money problems Jacobs was suffering from had made him distracted and impatient, although it did strike him as odd that Jacobs should have such debts in the first place. He didn't seem like a flamboyant spender.

And then, of course, there were the photographs. Who was that mysterious Russian who'd been trying to blackmail him? And why?

While all the other officers had been paired up and sent to patrol the grounds of the estate, Billings was left alone in the wardrobe, guarding the coats, hats and furs of the distinguished guests.

"It's because you're well spoken," CI Wright had told him. "If any of the guests should speak to you, you'll be able to answer back in correct English and without an offensive regional accent."

Billings knew that it was to his well-spokenness and proper middle class bearings that he owed his job at Scotland Yard. He was in essence a middle class man driven to a working class fate by lack of inheritance. But sometimes he wished he were coarse and rough like Clarkson. Perhaps he wouldn't have stood out so if he was. Perhaps he'd have been more accepted by his peers.

The orchestra was playing a waltz in the ballroom next door and Billings caught the occasional glimpse of swirling plumes and dresses through the crack of the door. It looked like a lively reception, but there was no life in the cold, dark hallway – other than the occasional appearance of an exhausted waiter carrying an empty tray back to the kitchen.

Close to midnight, after Billings had already been pacing the hallway for five hours, one of the guests emerged from the ballroom. A small, wiry fellow looking drunk and exhausted. He walked past Billings to the open front door, leaned against the doorway and took a few deep breaths of fresh air. His face was streaked with sweat and locks of red hair stuck to his clammy forehead.

He turned towards Billings. "Don't mind me, officer," he said. "I just need a bit of air. I have been swirling and twirling for the last two hours and that's never a good idea when your belly is full of champagne."

Suddenly Billings recognized him. It was Etherbridge. And Etherbridge recognized him too, because his eyes instantly lit up.

"I say, you're that chap, aren't you? That led us into the dungeons."

"I am Detective Sergeant Billings, sir."

"What a singular coincidence. What are you doing here?"

"Security Service, sir."

"How remarkable. I saw your boss only yesterday."

"My boss?"

"The other fellow we spoke to at the police station. Joseph or Abraham or..."

"Jacobs?"

"That's the one. Chief Inspector Jacobs. He came to our house to return this." Etherbridge showed Billings a large cameo ring on his finger. The ring was engraved with a picture of a Greek warrior. "It's the ring which was stolen from Lord Palmer," he said. "Together with a gold watch. I'd given them to him as a present. They don't really have much value, but as the chap went through all that trouble of retrieving them, I thought I might as well wear them tonight."

The cameo ring with the Greek warrior and the gold watch with the date palms! thought Billings. The very items Clarkson had been struggling to locate.

"I should tell Lady Palmer you're here,"

Etherbridge continued. "She may want to thank you. Although she's probably too busy chasing after the Prince of Wales. She came here in her mourning clothes, dressed up as the Queen, the silly thing! I'm sure her whole scheme will backfire. She's determined to meet the Prince of Wales, but he seems equally determined to avoid her. And who can blame him when she's dressed like his mother. I say, may I give you a cigar?"

Etherbridge kept nattering on, but Billings had stopped listening. All sorts of thoughts rushed through his head. How did Lord Palmer's jewels end up in the Russian counterfeiter's stash? How long had Jacobs known about them? Why did he wait until Billings was out of sight to return them?

Etherbridge tapped him on the shoulder. "You're not listening to me."

"I'm sorry, sir."

"I want to give you a cigar. As a token of my appreciation." He took a silver case out of his jacket pocket and pulled out a long cigar. "You're not allowed to accept money, but I'm sure your superiors will not object to a cigar." He placed the cigar in the detective's breast pocket and tapped it in place. "There. You can have that when your shift is over."

It had been the Prince's explicit instruction to leave the front door open at all times, in order for fresh air to enter the building and circulate around the rooms. It was past midnight and the frosty outside air had completely filled the room. Billings had been pacing the hallway for hours trying to keep himself warm. He kept pondering and worrying about Jacobs. Why was significant progress on the Lord Palmer case constantly being made when he was away? First there was the confession and now the identification of the jewels. It was almost as if Jacobs was deliberately sending him away all the time. Could Jacobs somehow be involved in all this?

Billings hadn't taken his morphine dose that day and he was shivering all over. There wasn't much he could do about that. The reception was going to last well into the small hours of the morning and he had to remain sober throughout. The only way of controlling his urges was to slip into the wardrobe from time to time and sniff the fumes from an ampoule he had hidden in his coat pocket. He was doing just that when suddenly he heard a man crying for help.

"Hello! Is anyone there? Please, I need help!"

Billings dropped the ampoule on the floor and

rushed out of the wardrobe, his nose still wet with morphine. A rough-looking man stood in the doorway, wearing mud-splattered clothes and looking anxiously around him. He was in his fifties with long, messy side whiskers and greasy hair. He wore an old black hat with a worn and frizzled brim and a long black leather coat which reached down to his ankles.

"Officer, please!" The man looked frightened. "Tha must come with me at once, there's been an accident!"

"What kind of accident?" Billings said. "Who are you?"

"I'm one of the grooms. My companion's been kicked by a horse. He's lying unconscious by th'road!"

"By the road? What road?"

"Th'road yonder!" The man pointed into the dark. "That leads to th'house!"

"What's he doing there? Why aren't the horses in the stable?"

"We were exercising it."

"In the middle of the night?"

"T'is a restless one this. It's not used to staying in an unknown stable and it were spooked by owt. Please, tha must come with me at once!"

"I can't leave this place unattended. Where are

the stable boys?"

"I don't know, officer. They're all gone."

"Have you been to the stables?"

"Aye!"

"There are other officers patrolling the grounds. You must go to one of them for help."

"There's no one there, officer. I've been runnin' around calling for help for th' last ten minutes. You're the first person I've seen."

Billings popped his head out of the door and peered into the darkness.Where is everybody? he thought. He couldn't see or hear a soul.

"Please, officer. Tha must come with me at once. My companion is lying on th' road dying while we're here talkin'."

"I should alert my supervisor." Billings turned towards the ballroom, but the groom grabbed his arm and stopped him.

"There's no time for that, officer," he yelled. "Come with me now, or my companion will be dead."

The groom ran out of the house and towards the drive. The sky was cloudy and moist, and the torches which illuminated the drive had all gone out. It was pitch black. Billings followed the groom towards some trees by the side of the road. A lone horse paced the lawn by the trees. It was saddleless and restless, and it kept shaking its head nervously from side to side. Then, behind the horse, by the side of the road, Billings suddenly saw a man lying on the ground.

"That's him, officer," the groom said. "Over there."

Billings rushed towards the wounded man and knelt down before him. He grabbed the man's arm and felt for his pulse.

"Hello, can you hear me? What's your name?" He looked at the man's face. He was young. Not yet twenty. His eyes were closed and there was a dark, sticky wound on his forehead. Billings loosened the man's collar and put his ear to his chest. The man's heart was beating. His body was shivering.

"We must get him inside where it's warm," Billings said to the groom. He got up and started lifting the man up by his shoulders. "You must help me. Grab his legs. I've got his shoulders."

There was no reply. Billings looked back towards the house. The man had gone.

"Hello? Where are you?"

He squinted into the darkness. All he could see were the illuminated windows of the reception rooms on the ground floor, but there was no sign of the groom. His heart started pounding again. Had he been conned after all? He laid the man back down on the ground and paced around in the darkness, looking for the groom.

"Hello? Where are you?" he called.

As he made his way back to the house, he suddenly heard a noise behind him. He turned back and saw the wounded man jump up on his feet.

"Hey!"

Billings made to go after him, but the man ran towards the horse, jumped on it and galloped away. Billings made a half-hearted attempt at chasing him, but it was futile.

"Damn it! Damn it! Damn it!" Billings ran back towards the house. "Where the devil is everyone!"

As he approached the house, Billings saw the groom's footsteps in the gravel. His boots had carried pebbles into the hallway and his dusty footprints led all the way into the wardrobe. Billings approached the wardrobe and looked in. Frock coats lay on the ground with the pockets turned out, and it was immediately apparent that there were some furs missing too.

Billings took a deep breath, put his hand on his trembling chest and hung his head.

This is the end of my career, he thought.

Suddenly three figures approached the house

from the drive. They were Detective Sergeant Cooper and Detective Constable Stanton and they were dragging a wounded young man between them.

"We caught an intruder!" called Cooper.

"Where the devil were you?" Billings asked as the detectives brought the wounded man into the hallway. "You were supposed to be patrolling the drive."

"We were at the gate," Cooper replied. "Caught this little ruffian trying to jump over the wall." He pulled the young man's head up by his hair and looked into his eyes. "That wall's much too high for your horse, boy!" he said. "Now sit down in that corner, while we get someone to take you to the police station." He pushed the young man down to the ground. The man winced with pain.

"There's another one," Billings said. "He has a companion."

"A companion?"

"They played a trick on me. Came here calling for help. Claimed to be one of the guest's grooms. Said his partner had been kicked by a horse and needed my assistance. He led me out there towards those trees. While I was attending to the injured man, his partner crept back in and stole some furs."

"You abandoned your post?" Cooper asked.

"What else was I to do? There was no one else around You were supposed to be patrolling the drive I couldn't find you anywhere. What the devil where you doing at the gate?"

Cooper didn't answer and turned to look guiltily at his partner. "Where is the other man now?" he asked.

"I don't know. Out there somewhere"

"You!" Cooper pointed at the wounded man on the floor. "What's your name?"

The man didn't answer.

He kicked the man in the ribs. "Oi! I'm talking to you!"

"I say, steady on, Cooper!" Billings interjected.

"What's your name?" Cooper asked again.

"Oswald," the man replied.

"Oswald what?"

"Oswald Crooke."

"And who's your partner?"

"He's my father."

Blood streamed from the man's forehead.

"What happened to your head?" Billings asked.

"My father hit me with a rock."

"Why?"

"To make it look like I'd been kicked by a horse."

Suddenly the man leaned forward and vomited right on Cooper's boots.

Cooper danced away from the splutters. "Jesus Christ!"

"He's got a concussion," Billings concluded. "We need to get him to a doctor."

"Doctor, my arse! A good hiding is what that hookem needs!"

"You two had better go and look for the boy's father," Billings suggested. "And try and retrieve those furs he's stolen, or we'll all be getting a hiding. I'll alert Chief Inspector Wright and get one of the waiters to clean up this mess."

Oswald Crooke was escorted to Dersingham Police Station later that night, but despite the fact that the whole Security Service was used to comb the vast estate until ten o'clock the following morning, the groom and the stolen furs were never found. CI Wright was forced to concede defeat and make his apologies to the Prince and his guests.

Meanwhile, Billings, DS Cooper and DC Stanton faced a bruising debriefing at the White Swan later that same day. Billings was reprimanded for not alerting his superior before abandoning his post, but Cooper and Stanton fared worse. It transpired that they had been playing dice at the gate with two Norfolk officers instead of patrolling the drive, and were given a week's unpaid suspension from the force.

The three of them were back on the train to London at five o'clock. They shared the same carriage and remained quiet and subdued throughout the journey, staring out the window and pondering their humiliation.

When the train stopped at King's Lynn Station, Billings picked up a copy of the evening's edition of the Norfolk Chronicle and read the following article:

Theft At Sandringham

Two sable cloaks and one mink scarf were stolen from Sandringham House last night during the Prince of Wales's annual Christmas reception. The sable cloaks belonged to Mrs Astrid Nielsen, the wife of the minister of the Danish church in Norwich, and Mrs Fenella Dixon-Wright of Tamblick Hall. The mink scarf was the property of Lady Alice von Trier. The furs were stolen by a pair of petty criminals known as Barnabas and Oswald Crooke. The villainous duo, who are father and son and originally hail from Lancashire, have been pickpocketing and burglering their way through the country for the last ten years and have already served time in several of Her Majesty's prisons. Oswald Crooke has been caught and is currently in King's Lynn hospital under heavy guard recovering from a serious wound to his head, but Barnabas Crooke is still at large. The Norfolk Constabulary believe he may be heading towards London, where he will undoubtedly hope to dispose of his stolen ware in a profitable manner.

Billings now remembered where he had heard those names before. It was at Whitehaven police station. "Barnabas Crooke and his son Oswald. Crooke by name and by nature," the Whitehaven inspector had called them. They were the men Sebastian got involved with after he'd been expelled from the priory.

CHAPTER FIFTEN

The Ruffian on the Bridge

Clarkson looked up from his desk, beady-eyed and sleepy, rounding off his night shift.

"'Ere, Billings, what you doing 'ere so early?"

Billings marched past him without replying and headed towards the filing room. He had arrived back in London at a little over one that morning and he hadn't slept a wink. So many thoughts and reflections raged in his head, battling each other for his attention, that no amount of morphine could silence them. At six o'clock in the morning, tired of tossing and turning, he got up, splashed some water on his face, got dressed and made his way to Scotland Yard.

He went to the filing cabinet and began ruffling through the files. He searched under 'R' for

'Russians', then under 'C' for 'counterfeiters', then under 'D' for 'Deptford.'

Clarkson followed him into the filing room.

"What are you doin'?" he asked. He leaned against the doorway with a mug of coffee in his hand and yawned. "You're not supposed to be in until after noon. 'Ow was Sandringham?"

"Where's the Russian counterfeiters file?"

"What do you want that for?"

"I need to check something."

"Jacobs has it."

"Jacobs?"

"He takes it home with him every night."

"Why?"

Clarkson shrugged. "'Ere, did you meet the Prince of Wales? What was he like?"

"Those jewels that were found in Deptford..."

"They've been returned now. Jacobs returned the last batch while you were away. I swear to God, Billings, if I read one more report about stolen jewels..."

"How did those jewels end up in Deptford?"

"Well, I don't know, do I? The Russians probably bought them."

"How were those jewels found?"

"I told you all about that, Billings. That was my doing. It's that man I'd spent the whole day shadowing. The one with the long red coat."

"The Cossack."

"That's right, the Cossack. A man called Bohdan Krymski. That was the lead the Russians gave us. He was suspected of running a counterfeiting operation in London and he led us to that warehouse. I told you all about this, Billings, but you never listen to me."

"So what happened to the counterfeiters?"

"Well, they were gone when we stormed the building. And they'd taken all their money with them. But they left behind the jewels. And then I spent three long, boring days collating reports, which is why I qualify for a share of the reward. Speaking of which, I went to visit Mr Boogledug yesterday."

"Who?"

"My goose. He is looking so fat and scrumptious, Billings. And huge. It's an absolute monster of a beast. This is going to be the best Christmas meal we've had in our lives. You *are* still comin', aren't ya?"

Suddenly a door slammed in the corridor and the detectives heard vigorous footsteps approaching them.

"Clarkson, my dear chap! Is that you?" It was the smug voice of Inspector Flynt, calling from the corridor. "And is that coffee you're drinking? I could simply murder a cup right now. I don't suppose you'd be so kind as to... Oh!"

Flynt appeared in the doorway of the filing room and was taken aback by the other detective's presence.

Billings nodded at him, but Flynt did not reciprocate the greeting and turned towards Clarkson. "I've just come back from Berkshire," he said. "Took the midnight train from Reading. Haven't slept a wink all night."

"Berkshire?" Billings asked intrigued. "Were you working on the Lord Palmer case?"

"Oh, that's right." Flynt suddenly turned his attention back towards Billings and looked him up and down. "Brendan's a friend of yours, isn't he?"

"Well, he's not really a friend."

"I hope not, because he's going to hang."

This was not what Billings wanted to hear. He tried hard to control the pounding of his heart. "Why do you say that?"

"I'm not sure I should be disclosing that to you."

"You can't have any evidence against him?"

"Nothing concrete, I admit, but..."

"But what?"

"I have probability."

"Probability?"

"There's no one else who could've done it."

"How do you know?"

"Everybody else has an alibi and no one else was spotted on the estate."

"Is that all you have? That's not enough."

"No, that's not all. I have other things too."

"Like what?"

"You know, Billings, you really shouldn't be questioning me like that."

"What else do you have?"

Refusing to answer the question, Flynt turned his back on Billings and continued his conversation with Clarkson. "How about that coffee, Clarkson?"

"Yes sir, I shall get you some."

According to the personnel file, Jacobs lived in Tavistock Square. It was a pleasant, quiet square in the centre of London, with a pretty green park surrounded by large, elegant houses. A little too large and elegant for a policeman's wages, thought Billings.

It was Jacobs's day off, which meant Billings wouldn't get the chance of speaking with him until the following day. This wouldn't do. Billings would have too much time on his hands and, sleep being impossible, he'd have nothing else to do but fret, worry and agonize. So he decided to pay

Jacobs a visit.

He took a deep breath before walking up the doorsteps and ringing the bell. What precisely was he going to ask him? How was he going to handle this? Damn it, he hadn't thought this through.

The door was opened by the maid.

"Good morning," Billings said, tipping his hat at her. "I'd like to speak to Mr Jacobs please."

"Who may I say is calling?"

"My name is..."

At that point an elegant young lady walked in from the drawing room. "Who is it, Mary?" she asked.

"It's some man asking for Mr Jacobs, ma'am."

"Don't let him in, Mary."

"I won't, ma'am."

The young lady joined the maid in the doorway, grabbed the door and pulled it towards her, so that there was only a small gap left through which she could communicate with her visitor.

"What do you want?" she asked.

"My name is John Billings, and I…"

"We settled this business with your people yesterday," the lady interrupted.

"Pardon?"

"The bill has been settled. You should check with your boss. Please do not disturb us any longer."

She was about to shut the door, but Billings managed to put his foot in the doorway and blocked it. "My name is Detective Sergeant John Billings," he repeated, this time with a little more assertiveness. "I am a colleague of Mr Jacobs."

The lady looked embarrassed. She had clearly taken him for one of the bailiffs. "I see," she said. "Well come in, Mr Billings".

Billings stepped into the hallway.

"My husband has a visitor at the moment, but I shall see if he can make some time for you." The lady made her way towards the drawing room, but stopped before entering. "You know, you really should have announced yourself sooner," she said, turning towards him. "Instead of making me believe you were somebody you were not!" She disappeared into the drawing, leaving Billings alone in the elegant hallway.

He looked around him. How could Jacobs afford to live in a place like this, he wondered. It really was a nice house. The hallway was spacious, with Greek-style columns flanking each door. The floor was tiled with black and white marble. There was a huge potted aspidistra – that great symbol of respectability – against one wall and a steam radiator on the other, strategically placed beneath the coathangers and the hatstand. A brand new, shiny top hat took pride of place at the top of the hatstand, like a fairy on a Christmas tree. Was it Jacobs's? He had never seen his boss wear it. Neither had he seen him wear that striking long red coat with the fur collar which hung conspicuously from the coat hanger. *Conspicuously,* he thought. Why did that word suddenly sound so familiar to him?

Jacobs popped his head from the drawing room. "Billings, what the devil are you doing here?"

"I need to speak to you, sir."

Jacobs came out and closed the door behind him. He wore a silk dressing gown over his clothes. Billings was taken aback by this unexpectedly flamboyant look. It didn't suit him at all. He looked comical.

"Well, what is it?" Jacobs whispered. He cast a sideways glance towards the drawing room, clearly anxious not to be overheard by his visitor.

"I need to speak to you about the jewels."

"The jewels?"

"I saw Mr Etherbridge at Sandringham. He said you'd returned the jewels to him."

"Well, what of it?"

"Those were the jewels which were stolen from Lord Palmer."

Jacobs looked confused.

"Whoever stole those jewels must have been involved in Lord Palmer's death," Billings explained.

"For heaven's sake, Billings!"

"I was trying to find out where those jewels came from this morning, but I couldn't find the report. Clarkson said you took it home with you."

"Flynt is dealing with the Lord Palmer case now."

"But you are dealing with the counterfeiters case and it now appears that the two are connected."

"This really isn't the time to discuss this, Billings. Today is my day off. I can discuss this with you tomorrow."

Jacobs was about to head back into the drawing room, but Billings grabbed his arm and stopped him.

"Could I just have a look at the file, sir?"

"No, you may not!"

"Why not?"

Suddenly the drawing room door opened and an olive-skinned man with long dark hair and a small goatee beard popped his head into the hallway.

"Is everything all right, Ezra?" the man asked with a foreign accent.

"Yes, yes. Everything is fine. Just help yourself to another glass of brandy. I'll be right with you."

The man glanced suspiciously at Billings before returning to the drawing room.

"You are being impertinent and difficult, Billings! I am not going to discuss this with you now. Just go home and see me in my office tomorrow." Jacobs re-entered the drawing room.

It wasn't until Billings had left Jacobs's house and was walking back to the Yard that he suddenly put two and two together. The conspicuous coat, the strange foreign accent. That was Bohdan Krymski! Jacobs was entertaining the leader of the Russian counterfeiting gang!

As Billings walked to work the following morning, he saw a man leaning on the railings of Chelsea Bridge. He had a rough-looking face with long greasy hair sticking out of an old black hat. He was smoking a cigarette and he was staring pensively ahead of him, not at the river but at the road. Billings thought that there was something suspicious about the man's manner. Why was he lingering on the bridge? What was he waiting for?

When Billings walked past him, the man crushed out his cigarette and followed him. He was still following when Billings got off the bridge and turned right towards Pimlico Pier.

Billings stopped just below Vauxhall Bridge and

bent down to tie his shoelaces. The man stopped also and gazed at the river. There was something vaguely familiar about that man, but Billings couldn't quite place him. Having tied his shoelaces, Billings continued on to Millbank Street and stopped again at the Victoria Tower Gardens to check whether he was still being followed. He was. Damn it, he thought. Who is this man?

He accelerated his pace and took some strange turns on his way to work. He turned right into Wood Street; then right again towards Great College Street; then left towards Dean's Yard and from there straight on towards Bridge Street. The man followed him all the way.

Billings stopped at the foot of Big Ben, to scan the masses of people who had gathered in the city. He couldn't see the man among them. Had his mad manoeuvring worked, he wondered. Had he been able to drop his shadow?

He smiled contentedly and continued to work when suddenly, out of nowhere, the man came running towards him and threw himself on top of him. He grabbed Billings by the collar, pushed him to the ground, and punched him in the face. Twice.

"That's for sticking yer nose in where it don't belong!" he said with the first punch. "And that's for locking up my son!" he said with the second.

He got up and ran away, cutting through the crowd of curious spectators which had gathered around them.

Billings was unable to open his eyes and remained on the ground, the pain pounding in his face and in his head. It took him a while to realise exactly what had happened. When he finally opened his eyes, all he could see was a swarm of people towering over him, looking down and fussing about him.

"You're gonna need that stitched up, sir," he heard a woman say. "We should get a doctor to look at your face."

"Have you checked your pockets, sir?" a man chipped in. "It wouldn't surprise me if he hasn't robbed you."

"I saw the whole event, sir," a gentleman stated. "If you need a witness, you must call on me. Let me give you my card." He took a calling card out of his breast pocket and handed it to him. But Billings didn't take it.

He pushed himself up. "Everyone please! Clear off!" He waved his arms in the air in an attempt to break up the crowd and catch a glimpse of his fleeing attacker. If he couldn't chase after him, he at least wanted to know who it was. But the crowd ignored him. They crouched down to help him up, pulling at his arms or wiping the blood off his face with their handkerchiefs.

"Let go of me! I'm fine!" Billings rose to his feet. "Everyone, clear off! Now!"

The crowd finally dispersed. Billings looked around him. There was no sign of his attacker. He wiped the blood of his forehead and staggered on to work, angry and humiliated. His sight was blurry, his face streaked with blood and his head pounding with pain.

"Good lord, what happened to you?" said the desk clerk as Billings stumbled into the building.

"Nothing! Leave me alone!"

Billings staggered into the gents lavatory where he splashed some water on his face. He lifted his head and looked at himself in the mirror. The man had made a real mess of him. He looked like a prize fighter at the end of a bloody match. Both his eyes were bruised and swollen and his right eyebrow had been cut. The man must've been wearing a sharp ring on one of his fingers. Why did he attack me? he thought. What did he mean by 'sticking my nose in' and 'locking up his son'? Then it struck him. The dirty long hair, the frizzled hat, the long leather coat. It was Barnabas Crooke!

The desk clerk entered the lavatory, with a breathless, panting constable behind him.

"This is PC Smith, sir," he said. "He saw the whole thing."

"Cor! Look at your face!" exclaimed PC Smith.

Billings ignored his last comment. "Did you chase after him?" he asked.

"Yes, I did, sir, but he got away. I chased him all across Westminster Bridge, but I lost him off Lambeth Palace Road. Do you know who it was, sir?"

"No, I don't," Billings lied.

"You should get that eye of yours seen to, sir," the desk clerk suggested. "Do you want me to call the surgeon?"

The door opened again and this time Clarkson walked in. "Cor blimey, Billings! Look at your face!"

"What am I, a freak show exhibit?" Billings yelled.

"Alright, don't get your dander up. Jacobs sent me to fetch you. He wants to see you in his office straight away. 'Ere, you should get a doctor to look at that eye."

Billings pushed past Clarkson and the others and stormed out of the lavatory. He marched up the stairs to Jacobs's office, ignoring the curious looks and snickers of the clerks he passed in the corridor.

Jacobs was sitting at his desk and screwed his face up as Billings entered his office.

"Good grief, Billings! You look like a squashed frog! What happened?"

"I don't know, sir." Billings grabbed a chair and sat at Jacobs's desk. "A man followed me to work from Battersea and lunged at me on Westminster Bridge. I didn't seen him coming."

"Do you know who it was?"

"I think it was Barnabas Crooke."

"Who?"

"The thug who stole the furs in Sandringham."

"Why was he following you?"

"I don't know. Maybe he wanted revenge for his son."

"His son?"

"Oswald Crooke. We caught him at Sandringham. The Norfolk Constabulary arrested him."

"Do you think that was the reason he beat you?"

"Yes... at least, I think so. He said something else when he punched me."

"What did he say?"

"He said, 'That's for sticking your nose in.'"

"What did he mean by that?"

"I don't know, sir, but I'd like to find out. There

should be a file on him. He's a known criminal."

"Don't worry, Billings. I'll handle this for you."

"If it's all the same to you, sir, I'd rather handle it myself. He attacked me in the middle of a crowded street. It's a matter of pride with me."

"Have you seen the surgeon yet?"

"Not yet."

"I suggest you do so now. That cut looks ugly. In fact, I suggest you take the rest of the day off. *I'll* deal with this thug."

Billings fell silent and stared suspiciously at his boss. Was he trying to get rid of him again?

"About yesterday, sir," he said, carefully.

"Not now, Billings."

"I really need to talk to you about this, sir. I am convinced that there is a connection between Lord Palmer's murder and the stolen jewels."

Jacobs frowned and let out a deep sigh.

"If you'd only let me have a look at that file, sir," Billings persevered. "I'm sure I'd be able to..."

"Billings, you're going to have to drop this once and for all, do you hear? I've given you enough warnings!"

"But I'm convinced Lochrane is innocent."

"Did you hear what I said?"

"Who was that man I saw in your house yesterday?" Billings asked suddenly. This took

Jacobs by surprise and he fell silent. "Was it Bohdan Krymski?"

"It's none of your business, who that was. This is a complicated case, Billings, and there are certain angles to it which are unknown to you."

"What was he doing in your house?"

"What do you think you are doing, Billings? Are you interrogating me?"

"I just want to get to the bottom of this, sir."

"You've been wounded, Billings. I order you to see the surgeon immediately and to take the rest of the day off. In fact, take the whole week off. I do not want to see you here again until you are fully recovered. Is this understood?"

"But sir, I..."

"Go now, Billings, or I will get someone to drag you out and escort you back home!"

Billings walked out of Jacobs's office, but did not go to the surgeon's room. Instead he headed straight for Clarkson's desk.

"You need to do something for me," he said, pulling the pen out of Clarkson's hand and splashing ink all over his cuffs.

"Oi! Careful!"

"Find out everything you can about this man."

Billings scribbled Barnabas Crooke's name on a piece of paper. "There should be a file on him. Then send a messenger to deliver the report to my address. Or better still, deliver it yourself." He added the address to the sheet. "But don't tell Jacobs. In fact don't tell anyone."

"What's all this about?" Clarkson asked. He frowned as he tried to remove the ink stains from his shirt sleeve.

"It's about the man who attacked me." Billings blotted the paper, folded it, grabbed Clarkson's hand and shoved the paper in it. "Bring the report to me as soon as you can. But don't tell Jacobs."

Clarkson looked worried and confused. "What's going on, Billings?"

"Jacobs has ordered me to take a rest and doesn't want me worrying about the attack. But I can't let it lie. It's a matter of pride with me. That's all."

"All above board then, is it?"

"Yes, Clarkson. It's all above board. Just don't tell anyone. I'm relying on you. Can I trust you?"

Clarkson nodded.

"Good man."

Mrs Appleby started fussing the moment Billings walked in the door.

"Oh my heavens, look at the state of you!" she cried.

Billings' eyebrow had been stitched. He felt a little light-headed now that the excitement of the moment had passed and wanted nothing more than to lock himself up in his room and lie down for a bit. But Mrs Appleby would not allow that.

"Oh no, you mustn't lie down!" she said. "That's the worst thing you can do. You might have a concussion. You come into the lounge, my dear. Let your poor old landlady look after ya." She grabbed his arm and pulled him towards the lounge. "You sit down in that armchair, my dear. I'll put some cold tea leaves in a towel and dab your eyes with it. That'll help bring the swelling down." She disappeared into the kitchen.

There was a knock on the door. Billings jumped up from his seat. Good old Clarkson, he thought. He ran to open the door. Jack stood in the doorway holding a letter out to him. Billings grabbed the letter from the boy's hand and paid him a shilling. He turned towards the staircase and was about to rush up to his room, when Mrs Appleby reappeared from the kitchen with a teapot in her hand.

"'Ere, where you going?" she asked.

"Sorry, Mrs Appleby. A letter just came for me

from work."

"You're not going to continue working now, are you?"

"Work never stops for a Yard man, Mrs Appleby." He ran up the stairs.

Barnabas Crooke was born in Bradford in 1838. He married Rebecca Yeoman in 1854. They had their first child in 1855, but it died two months later. They had another child in 1856, this one died in 1859. Their third child was born in 1857. This one survived and was named Oswald. The wife, however, died in 1862. Father and son moved to Whitehaven in '68 or '69. They both worked at Cranson and Son's Tannery Yard. Oswald spent three months at Peter Street House of correction for pickpocketing in 1870. He spent another five months there for stealing a gentleman's coat in 1872 and another full year in 1875 for burglary. Barnabas and Oswald left the employ of Cranson and Son in 1882 after it was alleged they had been stealing skins from the Yard. Neither are heard from again until 1885 when they are both sentenced to 8 months hard labour at Birmingham Prison for burglary (This was Oswald's fourth conviction - he was lucky not to have been hanged!) In prison Oswald seems to have attracted the pity of one of your lot – by which I mean Quackers [sic] – who arranged for him to be trained and employed as a boatman in the Grand Junction Canal. He's been ferrying between London and the Midlands with his father ever since, until he was arrested recently in Norfolk for trespassing at Sandringham, for which he was sentenced to six months hard labour (when are they going to hang this brute?. Their boat is called 'Ryckmer' and it was moored on the River Chess in Rickmansworth, at the time of Oswald's arrest. I should warn you that Jacobs has asked for a similar report (I really do hope this is all above board, Billings.) Don't worry about Jack, he's been sworn to secrecy. I had to pay him two shillings to buy his silence˙ (which I expect you to pay me back).

There was only one thing for Billings to do after he finished reading the report. He threw the letter on his bed, grabbed his hat and coat, ran out the door and hailed himself a cab.

There were about half a dozen narrowboats moored on the bank of the River Chess. Some laden with cargo (coal, flour, dye), some empty. The boatmen were hard at work. They were either carrying out repairs or rearranging their cargo, while their wives and children hung their laundry out to dry or tended the horses in the mews. But they all stopped what they were doing and stared at Billings as he walked down the towpath, scanning the boat names. Billings didn't know whether it was the sight of his bruised face which attracted this attention, or the fact that the boating community (or river gypsies as they were sometimes referred to) was notoriously insular, but he felt uneasy strolling amongst the silent, suspicious stares. He was relieved when someone finally spoke to him.

"Looking for anyone in particular, guv'nor?"

Billings looked up. A man sat on the roof of his boat, repairing and coiling a rope.

"I'm looking for the Ryckmer," Billings replied.

"The Ryckmer? Oh, you've just missed it, guv'nor. The Ryckmer left a couple of hours ago."

"Do you know where it went to?"

"Well, I saw her go down the Colne, but she was carrying no cargo." The man leaned over to the hatch and called out into the cabin. "'Ere, Ruthie! Where did Barney go off to this morning?"

"What?"

"Barney? Where did he go off to?"

A woman appeared from the hatch, holding a snotty-nosed, dirty-faced toddler in her arms.

"What you hollering about?" she asked.

"This man's asking after Barney. Do you know

where he went off to?"

"He went down to meet the Thames, didn't he? Gone upstream, where he always goes to when he's in trouble."

"How far would he have gone by now?" Billings asked.

The woman suddenly turned to look at him and jumped at the sight of his face. "Bloomin' heck, what happened to you?"

"I... um. I had an accident."

"Accident, my arse! You've been punched, that's what happened to you!"

"Never you mind what happened to him, woman! Get back in there and bring us some coffee!" The man pushed his wife's head back down into the cabin and turned towards the detective. "You *will* have some coffee, won't you guv'nor? Barney's long gone by now. What is it you want him for anyway?"

"I have business with him."

"Business, is it? Well, if it's business you have, I might be able to oblige."

Billings looked confused.

"You're looking to unload some ware, I'd wager," the man clarified. "We're all in the same trade here, guv'nor. I can take the ware off your hands just as well as Barney can. Now, come on.

Get on board and show me what you've got."

Billings concluded that the sight of his face and shabby clothes had convinced the man that he was a duffer, so he took advantage of this mistake, climbed on to the boat and sat on the roof beside him. He pulled out a golden locket his mother had given him from around his neck and showed it to him.

"Lets have a look at that then." The man grabbed the locket from the detective and turned it around in his dirty hands. "Well, it's not much, is it?"

"It's gold," Billings said.

"Gold *plated*," the man corrected. "And only lightly so. You got any more?"

"I have more at home," Billings lied.

"Well, I won't get more than a couple of sovereigns for this." He threw the locket on the detective's lap. "Sorry mate, not worth my while."

Billings picked the locket up and scrubbed the man's dirty fingerprints off it with a corner of his jacket.

"How can I find Barney?" he asked.

"You can't. He don't wanna be found. That's what he went upstream for."

"Why doesn't he want to be found?"

"What do you think? The law must be after him. But I'll tell you what, mate. If you really have more stuff, you might as well take it directly to Florence."

"Florence?"

"It's what Barney would've done with your loot anyway."

"And where can I find this Florence?"

The wife came out of the cabin again, carrying two mugs of coffee.

"'Ere Ruthie, where does Florence hang out these days?"

"How the devil would I know!" She handed the mugs out to the men. "You should go to the market in Spittalfields and ask around there. They'll know."

"What's her last name?" Billings asked.

"Whose?"

"Florence. What's her surname?"

The man and woman went silent and looked at each other.

"Florence is not a *her*, mister!" the man said. "Florence is a bloke!"

Billings instantly felt the mood darken.

"I told you, Archie!" the woman cried angrily. "I told you not to trust strangers!"

"Who are you?" the man asked. There was a sudden aggressive tone in his voice. "Everyone in our line of business knows Florence!"

Billings watched the two boatpeople stare at him with suspicious frowns on their faces.

"My name is John… um… Brown," he said. "John Brown."

"John Brown, my arse!" the wife cried. "You're a copper! He's a copper, Archie!"

"Are you a copper?"

"No, I assure you. I'm not."

"Oh Archie, I told you not to trust him! I hope you ain't said anything incriminating!"

"How do you know Barney Crooke?" the man asked angrily.

"I met him in Norfolk."

"Did *he* do that do your face?"

"What? No!"

"He did!" the woman yelled. "You're the one who's after him, ain't you?"

Billings looked around him nervously. The couple's angry cries had attracted the attention of the other boatpeople and they were all looking in his direction.

"I met Barnabas Crooke in Norfolk," Billings said. "At the White Swan in Dersingham. He told me he dealt in stolen jewellery and if I ever had anything for him I should look him up in Rickmansworth. Just ask for the Ryckmer, he said. Well, here I am, but he ain't here, so I guess I'll just…"

He turned away from the man and was about to jump off the boat, but the woman jumped off before him.

"Oh no, you don't!" she said, leaping onto the bank and untying the mooring ropes. "He's looking to run away, Archie! Don't let him!" She quickly pushed the boat away from the bank. Before Billings could do anything to prevent it, a big gap of water had emerged between him and dry land – too big for him to jump.

"Now tell me straight, mister!" The man picked a punting pole off the deck. "Are you a copper or not?"

"I told you, I'm not."

The man pushed the pole forcefully into the detective's stomach, causing him to stagger back towards the edge of the boat. "I don't believe you!" he said and gave him another blow, harder this time. It knocked the air right out of the detective and caused him to double over. A large crowd of boatpeople had assembled on the bank by now and watched as the man tried to push Billings into the water.

"I'm not trying to deceive you," Billings said, looking around him desperately for a way to get back on to dry land. "Just let me get off the boat and I'll be on my way."

"What's the matter? Can't you swim?" The man poked him again with the pole. "Well, there's only one way to learn, isn't there fellas?" He turned towards his audience, who all cheered and clapped, like children at a pantomime. Then, with one hard push, he thrust the pole right into the detective's guts and sent him flying overboard.

Billings emerged from the cold, murky water a couple of seconds later, gasping for air and splashing about him, desperately looking for dry land. The crowd on the bank was still cheering and clapping and laughing at him. Billings climbed onto the bank and, shivering and bruised, staggered back towards the station, leaving the ridiculing laughter of the boatpeople behind him.

CHAPTER SIXTEEN

The Foul Whiff of Corruption

Billings felt self-conscious walking onto the platform at Rickmansworth with his moist and muddied clothes. He worried that his suspicious appearance would attract the attention of the authorities. When the train arrived, he quickly climbed into the farthest carriage, sat down on the bench and curled up against the window. The mud on his clothes soon started to dry, but the smell of the dirty river had filled the carriage. This deterred other passengers from entering it, so he was left alone for the rest of the journey.

It was there in that slow-moving, pungent space that Billings collected his thoughts, assembled the facts and put them all together into a convincing narrative. It all made sense to him now. The death of Lord Palmer; the mystery of the Wild Man Of Sutton Courtenay; the disappearance of Sebastian Forrester; Bohdan Krymski and the Russian counterfeiters; the secretive behaviour of Chief Inspector Jacobs; the ubiquitous Barnabas Crooke. They were all part of the same long story and he had now finally been able to decipher in what manner they were connected. His problem presently, though, was knowing what to do with this information.

It was ten to six when he alighted at King's Cross Station. His clothes were still caked with mud and the dirt on his face did little to disguise the two blinkers on his head. But Billings was no longer concerned about unsettling the commuters with his appearance. Londoners were not easy to unsettle. Billings was invisible here. He was just another skipper, another shirker, another shivering jemmy begging for alms, and the commuters simply walked past him as if he didn't exist. He felt like a ghost, avoided and ignored by the masses, left to wander the darkening streets of London without really existing. Able to observe other people, but not able to interact with them. He felt strangely empowered by this. He had temporarily ceased being himself. He had finally been freed from consequence and responsibility. Billings took advantage of this new power and made his way to Tavistock Square. He finally felt ready for that confrontation with Jacobs.

Billings leaned against the park railings and stared impatiently down the road towards Endsleigh Place. It was a quarter past seven. Jacobs would be walking down that road any moment on his way back from work. Billings had chosen a good spot to hide in. He stood in a corner, far removed from the glow of the gas light, shielded from sight by the dark branches of a large chestnut tree. The mud on his clothes and face served as camouflage and made him completely invisible. A patrolling constable had circled the square twice during his beat and even he hadn't spotted him.

Suddenly Billings heard the clatter of horse hooves and he turned back to Endsleigh Place. A hansom cab rolled down the street and stopped right in front of Jacobs's house. Billings saw his boss step out of the carriage and pay the driver. Billings waited for the cab to leave, before jumping out of the shadow and rushing towards the house, where Jacobs was already unlocking the door.

"Mr Jacobs, I need to talk to you."

Jacobs jumped and cowered backwards when he

saw Billings approach him. He instinctively raised his umbrella in the air and was about to hit Billings with it, when recognition suddenly crept in.

"Billings? Is that you?" He squinted and looked into the detective's eyes.

"Yes. I need to have words with you."

Jacobs looked Billings up and down and laughed. "What the devil happened to you?" he asked.

"I fell into the river."

"The river? Where?"

"Rickmansworth."

"What the devil were you doing in Rickmansworth?"

Billings paused before answering. A moment of doubt crept into his head, but he clenched his fists and pushed on.

"I know that you are deliberately scapegoating an innocent man in order to cover the misdeeds in which you have become embroiled."

There. He said it. He felt the tension in his body ease and he unclenched his fists. But the storm had only just begun.

Jacobs laughed and shook his head. "You just won't give up, will you?"

"I went to Rickmansworth to look for Barnabas Crooke. I've worked it all out."

Jacobs remained unflustered and unmoved. "I suppose you had better come in, then." He opened the front door and stepped aside to let the detective in. "Come into my office and have some brandy. You look like you can use a good, stiff drink."

They were in Jacobs's study. Jacobs sat at his desk. Billings stood before him, like a chastened schoolboy in front of the headmaster. Jacobs looked down at his drink and fingered the rim of his brandy glass as he listened to Billings speak.

"I went to Rickmansworth to track down the man who assaulted me."

Billings looked around him. The room was decorated with beautiful and expensive porcelain vases which were displayed on side tables and which contained dried flowers. The walls were lined with grand bookcases which were filled with leather-bound volumes. Most of them looked like they had never been read. The room looked even grander than that of Mr Forrester.

"I didn't catch Barnabas Crooke, but I did learn some things about him. I learned, for instance, that he is a duffer. One of several in the country who sell their ware to Bohdan Krymski – better known to the criminal fraternity as Florence. Krym being the Russian word for Crimea and Florence

Nightingale being the most famous personage connected with that peninsula. The stolen jewels you found in Deptford were part of that ware. He intended to smuggle them back to Russia to sell."

"I know all about Bohdan Krymski," Jacobs interrupted. "What has any of this to do with me?"

"The discovery of the counterfeiters' stash couldn't have occurred at a more opportune moment for you, could it, Mr Jacobs?"

"Couldn't it?" Jacobs continued to look down at his glass and swirled the drink within it. "Why do you say that?"

"Because you were very much in debt at the time."

"Ah." Jacobs smiled wryly, but still would not raise his head and look Billings in the eye.

"I know the debts have now been paid off," Billings continued. "I learned this from a comment your wife made when I visited you yesterday and interrupted your visitor." Billings paused and stared at Jacobs, forcing him to lift his head and meet his look. "Who was that visitor, Mr Jacobs?"

Jacobs smiled. "I think you know perfectly well who that visitor was, Billings."

"Yes. I do. I recognized his long red coat which hung so conspicuously in the hallway. I remember Clarkson describing it to me. It was Bohdan

Krymski himself. You've been having dealings with Mr Krymski for a while now, haven't you? Tipping him off whenever an arrest was imminent. And receiving handsome rewards for your efforts. Handsome enough for you to be able to live in a house like this."

"No, that's where you're wrong, Billings." Jacobs finally downed the brandy he'd been playing with and slammed the empty glass back on his desk. "The rewards aren't handsome enough for *that*. No amount of pay-off is sufficient to support my wife's expensive tastes." He laughed bitterly. "But do go on with your story, Billings." He took the brandy bottle on his desk and refilled his glass. "What has any of this to do with Barnabas Crooke?"

"Two of the items which were found among the Deptford jewels are significant, because they link Bohdan Krymski's counterfeiting operation with the murder of Lord Palmer. The gold watch engraved with date palms and a cameo ring of a Greek warrior. These are the jewels which were stolen from Lord Palmer after he was killed. Whoever stole those jewels must have sold them to Krymski."

"And you believe that person to be Barnabas Crooke?"

"Yes. Crooke was known to Sebastian Forrester.

They met in Whitehaven several years ago. And Crooke had a boat – the Ryckmer – which he could have used to enter Lord Palmer's estate with, by accessing it from the river side. I believe Crooke may well be responsible for Lord Palmer's murder. Quite how the killing occurred and whether Crooke's encounter with Sebastian was premeditated or by chance, I do not know. But I do know that Lord Palmer's death was a serious inconvenience to Krymski. One which could jeopardize both his plans and yours, which is why it was necessary to incriminate Lochrane as fast as possible. This explains your eagerness to obtain a swift identification and the confession which you extracted from him. My constant digging for the truth became worrisome to you, which is why you made every effort to send me away. When that didn't work, Crooke was sent out to deal with me instead, although I like to think that that was on Krymski's orders rather than yours."

"But you do not have any proof for these allegations, do you, Billings?"

"Not yet, sir. But I can get it."

"So why did you not do so before confessing your suspicions to me?"

"I was hoping you'd do the honourable thing by confessing to all this yourself."

Jacobs burst out laughing. "Good old Billings! Our Quaker detective! Always so righteous and honourable, aren't you?"

"It is not my intention to threaten you, Mr Jacobs," Billings continued. "I want to help you rectify the situation before an innocent man is hanged. I don't believe you're a bad person. You've always been good to me and it is you I have to thank for my position in Scotland Yard. But your financial situation has made you desperate and desperation can lead you to do things which are foolish and reckless."

"Foolish and reckless?" Jacobs smiled mysteriously as he took a small key out of his jacket pocket.

Billings was put off by Jacobs's reaction, but he persevered. "You have dug yourself into a hole, Mr Jacobs, and I want to help you climb out of it."

"Well, that is very kind of you, Billings." Jacobs was still smiling and toying with the key in his fingers. "That's very gallant. And honourable. And altruistic."

There was a mocking tone to Jacobs's retort and Billings didn't know how to react to it.

"But then you are a Quaker after all," Jacobs continued. "And Quakers never do things which are foolish and reckless. Do they?"

"We try not to," Billings answered, unsure of where the conversation was heading.

Suddenly Jacobs lifted his hand and held the key between his thumb and finger. "Do you know what this is?"

Billings looked confused, but didn't answer.

"This is the key to all of your sordid little secrets."

Billing continued to look confused as Jacobs inserted the key into the desk lock and pulled out the central drawer. When Billings saw Jacobs take a large, brown envelope out of the drawer, he knew exactly what it meant and for a few seconds his heart stopped beating.

"Foolish and reckless, you called me?" Jacobs opened the envelope, removed the contents and displayed the pictures on the desk. There they were, those shameful photographs again. Billings couldn't bring himself to look at them and turned his face away.

Jacobs laughed. "Well, well, well," he said. "Who would have thought it? Our Billings. A mandrake. An invert. A pancy. I always wondered why you stubbornly chose to remain a bachelor, but this explains it. Our Billings is a sodomite."

"Those photographs are misleading." Billings still refused to look at the pictures. "Nothing happened."

"It doesn't look like nothing happened." Jacobs peered closer at the photographs. "What's that boy doing on his knees? Polishing your shoes, is he?" He laughed.

"I stopped him before anything occurred. You can't prove anything untoward happened when that photograph was taken."

"I don't need to prove that, Billings. I can prove you've been ordering obscene photographs. I can prove you've been frequenting a shop of ill repute. Whatever way you look at it, Billings, your career at Scotland Yard will be over, should this ever come out."

Billings didn't reply. He was still looking away from the desk, his face was red and his eyes filled with shame and disgust.

"Why don't you sit down, Billings." Jacobs' tone had changed now. There seemed to be a pang of sympathy in his voice.

"Please put those photographs away, sir."

Jacobs gathered the pictures, slid them back into the envelope and replaced the parcel in the drawer. "There. They're gone. Now grab a chair and sit down, Billings."

Billings walked towards the window, picked up a chair and placed it in front of the desk. He sat down in front of Jacobs, but continued to avoid his gaze.

"We all do things we're ashamed of," Jacobs said. "It's not easy being a police officer. Working ten, sometimes twenty hours a day for a measly wage. Being looked upon with hatred and suspicion by all. We work hard to catch criminals and collect the evidence, only to find all our efforts have been dismissed by the law courts and the criminal is set free. Free to rob again. Free to make more money with one act of deception than you and I can earn in a lifetime of service. It's a hard job, Billings. But there can be some rewards, if you look the other way. Who cares about counterfeit roubles, eh? Let the Russians catch their own criminals. I got the jewels back, didn't I? Surrender the British loot, I told Krymski, and I will cooperate. And he did. Those jewels weren't worth much to him anyway. It was the equipment he wanted. And the fake roubles. And the opportunity to continue making them in this country, unmolested by the police. That's where his profit lies. So where's the harm in that? Why should I not profit along with him? It's a victimless crime, Billings."

"It is not a victimless crime. Sebastian Forrester will hang unless we help him."

Jacobs frowned. "Brendan Lochrane was half-dead already," he answered gruffly.

"His name is Sebastian Forrester."

"Brendan, Sebastian, what the devil does it matter! That smelly wretch died many years ago! He's nothing but a walking corpse. We'd be doing him a favour, putting him out of his misery."

"He's a family acquaintance and his mother is relying on me to set him free."

"So you will jeopardize your career? Face the ridicule of your peers and the outrage of the public? Risk being sentenced to six months hard labour for committing acts of obscenity and sodomy? All for the sake of a distant acquaintance?"

"Sebastian Forrester is innocent. And I deserve all the punishment I get."

Jacobs went quiet and stared at Billings with a mixture of wonder and bewilderment. Billings sat hunched in his chair, staring at the ground. He hadn't looked Jacobs in the eye since the photographs were revealed. His left hand was trembling and everything about his appearance suggested dejection, shame, self-loathing. And yet... there was a defiant and determined look in his eye.

"Well, well, well. A principled man," Jacobs said eventually. "DS Billings, the Quaker detective.

With love for everyone. Except for himself."

"I cannot be bought," Billings said.

"You can't be bought, eh?"

"No sir, I cannot!" Billings got up from his chair.

"What are you doing?"

"I'm going home." He put the chair back by the window and walked towards the door. "I'm going to wash, I'm going to change my clothes, I'm going to take a shot of morphine and I'm going to sleep. When I wake up tomorrow, I will go to work as usual. If you haven't already confessed by then, I will knock on Superintendent McMurphy's door myself and I will tell him all. Good night, Mr Jacobs." And with that he left the room, leaving Jacobs looking puzzled and worried.

The first thing Billings noticed when he entered the cloakroom were Jacobs's coat and hat on the hatstand. Jacobs had arrived to work early. What could that mean? Did he come in early so that he could talk to the superintendent and confess his misdeeds? Or was he preparing another plot to further sabotage Billings's career?

With his heart thumping in his chest, Billings went over to Jacobs's office and tapped on the door. There was no reply. Billings knocked again, harder this time, but still there was no reply.

"Mr Jacobs?" he called.

His voice was trembling. He frowned. Pull yourself together, he thought. He cleared his throat and tried again. "Mr Jacobs? It's Billings."

Still there was no reply.

Billings turned the handle and pushed the door, but something was blocking it from the inside. There was a body on the ground, in front of the door. It was Jacobs, his bald head resting on the floor. Next to him lay his chair, which had tumbled over.

"Mr Jacobs, are you all right?" Billings cried, alarmed.

His cry attracted the attention of one of the clerks who was passing by the corridor with some files in his hands. "Help me!" Billings called to him. "There's something wrong with the Inspector!"

The clerk put his files on the floor and helped Billings bang repeatedly against the door, pushing Jacobs's body down bit by bit until there was enough room for Billings to squeeze through.

Billings knelt down beside Jacobs. He saw Jacobs's chest go up and down and he breathed a sigh of relief.

The clerk was still lingering in the doorway, looking alarmed and confused.

"Don't just stand there! Go get the surgeon!" Billings yelled.

"What happened to him?"

"I don't know. He must've had a heart attack or something. Just go."

As the clerk ran off to fetch the surgeon, Billings looked around the office. On Jacobs's desk, he suddenly saw the culprit: a small bottle of arsenic, half-emptied. Also on the desk were two envelopes, carefully placed in plain view on either side of the bottle. One was a large brown envelope, the sight of which instantly made Billings's stomach turn. He picked it up and opened it with trembling hands. Inside were the glass plate negatives which were used to make the compromising cabinet cards. A handwritten note slipped out of the envelope and floated onto the desk. *'Never let yourself be bought'* it said, in Jacobs's spidery writing. Billings returned the negatives in the envelope and stuck the parcel in his satchel. He picked up the second envelope. It contained a letter, also written by Jacobs, in which he clearly and methodically detailed all his dealings with Bohdan Krymski and his attempts at scapegoating Sebastian.

Billings and the clerk stood in the superintendent's office, watching McMurphy read the letter.

"I understand that it was you who urged him to write this letter?" McMurphy said, looking up from Jacobs's letter.

"Yes, sir," Billings replied. "I saw him at his house yesterday."

"And what did you talk to him about?"

"Well, I told him I knew about his plot with Bohdan Krymski. And I urged him to confess to it to you."

"Why?"

"Because an innocent man's life was at stake. How is Mr Jacobs, sir? Is he all right?"

"Never you mind how he is!" McMurphy turned towards the office clerk. "And what about you?"

"What about me, sir?"

"Are you involved in this plot?"

"Plot, sir?"

"This blackmailing plot?"

Billings's heart leapt at the mention of that word. It had never occurred to him that his meeting with Jacobs could be construed as blackmail.

"No, sir. I have nothing to do with this!" The clerk gave Billings a nasty look. "I was merely passing by when the sergeant called for my assistance and..."

"Please, sir," Billings interrupted. "I wasn't trying to blackmail him. I was merely trying to..."

"Be quiet!" McMurphy slammed his fist on his desk. "You can go now," he said to the office clerk. "I'd like to talk Sergeant Billings on my own."

"Yes, sir." The office clerk gave Billings one last nasty look before leaving the office.

"Please, sir. You must tell me how Inspector Jacobs is doing," Billings asked again. "I am very concerned."

"He's having his stomach pumped out as we speak."

"I never expected he'd do something like this."

"What *did* you expect? Or should I ask how much?"

Billings frowned. "I am telling you, sir. It had not been my intention to blackmail him."

"Well, then what *was* your intention?"

"I had discovered that Inspector Jacobs had become embroiled in an illicit plot with Bohdan Krymski and I wanted to give him the opportunity to explain himself before alerting you."

"This... um..." He picked up a file from his desk and scanned through it. "Sebastian Forrester – aka Brendan Lochrane – aka The Wild Man of Sutton Courtenay. This is a friend of yours, I believe."

"He is a family acquaintance."

"He confessed to killing Lord Palmer."

"That confession was induced from him by Inspector Jacobs. He retracted it later."

"That's right. That's what this is." He held up a bunch of papers. It was the letter which Sebastian had written in his prison cell. The six or so tightly packed pages which explained how he had turned from a passionate young man to a wretched recluse. Billings had been desperate to read his account ever since he had encouraged him to write it, but Jacobs had kept it locked in his drawer all this time.

"Didn't you visit him in his cell the day that this was written?" McMurphy looked at the date on the letter. "Friday, December the first?"

"That's right, sir."

"And wasn't it upon your recommendation that he wrote it?"

"I knew that his confession was false, sir. I knew he couldn't have killed Lord Palmer. There was no reason for him to do so."

"Then why did he confess?"

"It's complicated, sir. Sebastian has a self-destructive streak about him, which..."

"Sebastian, is it?"

"I meant Mr Forrester, sir. He was down and out

at the time and death must've seemed like a relief to him."

"And what made him change his mind?"

"I believe it was seeing his mother."

"His mother?"

"She came with me to his cell."

McMurphy looked at the file again. "His mother is Cecilia Forrester. Wife of Frederick Forrester. Who also happens to have been your guardian."

"That's right, sir. They looked after me when my parents died."

"I see."

McMurphy tapped his fingers on his desk as he looked at Billings. It was clear that he didn't know what to make of all this. Billings just stared back, earnestly.

"This arsenic, then," McMurphy said. "Where did that come from?"

"I don't know, sir."

"You believe he took it himself?"

"I do, sir."

"And why would he do that?"

"I believe he felt ashamed, sir."

"Ashamed?"

"He is a proud and honest man, sir."

"Not *that* honest, Billings, if your accusation is true."

"He must've felt very desperate, sir, to have agreed to Mr Krymki's proposition. We all have our weaknesses."

"Well, I suppose we will just have to wait, won't we? Until Jacobs recovers – which his doctors have assured me he will – and see what he has to say about all this."

Billings breathed a sigh of relief.

"As for this Barnabas Crooke, I suppose we had better alert the Berkshire Constabulary and the river police and see if they can pick him up. And we had better alert the magistrate too and let this Mr Forrester go. Because I agree with you, it doesn't look like we have enough of a case against him. But as for you, Billings... I don't think you've handled this at all well. You should have come to me if you had any suspicions. You should never have let it come to this."

"I realise that now, sir."

"You can go home now, Billings. I am suspending you until we have cleared this whole thing up, and that won't be until after Jacobs has recovered."

Billings turned to exit the office, but then he hesitated and turned back to face McMurphy.

"Sir, I was wondering..." He stopped. (Was he being tactless?)

"Well, what is it, Billings?"

"May I read Mr Forrester's letter?"

CHAPTER SEVENTEEN

Statement written by Sebastian Forrester,
Tuesday 2nd December, 1890

I found myself wandering the streets of Whitehaven in the summer of 1880. It is not necessary for you to know how I landed there, suffice to say that this was just one stop in a much longer journey, the route and destination of which were in the hands of a greater power and completely unknown to me. I remember stumbling through the cobbled streets of the West Strand, penniless and mute, listening to the rhythm of the surf crashing against the shore. In the whisper of the wind and the waves I suddenly heard a voice calling me. It was the sea. "Climb onto my waves," it said, "and let me take you to paradise."

I was younger then – and passionate and ignorant and desperate to do something glorious – but I was also ill (I recognize that now). The infection in my mouth had given me a fever and I was burning up and sweating profusely. What I then considered to have been a religious experience, I now know to have been mere delirium.

I must have collapsed at that point and fainted, because the next thing I remember is waking up on a pile of skins in a small brick room with four unknown men staring down at me and muttering words of concern.

"He's awake!" I heard the oldest of the four say. He had a large red head with small round spectacles and cheeks which trembled every time he moved his face. "You fainted, good man," he said to me. "Just out there, by the pier. What is your name?"

I put my lips together and was about to utter 'Brendan' when I suddenly remembered that I had no tongue. It had been three or four days since the episode occurred in which I lost my tongue, but only now did I feel the first pang of regret.

"He's thirsty," the man concluded and turned to the young labourer standing behind him. "Go fetch some water for the patient." He turned back to me. "My name is Jonas Cranson." He put his arm around a younger version of himself. "And this is my son, Philip. We are Cranson and Son. This is our tannery you're in."

I suddenly noticed the foul smell of smoke, bait and rotting skins wafting in the air.

The young labourer returned with a cup of water. I hadn't realised how thirsty I'd been until the sight of water put my instincts into action and made me yank the cup off his hands and pour the contents down my throat. The four men looked on silently as I drank. "He wants more," said Cranston watching me tip the cup over my face to let the last drops of water slide into my mouth. "Well, go on, get him some more!"

The young labourer took the cup back off me and shuffled out of the room. He must've been only fifteen or sixteen, with shifty eyes and a slouched back. Years of put-downs, reprimands and humbling had taken their toll on his thin body.

I downed the second cup of water as avidly as the first. As soon as I felt the hot, throbbing flush in my head ease away, I placed the empty cup on the ground and pushed myself up. I don't know whether it was the stench of the tanning liquor, or being confined in that small brick room with four strangers towering and fussing over me, but something made me want to get up and walk out of the room.

"Hey, what are you doing?" Cranston said. "Don't get up, good man. You're not well."

I ignored him and stumbled past the large pits in the yard where the skins were soaking in their liquor and out the door. The fresh sea breeze hit my face and in the roar of the waves crashing against the pier I heard that call again. A strange instinct led me back to the pier, and there I sat, still and upright, listening to the meditative rhythm of the ebb and the flow and longing, like St Brendan of Clonfert, to be set adrift on this watery desert.

I was still there the following morning, shivering on the outside but flushing hot inside, when two men approached me from behind.

"It's him, Da! Look!"

I turned around and saw the two labourers from the tannery approach me, the put-upon boy and his father.

"Ayup, what's tha doin' here?" the father asked, squatting down before me and looking me in the eyes. "Tha'll catch thy death, tha will, sitting out here. Looks like tha art halfway there already."

"Look Da, money!" The boy was pointing at some coins which had miraculously appeared on the ground before me. How did those coins get there, I wondered? Had an early morning stroller mistaken me for a beggar and thrown the coins at me?

"And tha should be careful with that and all," the father said, picking the coins up from the ground. "Hast tha not got a pocket tha can keep them in?"

I was wearing the clothes given to me by the Whitehaven police, as I had none of my own: a pair of woollen trousers, a shirt, and a long, ragged frock coat with no pockets.

"Och, well. I'll keep them for thee, then." He put the coins in his own coat pocket. "Tha should be more careful, man. 'Tis a nasty place tha hast landed in. Full of robbers and bandits and thieves. Eh, Oswald?"

The boy laughed.

"Why doesn't tha come with us? We've got a bed. And this'll do nicely for the rent." He tapped the coins in his pocket. "Come along. I'll make thee a nice cup of hot grog. That'll warm thee up."

Father and son pulled me up by the armpits and dragged me down the road.

"The name is Crooke, by the way," the father said, taking my hand and shaking it. "Barnabas Crooke. But tha can call me Barney."

There is a certain quality to my face which has always attracted the pity of others. I have often heard people speak of my 'melancholy eyes'. Perhaps it's the shape of them, or the colour, but there is something about them that moves people to care for me. I have taken advantage of this all my life; my mother, Mr Crickshaw, Janie Drew, they have all put up with things they would otherwise not have tolerated.

Barnabas Crooke made good use of this too. He had me sit on street corners all day long and beg for money. He would place me at various points all over Whitehaven. Mondays and Tuesdays, I sat on the corner of Queen Street and Lowther Street. Wednesday and Thursdays, I sat outside the tavern on Tangier Street. And Fridays and Saturdays, I sat against the wall of the small pavilion in Duke Street. I didn't mind. I was happy to sit still all day, ignoring the discomforts of the weather, staring ahead of me and meditating, only moving on when I was told to do so by the police. I earned mostly pennies and farthings, but occasionally there'd be a shilling or even a half crown. I could make up to six shillings on a good day, just by sitting still and looking pitiful. Crooke would pocket the money and in exchange he'd give me a bed and a warm meal every day.

Crooke lived in a crowded collier tenement on Mount Pleasant, right at the top of a flight of stone steps which led from the docks to the high land. We shared a small, dark room, furnished only with a stove and two iron beds. I slept in one bed and Crooke and Oswald slept top to toe in the other. It was a smelly room. The stench of the tanning liquor (which was composed of lime water and dog dung) clung to the tanners' clothes and they brought it back into the room with them every night. But I soon grew accustomed to their smell and they grew accustomed to mine. We were an odd and dirty trio, but a peaceful one. We only came home to sleep. Crooke spent his evenings in the tavern and Oswald was up to no good on the waterfront. As for myself, when I was not begging (at the time I didn't think of it as begging) I was on the moorland, constructing a currach.

My desire to set out to sea had not left me. I had studied St Brendan's Navigatio in my previous life and was very clear about how to construct the vessel which led him to the Isle of the Blessed. I had already assembled some timber to build the frame and all I needed were a dozen or so oak-soaked hides to stitch together. Crooke, of course, was in a good position to provide me with these and was willing to do so. Obviously I knew that he would be stealing them from his employer, but I could overlook that. This was providence. God had not introduced me to the acts of the Irish sea-faring monks for nothing. Nor was it coincidence that I woke up in the courtyard of a tannery.

I don't know what Crooke got out of my company (other than a few shillings). I suppose I must have been a distraction from his mundane existence and he was intrigued by my nightly labours. He and Oswald would often join me on the moorland and watch me work. Sometimes they'd even help out. Soon it wasn't just the Crookes who'd watch. The slum's children, who were constantly hanging around the steps and alleys of Mount Pleasant like gannets on a sea rock, would come up and watch me work with curious delight. They looked on with wonder as I stitched the skins together and strapped them to the frame, all the while guessing as to its purpose.

"Is it a tent?"

"No, it's a kite. It's a really big kite."

"I know what it is! It's a hot air balloon."

"It's a tent, dummy. He's building himsen a tent."

It took me five months to complete the boat. On a cold November night, when everyone was asleep, Crooke, Oswald and I descended down to the dock carrying the currach over our heads. I was feeling nervous about my adventure and I didn't want great crowds of people waving me off. After all, the currach had not yet been tested and it might sink the moment I stepped into it (although I had smeared the skins repeatedly with sheep wool grease, which should have made them waterproof). I also didn't want large crowds to attract the attention of the authorities, who might have stopped my expedition.

Crooke and Oswald watched with a bemused expression as I climbed into my ramshackle vessel and rowed off to meet the waves. What must they have thought? 'There he goes, the poor, mad bugger. Off to meet his death.' Well, death was on my mind. Of course it was. I knew perfectly well that many an Irish monk had sailed into oblivion, led astray by the winds and the currents. But like me, they must have felt God had a bigger plan for them and would see them safely to their destination – whatever that might be.

The night was cold, but the wind was smooth and the sea was calm. My sail billowed gently as I left the protection of the pier and the boat started skipping over the waves, almost hovering over the sea. There was another pang of doubt and regret as I looked back and saw the shoreline move farther away from me and the figures of Crooke and Oswald becoming rapidly smaller. I quickly sank down into the hull of my boat and turned back towards the stars and the dark horizon, biting my lips and fighting my tears. Never look back at a burning bridge, I thought. No good can come from that, as Lot's wife would surely testify.

Although the sea remained calm throughout the journey, the boat was so light and flexible that it twisted and curled over every single wave, making me profoundly sick. I spent six nights on that boat, most of them curled up on the floor in a puddle of my own vomit. It was agony. After three days of nausea, my whole body had stopped functioning. I lost all sensation in my limbs and was barely able to move. The spray of the waves kept splashing over my face as I lay half-conscious in the hull, making my skin sticky and salty. And the seagulls kept circling over the boat and screeching. Every now and then a daring gull would come down and land on my disabled body, like a vulture on a carcass, to pick up a morsel of my throw up. I drank little and ate less. I had taken enough food and water to last seven days; seven leather flasks of drinking water and a basket full of dried bread and biscuits. I was able to collect rain water on the tarpaulin, in case the journey should last longer than expected, and I had a hook and thread for catching fish or gulls. But all this proved unnecessary, because on the seventh day of my journey, my boat was hurled onto a rock off the coast of Whithorn and I was thrown out of the vessel and onto a rock pool, where I was rescued the following day by a local fisherman.

I remained in Whithorn for ten years, living among the fishermen, sailors and dock workers. I waited patiently for the first five years for another sign from God, for an indication of my purpose in this desolate outpost. But none came. God had become silent and I was left stranded, spiritually and physically. After five years of waiting, doubts finally started creeping in. Had I misinterpreted everything? Had this powerful yearning to leave behind my life of comfort and follow God's call been nothing more than a fantasy? Had this been nothing more than the usual restlessness of youth? If so, then all my sacrifices (by which I mean not only the loss of my tongue, but also the loss of my family and my position) had been for nothing.

I tried desperately to regain those glorious old passions again by committing acts of random asceticism (at one point I even drove a nail into my palm), but it was all in vain. The passion was missing and had been replaced by feelings of uselessness, frustration and regret. Something someone once told me came to mind:

'Real suffering doesn't come in one intense sweep. It is a slow, creeping thing which gradually engulfs you and traps you for the rest of your life.'

It was a dark episode of my life and it pains me to remember it. There is one person in particular — whose name I do not wish to mention in this report — who has been wronged and mistreated by me and who deserved better. Should the contents of this report ever come back to her, and I hope that they will, I want her to know that I am sorry. All I can say is that hope is a desperate thing. Man clings to it for much longer than he should and it took me ten years to realise that.

One morning I was wandering along the harbour, recovering from a hangover. I hadn't been home all night and the thought of doing so filled me with dread. I still had a couple of shillings in my pocket and when I saw the Liverpool ferry getting ready to depart, I suddenly felt the urge to board it. So I did. I left that same morning, suddenly and unexpectedly, without telling anyone. Escaping once again a life which had become dead, dull and unbearable.

I wandered throughout the country for a number of months, slowly edging southwards, sleeping in sheds and haystacks, indulging in the charity of others and working wherever I could. I wanted to return home, to the life which I had left behind, but I didn't dare. I was ashamed. Ashamed of the wretch that I had become.

Ashamed of the pain and grief I had imposed on my parents. They must surely have assumed me to be dead by now and they must have adapted to life without me. My appearance could only cause greater upheaval and further grief. And yet... I did so long for home.

By January I had drifted down to the Thames Valley in Berkshire. It was just outside the village of Appleford when I picked up a discarded newspaper from the street to line my coat with and saw Lord Palmer's advertisement. He was looking for a hermit to live on his estate and was offering three shillings a week and a hundred-pound bonus after completing a full year. It was providence. God had finally spoken again and had offered me a way out of my predicament. I could pull myself together with a hundred pounds. Find some treatment for my putrid wound. Set myself up in some sort of business, so as not to be reliant on charity. I might even bring myself to be reunited with my parents.

And so I went to Sutton Courtenay to apply for the position. I was nervous. I had been someone others would shriek away from or look upon with a mixture of pity and disgust for so long, that I no longer knew how to interact with people. But Lord Palmer took a shine to me despite my wretched appearance (or probably because of it) and I was given the job.

I can't deny that it was hard. I was used to living like

a stray cur in the privacy of my own degradation, but to do so in plain sight of others, and for their amusement, was a humiliating experience. But I consoled myself with the notion that this was the lesson which God had wanted me to learn. I had reached rock bottom and could only rise from this a wiser and more enlightened man.

One month before the completion of my contract, I started preparing myself for my reincarnation and wrote to my parents. It was a short letter. I did not want to give away too many details of my life. I just wanted to let them know that I was still alive and that I was hoping to be reunited with them. I gave the letter to the gardener who posted it for me. I was planning to write more letters later. I wanted to prepare them slowly. It would have been too much of a shock for them to become acquainted with my extraordinary history in one go. But alas! Tragedy struck before I was able to write to them again.

As I was chopping wood one morning, I heard someone calling in the woods. I went down to the river and saw a narrowboat floating gently by, with two figures of my past standing on it and grinning broadly at me.

"Ayup, look who it is!" one of the figures called.

It was Barnabas Crooke. And his son Oswald was standing at the back, punting.

"So it is thee!" Crooke said. "I heard down th'river

that tha were living in th'estate of some rich lord. 'A tongue-less wild man' they said. 'Well,' I thought, 'that can only be our good friend Brendan.' And here tha art."

While Oswald moored the boat, Crooke jumped off, ran towards me and grabbed me in his arms. "So tha survived then?" he said, patting me on my back.

I remained standing still, shocked and frozen. I had a foreboding that this unexpected visit could only lead to tragedy.

"I was sure tha'd drown," Crooke continued. "We got a boat too now." He pointed proudly to the narrowboat. "They loaned it to Oswald. He put on a great show there in Birmingham Gaol, with his sad eyes and lost lamb routine. He learned a lot from thee, did Oswald. So where's this posh house, then?"

He let go of me and walked towards the bridge which crosses onto the garden. When he got a good view of Sutton House, he stopped. "Stone me! Is that it?" he said. "Tha hast it made, tha has! Art tha allowed in?"

I shook my head.

"They have tha living out here, have they?"

I pointed towards my cave.

"But tha can get into th'house if tha wants, right?"

I shook my head.

"Tha could let us in. At night. Tha could leave a door open for us so we can slip in?"

I shook my head again, but he kept ignoring me.

"That door, there." He pointed towards the servant's entrance. *"I wager that's the kitchen door. Is that locked at nights?"*

I didn't know, but I nodded.

"Dost tha have a key?"

I shook my head.

"Can tha get one?"

I shook my head again.

"What's the matter?" Crooke suddenly looked at me with a suspicious frown. *"It's me. Barnabas Crooke. I saved tha life back in Whitehaven, remember?"*

I kept looking at him, pleadingly. I wanted to tell him that I had nothing to do with the house, that I never ventured out of the woods, that I could be of no use to them and that they should go.

"Tha wants the whole loot for thyneself, doesn't tha? Tha greedy little bastard!"

"Hey, Da. Look at this!" Oswald was holding up the hatchet I used to chop wood with.

"Oh, that'll do just fine." Crooke took the hatchet off his son. *"We could break down the door with this."*

At this point, Lord Palmer suddenly appeared. He was taking a shortcut to the fair in Abingdon when he stumbled upon us, taking us by surprise. We all froze on the spot and stared at each other for a few seconds, before Lord Palmer finally spoke.

"What's this? Poachers, is it?" He kept looking back

and forth between Crooke and Oswald, the hatred in his eyes growing by the second.

"Good morning, sir," said Crooke, tipping his hat at him. "We were just passing by on our boat and we ran out of kindling. I were just asking thy man here whether we could get some dead wood from…"

"Green!" Lord Palmer yelled angrily. "Bring me my shotgun. I have a gypsy parasite here!"

"Here, who's tha calling a gypsy parasite?"

"You are trespassing on my property," Lord Palmer shouted, "and that's a criminal offence!" Suddenly he grabbed Oswald by the shoulders and pushed him against a tree. "Now you will stay right here until my man arrives with my shotgun. Then I will personally frogmarch you all the way to Abingdon Police Station !" He called again for the gardener.

"Maister, tha hast gone too far!" Crooke approached his lordship and tried to wrestle Oswald away from Lord Palmer's grip. "Take tha hands off me son!"

"Speak English, man! I can't understand a word you say!"

"Let go off me son now, tha hears?"

Crooke then started waving the hatchet in the air, which further enraged Lord Palmer.

"You put that thing down this very instant!" he yelled. "I will not be threatened in my own land by a pair of thugs!"

"I ain't gonna warn tha again, maister! Let go off me son!"

"It's not 'mister', it's 'Lord'! You'll have the decency of calling me 'sir', you impudent rascal!"

This was too much of an insult for Crooke. He swung the hatchet in the air and hit Lord Palmer with it on the back of his head. He hit him with the blunt side, but it was a powerful blow and Lord Palmer fell on to his hands and knees, yelping like a dog. Without a moment's hesitation, Crooke then turned the hatchet around, took another sweep and dug the blade right in-between Lord Palmer's shoulder blades, causing him to collapse face down on the ground.

"Quickly Oswald, grab what tha can!" He knelt down beside the body and ruffled through his pockets. Oswald joined in. They took a gold watch out, pulled a ring off his finger and found some bank notes in his pocket. Then they got up and ran back towards their boat.

Crooke suddenly stopped and turned towards me. "That hast better come back with us," he said.

I remained frozen on the spot, staring at Lord Palmer's body with horror. He was still alive then. I could see his eyeballs rolling frantically up and down, as if he were having an epileptic fit.

"Art tha coming, or what?" Crooke called.

I shook my head.

"Well, suit thy self," and he jumped back on to his

boat.

I realised shortly afterwards that I had made a mistake. I should've gone with them. I knew that this murder would be blamed on me, but when I turned around to face them, Crooke and Oswald had already pushed off and were floating downstream. I ran after them, waving frantically, begging them to stop, but it was too late. They simply shrugged and refused to turn back.

All sorts of thought and emotions flashed through me at that moment. Why did this have to happen now? Why did God raise my hopes, only to dash them again so cruelly? What game was He playing with me? But then it struck me. Of course! How could I have been so stupid! It wasn't enough to abandon my worldly possessions and elope to the Lake District! It wasn't enough to cut off my tongue or to suffer an excruciating boat trip! I was responsible for the loss of two lives, that of Janie Drew and her unborn child! I deserved all of this. And much worse. Although I continued following the boat, I knew I had no hope of escaping. Lord Palmer's body would soon be discovered by the gardener and the police would be called in. I'd be tried and hanged.

I lost all hope of ever being reunited with my parents and of recovering my old life. My life was over now. Finally, after all these years, I gave myself over completely to the will of God. I had only a short time left to live and this time would truly be spent 'as though crucified; in struggle, in lowliness of spirit, in good will and spiritual abstinence, in fasting, in penitence, in weeping'.

It wasn't until I had wandered down the winding river all the way to London that I was finally picked up by the police. I don't need to write what happened after that. I've been behind bars ever since, preparing myself for my final fate. I was ready to hang until suddenly another figure from my distant past re-entered my life. This time it was John Billings, my father's ward. He's the one who convinced me to write down this narrative. I don't know whether this will save me from the gallows – and I don't care if it doesn't – but at least the truth can now be known.

Epilogue

The first five days of his suspension Billings barely left his room. There had been too many strong emotions, too many unsettling revelations, which had kept him bound to his bed (and to his morphine). But on the week leading to Christmas, he finally decided to pull himself together.

He climbed the hospital steps, a bag of fruit in his hand. His heart pounded in his chest as he approached the ward. What was he going to say? Would Jacobs even want to see him?

A group of people were gathered by Jacob's bed. Mrs Jacobs sat beside her husband and Superintendent McMurphy and his assistant stood at the foot of his bed.

Billings stopped in the doorway. It felt inappropriate to barge in. He turned around, sat on a bench in the corridor, and waited for them to leave. He could hear them talking in the ward.

"Did he ask for money?" McMurphy asked Jacobs.

"No, he didn't ask for money."

"Was there an implicit understanding that Detective Sergeant Billings would withdraw his accusations if you paid him some money?"

"No, sir. There was no understanding between me and Billings. Billings is entirely blameless in this whole affair. It was me who was in the wrong. Me. Just me."

"How much money did Bohdan Krymski offer you to tip him off?"

"He offered to pay my debts, which amounted to five thousand pounds. This was a loan which I would have to pay back gradually from the rewards received for foiling his counterfeiting operation and the salary increase which might result from a possible promotion."

"Promotion?"

"I assumed there might be a promotion in it for me."

"There's not going to be a promotion now, Mr Jacobs. Damn it, man! This is the Turf Fraud Scandal all over again!"

"I think he knows that!" Mrs Jacobs chipped in.

"There's no need to rub it in!"

"Be quiet, Winnifred."

"But he's talking to you like a common criminal!"

"Be quiet, I said."

"How did this understanding between yourself and Krymski come into existence?" McMurphy asked.

"It appears that Krymski was spying on us at the same time as we were spying on him. When he realised we had discovered his warehouse, he came to my house to make his proposition. I was in too desperate a position to refuse."

"How did he know about your debts?"

"He has an informer at the bank."

"So in what manner is the murder of Lord Palmer connected to this case?"

"Lord Palmer was killed by one of Krymski's associates."

"Barnabas Crooke?"

"Yes. He's something of a loose cannon. The murder wasn't planned. In fact it was a downright inconvenience."

"So when Detective Sergeant Billings accused you of deliberately scapegoating Sebastian Forrester, he was right?"

"Yes. Except I didn't know his name was

Sebastian Forrester. I thought he was just a homeless vagrant."

"And did you think that that would make him more expendable?"

Jacobs didn't answer.

"How's your health?"

"Not very well, sir."

"The doctor tells me you have lost the use of your right arm?"

"Partially."

"And you are having difficulty walking?"

"The arsenic has affected my balance."

"The doctor says you might never recover."

"No."

"We can't have you back in the force unless you do."

"I realise that."

"And you probably won't qualify for a pension after what you have done."

"I am aware of that too."

"So what will you do, then?"

"I shall just have to sell up, won't I?"

Billings heard Mrs Jacobs break out in tears. He felt uneasy. His hand was trembling and he had a horrible feeling in his gut. Was he responsible for Jacobs's predicament? Should he have foreseen this outcome? He got up, put the bag of fruit on the bench, took a calling card out of his pocket, left it beside the bag and marched out of the building.

A letter lay waiting for Billings when he returned home.

Dear John,

I am sorry that it has taken so long for me to write and thank you, but this has been a tumultuous time for all of us. I am afraid that I shall have to start the letter with some bad news. Mr Forrester has died. He died two days ago with me and Sebastian by his side. Although he has been unconscious and confused a lot lately, he did have a moment of clarity when Sebastian grabbed his hand and held it in his grasp. Neither father nor son could speak, but I could see Mr Forrester's eyes well up with love and gratitude and I knew that he had recognized him. It was shortly afterwards, in fact, that he died, but I am so glad that God has allowed him to see his beloved son one more time before he passed away.

The other sad news is that Sebastian has gone away again. When I went up to his room yesterday, his closet was empty and he had left a short note with an apology behind on the table. Please do not be sad for me. In a way I am glad that he has gone. It was clear to me that he felt uncomfortable being home. He was very unsure about himself and his inability to speak and the odour from his mouth made him very reluctant to leave the house and interact with our friends (who have all been very kind and welcoming towards him). He was also very restless. He slept little and paced about his room a lot. He mentioned in his letter that he had gone to the continent. I don't know what he will do, but at least I know he's still alive and that he knows where to reach me when he needs some money.

Mr Forrester's funeral will take place on Thursday, the day after Christmas. You will come, won't you? You are the only family I have left.

Yours lovingly,
Cecilia Forrester

Billings dropped the letter on the floor and fell on his bed. He rolled up his sleeve and injected another dose. It was the second dose of the day. It was still only three o'clock.

"God, we thank you for this food. For rest and home and all things good. For wind and rain and sun above – but most of all for those we love."

Billings looked around the dinner table as Clarkson recited his prayer. Clarkson sat at the head. His wife sat to the right of him and his two children to the left. They all had their eyes closed, their elbows on the table and their hands wrapped beneath their chins. Their happy faces glowed warm in the candlelight. A large crisply browned goose on a bed of roasted vegetables lay in the middle of the table and the smoke which rose from it smelled very appetising. The Clarkson family looked idyllic, like a picture on a Christmas card. Billings sat at the other end of the table, a little removed from the family, feeling awkward and out of place.

Clarkson finished his prayer, opened his eyes and stood up from the table. "Right, everyone on your feet," he said.

The diners looked at each other unsurely.

"Well, come on. Up you get," Clarkson repeated.

"What for?" his wife asked.

"Never mind what for. Just do as you're told. Come on, all of you. On your feet. You too, Billings."

They got up.

"We've thanked the Lord, now it's time to thank Mr Boogledug."

"Who's Mr Boogledug?" one of the children asked.

"Mr Boogledug is a very special friend of mine."

"Oh Samuel, you're being silly!" Mrs Clarkson laughed and sat back down again.

Billings felt like sitting down too, but he didn't want to ruin Clarkson's joke, so he remained standing.

"In fact, it's Mr Boogledug we have to thank for this special meal," Clarkson continued. "If it weren't for Mr Boogledug, we'd have nothing to eat this Christmas, except for some roasted carrots and parsnips."

The children stared at their father with doe-eyed wonder and hung on to his every word. Mrs Clarkson stifled a laugh.

"Daddy don't make much money at Scotland Yard," Clarkson continued. "Unlike our friend Billings." He winked at his colleague. "He's a sergeant, but Daddy's just a constable and I only earn a couple of shilling a week. And that ain't much. So there I was, wandering around Clapham Common, wondering what to feed my family this Christmas, when suddenly I saw Mr Boogledug, pecking and picking and fluttering about on the lawn. He was an 'andsome chap. Strong and sturdy and fat. So I walked over to him and I said 'Sir,' ... "

"'Sir'?" Mrs Clarkson interrupted with a smile on her face.

"Yes, 'sir'. I'm always polite when I talk to

strangers. 'Sir,' I said. 'I've got a bit of a problem. It's Christmas coming soon and I ain't got nothing to feed my family. I was wondering whether you could help me?' 'And why would I want to help you?' Mr Boogledug asked. 'Well, I'm an 'ard-working man,' I said, 'and I've just spent the last few days and nights sitting in a dark little office, nearly blinding myself by reading and collating reports about stolen jewels."

Mrs Clarkson burst out laughing. Clarkson ignored her and continued. "And I did all that just so that I could give my family, who I love more than anything in this world, the most scrumptious meal they've ever had in their lives. So I was wondering if you could help me out?' 'Well,' said Mr Boogledug, 'you sound like a good and honest man to me and I'd be more than happy to help you out.' And so he did. It was Mr Boogledug who provided us with this scrumptious fowl which your mother has cooked for us so deliciously. Well, what do you think of that, children? That was nice of Mr Boogledug, weren't it?"

The children nodded.

"And I think it's only right and proper that we should thank him, don't you?"

The children nodded again.

Clarkson picked up the poultry knife and fork.

"Now, look down at the goose and say 'Thank you, Mr Boogledug.'"

"Why do I have to look down at the goose?" one of the children asked.

"Because you should always look someone in the face when you thank them. It's good manners. Go on. Look down at the goose and say 'Thank you, Mr Boogledug.'"

"You mean Mr Boogledug is the goose?" the child asked.

"That's right. Mr Boogledug is the goose. Thank you, Mr Boogledug." He plunged the fork and knife into the goose's breast. The children shrieked with horror and Clarkson and his wife rolled about with laughter.

Dinner was over and Mrs Clarkson and the children were in the kitchen, clearing up. Clarkson sat at the end of the table, huffing and puffing and rubbing his recently filled belly. Billings observed how different he was surrounded by his family. He looked proud and contented – even quite handsome. Did he always come home to a house filled with laughter and companionship, he wondered.

"You all right there, Billings?" Clarkson asked.

"Yes, thank you."

"You enjoying yourself?"

"Yes, I am."

"You sure? 'Cause you don't look it."

"Oh, I am. I am."

Clarkson was right. Billings had been distracted all day. He couldn't get the events of the past month off his mind. He kept thinking about Jacobs in hospital. And Mrs Forrester all alone in that cold, large house. How where they spending *their* Christmas?

"I think I'll go outside for a while," he said, getting up from the table. "Get some fresh air."

"Good idea," Clarkson replied. "I think I'll go to the john myself in a while. Make some room for the Christmas pudding."

Billings stepped out of the door and felt a cold, fresh breeze caress his face. He took a deep breath and looked around him. The street was deserted, but there were candles burning in every window and he could hear laughter and singing behind every door. He decided to stretch his legs and started pacing down the cobbled lane towards Clapham High Street. From there, he continued his walk and wandered all the way to the common. He listened to his footsteps over the frosty cobbles. He was reminded of his long walk through the fens of Cumberland and he felt that same peaceful feeling engulfing him. Not wanting that feeling to end, he continued walking. He walked over the common all the way to Battersea. Before he knew it, his feet had dragged him back home.

He was tired now and his stomach felt heavy with food and alcohol. He went inside and stumbled up the stairs, avoiding Mrs Appleby who was celebrating Christmas in the lounge with her sister. He locked himself up in his room, fell onto his bed and dozed off. He woke up several hours later with a syringe dangling from his arm and a gentle knocking on his door.

"Mr Billings? Are you there?"

It was Mrs Appleby.

"He's probably doped on that morphine again," he heard her tell someone. Who was she talking to? Was it Clarkson? He suddenly felt bad for abandoning Clarkson's party without saying goodbye.

"Mr Billings!" Mrs Appleby continued. "I ask you! Christmas Day and he just locks himself up in his room. It's a right shame, the way that man carries on!"

Why did he do it, thought Billings. Why did keep pushing people away only to complain later that he was feeling isolated?

"Oh well, let him be." He heard Mrs Appleby

walk back down the stairs. "Best check up on him again tomorrow morning, see if he's all right."

Billings remained in his room all night, haunted by thoughts of Jacobs and Sebastian. Two lives, completely ruined. Not by misfortune or circumstance, but by their own reckless hands. Why did they do the things they did? He was reminded of that quote from Robinson Crusoe, the one which had so impressed him when he read it. *'It is a secret overruling decree that hurries us on to be the instruments of our own destruction. Even though it be before us we rush upon it with our eyes wide open.'*

Other Books by Olivier Bosman

D.S. Billings Victorian Mysteries
Death Takes a Lover
Something Sinister
The Campbell Curse
Anarchy

Gay Noir

www.olivierbosman.com-

ABOUT THE AUTHOR

Born to Dutch parents and raised in Colombia and England, Olivier is a rootless wanderer with itchy feet. He has spent the last few years living and working in The Netherlands, Czech Republic, Sudan and Bulgaria, but he has every confidence that he will now finally be able to settle down among the olive groves of Andalucia.

He is an avid reader and film fan (in fact, his study is overflowing with his various dvd collections!)

He did an MA in creative writing for film and television at the University of Sheffield. After a failed attempt at making a career as a screenwriter, he turned to the theater and wrote and produced a play called 'Death Takes a Lover' (which has since been turned into the first D.S.Billings Victorian Mystery). The play was performed on the London Fringe to great critical acclaim.

He is currently living in Spain where he makes ends meet by teaching English .

Made in the USA
Columbia, SC
16 July 2021

41954236R00217